Nascent Witch

Books by Melissa Bobe

NASCENT WITCH

SIBYLS

Nascent Witch

MELISSA BOBE

THE HIVE PRESS ● NEW YORK

NASCENT WITCH

A Hive Press Book

Cover art & design by Melissa Bobe

For everyone who has

planted lavender for luck
wished to float as light as a feather
longed for lucky cats to cross their path
believed in full moons, midnight, and sisterhood

and who now worries that magic may have left their life:

May this book bright your cheeks, warm your heart,
and remind you of the magic that is always there
even when you can't quite seem to find it.

One

"You know," Sela Glaser said offhandedly to the woman ringing her up at the register, "you'd think guys would have better things to do than stalk a girl through a bookstore, but I guess not."

The woman stopped typing, giving Sela an alarmed look. "Was he fortyish? Balding? Did you hear him undo his belt at all?"

"Um, no, no, and definitely no. Please tell me that's not a regular you've just described?"

"Friday Night Pervert," the woman confirmed as she started to bag up Sela's things. "I was worried he might have added Wednesday morning to the schedule."

"So, instead of sending dick pics to the unsuspecting women of Coffee Meets Bagel," Sela went on, handing over a twenty, "this guy unleashes his charms on your...biography section?"

"Cooking and baking. Occasionally travel—he tries to be well-rounded."

"Nothing is sacred."

"Tell me about it." The woman gave Sela her receipt and change. "Sorry for whoever was bothering you, though. Have a better day."

Sela had been trying to "have a better day" since she'd finished college six years before. She glanced behind her as she left the store just to be safe, but the guy in the leather jacket was nowhere in sight. The only thing accompanying her was the gift for the baby shower she couldn't attend of a coworker she wasn't even close to who was going to have yet another baby that Sela would pretend to find cute.

"It's not that I object to babies," she remarked as she got into her car. "I just prefer cats."

Her phone pinged a distinctive bell tone she'd assigned to reminders for short-term hustles. Anything baby-sitting, dog-sitting, or house-sitting got the bell. Jobs beyond sitting—secretarial, temping, and the like—got a trumpet. Interviews for full-time positions received a gong, marking them as the death-match they almost always were.

"Whatever it is, I'm on my way," Sela sighed as she threw the gearstick into drive.

A split-second later, she slammed her foot on the brake as a grey-and-brown blur flew in front of her car.

"For fuck's sake, I do not need to end this morning by killing a raccoon."

She pushed a mess of auburn waves out of her face, reminded herself that if she couldn't afford a salon she needed to learn to trim her own hair, put the car in park, and got out fearing the worst.

"You can't possibly have just said 'raccoon,'" an agitated voice remarked.

Sela froze in her examination of the front of her car and looked around, worried that the creep who'd been following her through the bookshop had indeed stalked her outside. But there was no one nearby. A mother and her toddler were heading towards the parking lot, but for the moment, Sela was alone.

Checking under her wheels once more to make sure she hadn't killed anything cute and fluffy, she started to get back in the car, telling herself, "You need to get a grip, Sela."

"No argument here." A grey-and-brown cat with amber eyes and—no denying it—a pissed-off expression on its face leapt onto the hood of her car. "A raccoon? Do I look remotely like a raccoon?"

She managed not to scream, though her feet brought her a good distance backwards without Sela even trying to move them.

The cat looked at her with more attitude, if that were possible. "Oh, I'm sorry—*raccoon* got your tongue?"

The talking cat was mocking her. Something in her wanted to sass it back, but then a different and more dominant part of her brain reminded Sela that, mocking or not, cats shouldn't talk at all.

"You're talking," she managed.

"And you need a haircut. Are we done stating the obvious?"

She flushed, even as she realized on some level that it was ridiculous to be embarrassed about the state of her appearance in the presence of a talking cat.

"Okay, okay." The cat gave an eye roll, which was astonishing to see on a non-human face. "I know I'm being rude. We can start over. I even forgive you for almost running me down with this...lovely...Toyota."

Sela found her voice. "Are...are you judging my car, now?"

"Well, I'm sure you're probably budgeting for something newer—"

"What the fuck is actually happening? I'm talking to a cat that doesn't like my car?"

"*Not* a cat," the cat countered. "A familiar. A witch's familiar."

"I'm sorry: what?"

"I'm not a cat." His tail swished, a gesture Sela recognized as one of feline agitation. "I resemble a cat, but I belong to an entirely separate class of animal. Cats are relatively stupid and vain. And they vomit everywhere."

"My cat doesn't vomit everywhere," she found herself arguing, though she was barely processing the ludicrousness of this conversation.

"Ugh, you have a cat?" He shook his head in a manner that was not even close to feline. "I'd really been hoping for a two-roommate situation."

"Situation? Roommate?" Sela found the extent of her patience. "Dude, *what are you talking about*?"

The cat sighed. "You're Sela Glaser, right?"

Disturbed that the talking cat knew her name, Sela nodded.

"And you're about to turn twenty-eight, yes?"

She nodded again.

"Hi, Sela. I'm Sable. You're a witch about to come into your powers, and I am your familiar."

Now, instead of doubting her sanity further, Sela felt a tug at the back of her mind, a combination of memory and nostalgia that whispered triumphantly: *I knew it.* It was a flash of feeling that extended into her past, way back to high school when she and her friends had spent evenings casting spells, trading crystals, reading tarot cards, and giggling over pots they'd taken from their parents' kitchens to serve as makeshift cauldrons.

She pushed those memories aside. If temping for six years didn't make a girl a skeptic, Sela didn't know what did. "I'm sorry, are you sure you have the right person?"

The cat who had called himself Sable rolled his eyes again. "Are you serious? What, is my presence not magickal enough for you to believe that you're a witch?"

She hesitated as she tried to focus not on a happy past, but what was until a few minutes ago her very dreary present. "Nothing special has happened to me recently. Or ever."

"That's why I said you're *about* to come into your powers." He seemed to regard her with less snark for the first time. "It's not bullshit. I promise."

"Okay," Sela said after another minute of taking in this bizarre new reality, "so, you're Sable. One hundred percent familiar and…totally unfamiliar."

"That's me." He jumped off the hood of the car, hopped in through the still-open door, and settled himself on her passenger seat. "So, where are we headed?"

Two

A witch, Sela thought to herself, giddy with excitement despite the persistent cynicism she'd cultivated over the last several years. After all of the dead-end jobs, disappointed hopes, disgusting living situations, and horrific first dates, having her adolescent dreams come true seemed, well, a pretty magical turn of events.

And what adolescent dreams they had been. She'd been part of a "coven," as she and her friends had called themselves. Really, they were a group of girls obsessed with occult shops and flowy dresses, and with the idea that they were doing something a little on the forbidden side. Sela was one of two coven high priestesses, the others being Maria Gonzalez, Sela's bookish and beautiful then-best friend, and Kendra Reilly, who had a huge house with a cavernous basement that the coven used for casting circles.

"Please tell me you're deep in thought about getting us something to eat."

Sable's voice cut through her thoughts, and Sela blushed at the youthful memories she'd been dwelling on. What was happening to her now wasn't childhood witch games with friends: this was real and present magick, if what Sable had been telling her was true.

"Uh, do you have any preferences?"

"Isn't that a drive-thru just ahead?" Sable pointed up the street with one tawny-grey paw.

"You want tacos?"

He gave her a cutting look. "What, am I supposed to beg for a can of ground-up meat, fish, and whatever the hell else you feed your housecat?"

"I just meant that it's a little early for beans and hot sauce," she said, holding a hand up defensively. "But whatever—tacos work."

As they waited in the drive-thru line, Sela tried to stay quiet in an effort to avoid offending Sable again, but that was a losing battle. She was a witch! How could she not be bursting with questions?

"Okay, so you look like a cat, but you're not a cat," she blurted. "Why aren't you a cat?"

"I have to look like something, don't I?"

Sela paused to think about this. "That does not help me understand anything."

"Maybe if you stopped comparing me to useless domesticated mammals, I'd have more satisfying answers for you."

Sela wondered if all familiars were this prickly. "Look, you just dropped this 'yer a wizard, Sela' truth-bomb on my head in the middle of my Wednesday. Could you maybe give me a moment to have all of the questions about how my life is going to completely change?"

He sighed. "Sorry, I'm not trying to be an asshole. You're just kind of hitting a nerve."

"Cats? Are cats the nerve?"

"Not acknowledging me as a witch's familiar is the nerve," Sable responded, struggling to keep his voice just this side of agitated.

Sela turned her attention to the drive-thru menu. Even though she was hungry, the full lunch deal was way too expensive. She'd have to get a small burrito and leave it at that.

"What do you want?" she asked Sable.

"The chalupa with the crunchy stuff."

Sela made a face as though she didn't know what her feline-sized companion was talking about, hoping he might take a hint.

"You know," he added, "the one with the special sauce and the sour cream."

Great, I get a prickly familiar who orders the most expensive things on the menu. "Are you sure? That's like as big as you are."

This was apparently the wrong comment to make. Wincing at Sable's intense glower, she relayed his order into the speaker.

"Is that all?" the drive-thru attendant wanted to know.

"Just that and a kid's taco."

"That's it?"

"Yep." *I'm way too broke to buy anything else thanks to Mister Fancy-Pants Chalupa over here*, she thought to herself, trying to forget she hadn't eaten breakfast that morning.

As they rolled forward, Sable remarked conversationally, "Not much of a lunch person?"

"I don't even know what a familiar is." She decided to bring them back to the previous topic of conversation; they could have it out over his expensive taste later. "For that matter, I'm not sure I know what a witch is. Are we talking *Charmed* or *Sabrina*? And which versions—originals or reboots?"

"Try to leave Hollywood and witch novels out of it," Sable advised. "Most of them are dead wrong, and even the parts they get right are all screwy."

"They got the part about you looking like a cat right."

The words were out before Sela could stop them. Was it her fault she had a snarky familiar who made her want to give as good as she got? Besides, she was hungry.

"Your cat is going to be an issue, you know," Sable replied testily. "Cats don't care for me any more than I do them."

"Must be your winning personality."

"It's actually *your* fault, since it's your mark that I'm walking around with. If your cat isn't already territorial, a magickal creature strolling into his home sporting an indelible link to his owner is definitely going to make him want to piss on all the furniture."

At that point, they'd reached the drive-thru window and Sela had to reach forward to pay. A bored-looking guy a few years younger than her handed over the food, then noticed Sable and gave Sela what she felt was a more judgmental look than necessary.

"Is it my fault some cats piss on all the furniture if you don't take them with you everywhere?" she snapped at the kid, using her familiar's own words against him. Then she quickly hit the gas so the drive-thru attendant wouldn't hear Sable's indignant response.

They bickered the rest of the drive home, though Sela managed to get bits of useful information out of Sable. She learned that the mark he'd mentioned was a magickal seal she'd apparently been born with (although Sela had a hard time believing she'd been magickal all these years and hadn't gotten a single decent job or long-term relationship out of it). She didn't quite understand what the seal did; Sable waxed poetic about how she'd have to learn to uncover it over time, whatever that meant. She found it a little hard to pay attention to what he was saying as he munched away on the delicious-looking chalupa.

They made their way up the staircase to her apartment, which was located above a restaurant.

"Sorry if it smells a little greasy," she apologized as she unlocked the door.

Sable made a relaxed gesture she'd started to recognize as a shrug. "We can work a spell for that once you're initiated."

Sela froze in the doorway, astonished. "We can?"

"Well, why not? You're going to be a witch, aren't you?"

But before she could say anything else, a blood-curdling, inhuman scream came from the middle of the living room.

Pluto, Sela's slinky black rescue cat who usually came to greet her at the door with love and affection, was staring daggers at Sable. Every inch of his typically silky fur was standing on end, and his body had gone rigid like he'd stuck his paw in a socket.

"Hey, sweet boy!" Sela tried enthusiastically in a soothing voice, hoping that might calm Pluto down.

Further screaming commenced.

"Do you want to continue trying to defend this species to me?" Sable shouted over the din.

"Maybe if we go sit quietly on the couch," she yelled back, stepping into her apartment.

"I don't think that will work…"

Sure enough, as soon as Sable had passed the front-door threshold, Pluto took several violent hops towards him, still fluffed out and screaming bloody murder.

"What do we do?"

Sable rolled his eyes. "*You* have to promise not to laugh." He drew himself up into a standing posture and began shouting at Pluto, "Bad kitty! That's a *bad kitty*! No!"

Pluto spat once, then tore underneath Sela's sofa, where he reverted to yowling pitifully. Meanwhile, Sable returned to all fours and began smoothing his whiskers as though they were a mustache he'd ruffled by mistake.

"Okay. What the fuck was that?"

Sable walked fully into the apartment with a flick of his tail. "I've found the best way to get housecats over my unfortunate resemblance to them is to make them aware of how we differ."

"Well, now that that's done," Sela said, sweeping her arm out, "welcome, I guess. In comparison with some of the other shit-holes I've lived in, it's actually pretty nice. I get a good deal on the rent for putting up with noise from the restaurant."

Between the high ceilings, wood floors, large windows in the bedrooms, and exposed brick in the living room, the apartment really was a steal. Sela had been thrilled to find such a spacious place, and her landlord had been just as happy that someone was actually willing to live above a loud business. She hadn't bothered to mention at the time that tuning out restaurant bustle was nothing after all the waitressing she'd done over the years.

Sela liked to think she had managed to make the place hers: paintings and collages hung along the exposed brick, detailed quilts cozied the sofa, pottery filled with odds and ends brightened coffee tables and countertops, and soaps in shades of lavender, peach, and mustard graced the edge of the kitchen sink. The one-wall kitchen was sequestered from the airy living room by a wraparound counter-island that created a small dining nook, which Sela had decorated with candles and more pottery.

She had made all of the home accents herself. She remembered the abject distaste on her undergraduate advisor's face when he saw the first collage made of natural mixed media Sela had constructed in the fall of her senior year.

"If you want to teach craft classes for old women at a community center to make ends meet between gallery shows, that's your business," he'd told her. "But this kind of hobby doesn't belong in my classroom."

Yet Sela had been inspired in a way she still didn't quite have words for. Natural materials seemed second-nature to her, and she couldn't help herself from incorporating them into her work. So when the time came for her to create her senior project, the giant mural her thesis committee had expected evolved into a natural mixed media triptych, which for Sela's advisor was the final straw. Her GPA dipped, her references evaporated, and she left school without any prospects, never mind a plan for the future.

"Greasy smell notwithstanding, it's nice."

Sable's voice again brought her out of her thoughts, and a smile spread across Sela's face. "Yeah?"

"Do you sleep on the sofa?"

"Oh, there's more." She led him towards her bedroom, across from the apartment's tiny windowless bathroom. As she pushed the door open, she warned, "It's not very big compared to the living room."

Sable hopped onto Sela's bed to survey the space. She saw him take in the tapestries she'd hung to brighten up the plain white walls, her small dresser and full-length mirror, and the sprawling windows, the rightmost with its swinging security gate blocking access from a fire escape. Her narrow closet was ajar, a mess of clothes sticking out of it that she was sure Sable would snark at.

Instead, though, he nodded to the door on the other side of the room. "Where does that lead?"

Sela hesitated. "The second bedroom."

"And you're not showing it to me because…it's where you keep the bodies?"

She sighed. "Will you judge me for having an aversion to a room in my own apartment?"

His tail flicked. "No judgment. But in addition to being your magickal counterpart, I'm also your new roommate. I kind of want a full tour, if that's okay?"

Sela reluctantly walked over to the door, which stuck a little. It had been so long since she'd opened it.

Sable sprang off the bed and trotted into the room ahead of her, saying over his shoulder, "Remember, familiars are confidants. Who am I going to tell your business to: that deranged cat in your living room?"

The second bedroom was a few degrees cooler than the rest of Sela's apartment. A bulb sparked and died as she switched it on, so they only had the late afternoon sun glowing through the windows for light.

A massive ebony table occupied the center of the room. Sela had been so proud when she'd saved enough to buy it from a local carpenter who, like her, was dabbling in work both practical and beautiful. Complementing the table along the length of the right-hand wall was an enormous black breakfront with a base that sported five neat rows of small square drawers reminiscent of an apothecary cabinet.

When Sela had still been making art, she'd filled the drawers of the breakfront with shells, stones, pressed flowers, and other natural elements, some of which remained scattered across the top of the table. But it had been a long time since she had made such efforts, what with student loan reminders coming with ever-increasing frequency and job after job occupying her every moment.

Beyond the table, mounted on the wall and framed by two windows, was the reason Sela had been so reluctant to enter the room: the triptych that had been her senior project. She remembered so clearly the day she had found the sprawling tree trunk that would become its three panels. She'd had to flirt with and pay a guy studying wood sculpture to help her unearth the trunk and cut it into three neat slices.

"You know, it's most likely rotted through," he'd told her, obviously more interested in the neckline of Sela's top than the task at hand.

"I'll pay you even if it turns out it is."

But her instincts about the tree trunk had been right, and three beautiful panels without any evidence of rot were the end result. Sela had begun her work with a kind of reverence: this was her first foray into a piece that was entirely natural, without the familiar stretched and ready canvas beneath her hands.

"Maiden, mother, crone," Sable murmured as he regarded the triptych now. He'd leapt up onto the ebony table and was tracing every woven branch, every twist of sand on the panels with pensive amber eyes.

His words brought back echoes of chants recited by her childhood coven, the laughter of girls ringing in Sela's ears as she recalled sneaking out into the night to gather stones and flowers; lighting candles and incense in Kendra's basement as they passed around ceremonial cakes rich in spices; Maria whispering ideas for new spells into Sela's ear as they held hands and called the corners under many a brilliant full moon.

She realized that yes, there was some continuity between those bright moments in her adolescence and what she'd communicated within the triptych. The vibrant stains she'd sealed into the wood, the applied mosaic of shells, sea glass, sand, and clay—all of it breathed a narrative, an evolution from youthful whimsy into certain power into eventual wisdom.

Real high hopes for a future that never came, she thought wistfully. *If only I'd known.*

"Sela," Sable turned, the table putting him eye level with her, "did you by any chance know you were a witch? I mean, you haven't practiced magick before, have you?"

"Of course not."

The tarot readings and homemade spells she'd said with her friends couldn't possibly count, she knew. Sable would probably never let her hear the end of it if she told him about what was really just the play of young girls. But part of her felt guilty, like she'd just lied to him, somehow.

Before she could say anything else, Sela's phone pinged and a sinking feeling rose in her chest as she read the words on the screen: *Where are you?? Is this even the right number?*

The dog-sitting appointment she'd booked for this afternoon had started twenty minutes ago, and it was completely across town.

"Shit." She turned and ran back through her bedroom, Sable close at her heels.

"What is it?"

"I am super-late to a job, so I need to ditch you for a bit."

"What do you *do*?" he asked, a whiskery eyebrow raised.

"A lot of things that I can't get into now—like I said, I'm late."

"Well, why are you late?"

Her brown eyes narrowed. "Because I was buying *somebody* a chalupa." But before Sable could snap back at her, she held up a hand. "Look, I've got to run. I'll be back within an hour or two. Do you think I can leave you alone with Pluto without the two of you killing each other?"

"I make absolutely no promises," Sable replied as she ran out the door, and she heard a low hiss coming from under the sofa.

"Glad we're all getting along famously," she muttered as she jogged down the stairs to her car.

Three

"I just don't understand what kind of a dog-sitter can't be on time."

Sela gave what had to be her fifth apology to her new client, Courtney, a woman whose house rivaled in its lavishness many of the architectural wonders Sela had been required to study in art history. And while Sela understood to an extent the woman's irritation with her lateness, she really didn't get how anyone could be so cranky with a three-car garage, original wood paneling, floor-to-ceiling windows, and a home media center that could probably pay off the entirety of Sela's student loans and then some.

While dog-sitting was usually one of the more relaxing jobs Sela relied on, she already sensed that watching Porter, Courtney's toy poodle, might be a different story. For one thing, the minute Sela had entered the house, he'd run up to her and peed on her leg like she was a human fire hydrant. And for another, this was just a consultation—she wasn't even getting paid for her time until the actual dog-sitting started the next day.

"I'm honestly a little reluctant to continue with our arrangement after this, Stella," Courtney went on, shaking her head as she lifted Porter for what Sela felt were unnecessarily mouthy kisses.

"This was an incredibly unusual day for me." Sela resisted the urge to correct Courtney for calling her by the wrong name, knowing she couldn't afford to lose even one job she had lined up for the week. "As I'm sure my references told you, I'm always punctual. This will not happen again."

"It had better not," Courtney sniffed. "Well, I suppose I should show you what you'll be doing. Come, Stella."

She did everything but snap in Sela's face like she was a dog herself, and Sela had to fight the urge to see if the woman's peroxide-bleached hair would come off with a good tug of her high ponytail.

Money, she thought to herself. *You need money.*

She was shown Porter's daybed as well as the two evening poofs that he needed available at all times for naps. Courtney pointed out multiple fancy water bowls and pet fountains, a thermostat under which was written the variety of climates appropriate for Porter, a trunk full of dog toys, and a particular book of poetry from which Porter liked to be read. There was also a walk-in closet devoted entirely to his wardrobe.

"Make sure you dress yourself to match Porter's jacket and leash whenever you're walking him," Courtney instructed Sela, who wasn't even sure she owned any clothes that would go with the rhinestone-studded ensembles in Porter's closet. "And you'll have to change outfits if your morning clothes don't also complement his evening ensemble. He should never wear the same outfit twice in one day."

As they made their way into the kitchen, which all but sparkled with its immaculate granite counters and polished tiles, Courtney continued, "Now, Mary Beth told me that you were very good about staying on top of all of Annabelle's dietary restrictions. I assume you'll do the same for Porter?"

Mary Beth was one of Sela's references, a frequent client of hers, and Annabelle was Mary Beth's seven-year-old daughter—her *human* daughter, who couldn't ingest wheat or dairy.

"Um, does Porter have any food allergies?"

Courtney smiled fondly at the dog in her arms. "No, he's much too smart for that." She glanced back at Sela sharply. "But he is on a strict rotation. I've labeled his food in the order he'll want to eat it."

The massive refrigerator contained an entire shelf devoted to sealed cans of dog food, which Sela wasn't about to tell Courtney probably didn't need to be kept cold.

"After you heat the food, make sure it goes back down to room temperature before serving him. Here are his breakfast and dinner bowls." Courtney gestured to two crystal bowls on a counter that were probably large enough for Porter to bathe in. "And Stella, don't mix them up. He won't eat a meal out of the wrong dish."

Sela blinked at the identical crystal bowls and nodded. "Of course."

By the time she was exiting Courtney's home after an hour and a half of meticulous instruction and several instances of being called the wrong name, Sela wasn't even sure she knew who she was anymore. Was she now Stella, caregiver to the world's pickiest toy poodle? Would anyone ever see Sela Glaser again?

"Stella!" Courtney called, and automatically, Sela turned around with a friendly wave to bid her new employer goodbye. But instead of a farewell in response, Courtney shouted with a warning frown, "If you expect to be paid, you won't be late again!" And she slammed the door.

Sela sat heavily in her car, wincing at the stink of Porter piss soaked into her jeans that became even more potent once she'd shut the door behind her. She had to take a few long breaths before she could even bring herself to turn the car on.

It wasn't that this was the worst she'd ever been treated on a job; it certainly wasn't one of her finer moments, but people had been meaner. But there were only so many years of stress and demoralization a person could take, and Sela was starting to feel that she was getting to the end of her rope. A witch? Not likely; Sable might be a talking cat or whatever, but there was nothing magical about her life at all.

The revolting smell of dog piss filling her nose, Sela glared at the perfect, six-bedroom miniature mansion she'd just left. Without really thinking about what she was saying, she muttered, "How's this for a spell? *What you've said and done this eve will break apart this lovely home; your sense of safety soon shall leave as days of devastation come.*"

A strong wind kicked up and sprayed pebbles from the road across the hood of Sela's car.

She shivered. *Where did that come from?*

But as she tried to understand why she'd said the words that had just come out of her mouth, movement a few houses down the street caught her attention.

There was a man wearing a brown leather jacket and jeans standing in the road. He was alone—no dog to walk or car to unload—and if Sela didn't know better, she'd think that he was staring straight at her. But there was no way he could see into her car from that far away, and it wasn't like she knew anyone other than Courtney and Porter in this neighborhood.

The wind blew again, a few errant leaves from the tree above now trailing down her windshield, and Sela shook her head.

"It's just all this witch shit messing with me," she explained to no one.

She pulled the car into a U-turn and headed back to Sable and Pluto, hoping they'd managed to not to destroy her apartment—or each other—while she'd been gone.

Four

"What in the name of hell happened to you?" Sable demanded the minute Sela got home.

"Dog-sitting job."

"That explains the smell, I guess."

She didn't even have the heart to snark back at him. "I'm going to hop in the shower before bed."

"Um, aren't you forgetting something?"

Sela blinked. "My dignity? Because that ship sailed a long time ago."

"Food," Sable told her, and when she didn't respond right away, he continued, "for yourself. And for me. And for that psychopath hiding under the sofa."

She smirked. "You want me to feed Pluto?"

"Even psychos don't deserve to starve to death."

Sela sighed. "Shower first, then I see what's in the fridge."

As had been her routine since she'd started juggling her many odd jobs, Sela mixed bergamot and eucalyptus oils in the aromatherapy burner on the sink, ran the shower at an almost burning temperature, and scrubbed away the day. She cleaned her hair with a lavender shampoo she'd cooked up herself, complete with coconut and rose oils to keep her long waves healthy (though as Sable had pointed out, what she really needed was a trim).

By the time she'd dried off and put on the pajama pants and tank top she was going to sleep in, she felt almost like herself again.

"I'm so glad you no longer smell like dog urine," Sable greeted her as she emerged from the bathroom.

Ignoring this, she told him, "I've got work pretty early and I need to knock out soon, so dinner is going to have to be quick." She browsed through the fridge, finding mostly salad dressings and other condiments, and some questionable cheese. "I hope you're okay with tuna sandwiches, because I apparently need to go grocery shopping."

"Tuna's fine," Sable replied, "but we should talk for a bit before you go to bed, especially since your Nascent Eve is going to be here before we know it."

She glanced over her shoulder in confusion as she set out a mixing bowl for the tuna. "My who-the-what now?"

Sable climbed onto one of the chairs in the dining nook of her kitchen, and Sela found she was strangely pleased that someone would actually be sitting across from her during dinner tonight—even if the food was far from glamourous, and even if the company was her prickly new familiar.

"Your Nascent Eve," Sable explained, "is the fancy term we use for the day your powers awaken."

"Isn't that just my birthday?"

"The Nascent Eve doesn't necessarily fall on the witch's birthday, though it's almost always around the start of her twenty-eighth year. Usually, you're looking at a few days to a week before or after. For some witches, it can even be a month, though that's less common."

Sela thought about this. "So one day soon, just…boom! I have powers?"

"There will most likely be indicators leading up to the 'boom,' as you so eloquently put it. And no crust on my sandwich, please."

She almost asked if he was serious, but didn't want to interrupt their discussion of her Nascent Eve, even if Sable was once again proving ridiculous about food. As Sela sliced the crusts off of his sandwich and moved them over to her own plate, a thought occurred to her.

"What if I have work?"

He raised a whiskered eyebrow. "Um, you do what most people do around their birthdays: call out sick."

As she set their sandwiches down and sat across from Sable, Sela suddenly remembered that her birthday would include the arrival of more than just her powers.

"Shit! I totally forgot: Natalie's coming to visit for my birthday."

"Natalie?"

She slapped a hand on her forehead. "My mess of a baby sister."

Sable looked surprised. "I didn't picture you with a sister. And she's a mess because…?"

"Ugh, I don't know." Sela considered how to explain Natalie. "So, I'm the mediocre one, right? And she's the one who bounces from glamorous job to more glamorous job, all while partying way too hard because it never catches up with her looks, somehow."

"How could anyone possibly have more jobs than you do?"

"Uh-uh, not like me." Sela shook her head. "I've got a bunch of steady hustles but I can't get anything full-time, no matter how hard I try. Natalie finds *careers*, even though she's in school. She gets all of these amazing internships and fellowships and whatever else it's called where you run around making important people coffee—unless, of course, you're really talented. And since she's really talented, she always ends up doing awesome work."

Sable munched on a bite of tuna sandwich. "I'm failing to see the issue here? It sounds like she's doing great."

Sela shrugged. "I mean, it seems to be great for the ten seconds she decides to stay in the job, until it's time to move somewhere else because she's bored, I guess? Or, you know, she's slept with the boss—whichever happens first."

"Ouch." Sable winced. "Remind me never to ask what you really think of me."

"I'm not slut-shaming my sister, okay? I just hate how the worst kind of people always seem to find their way into her heart, and then once they're done with her, she has to make a sharp turn in a completely new direction because she can't handle the loss."

Sela remembered years before, when Maria had pulled her aside after one of their classes and asked, "Is everything okay with your sister?"

They'd been in their senior year of high school, and Natalie in the sixth grade.

"What? Why, what's wrong?"

Maria hesitated, frowning. "Look, I know Natalie was being bullied by those girls about her weight earlier this year, but...well, you know my cousin Elias is in her class, right?"

"Yeah?"

"He told me that she's been hanging around this kid who, you know, kind of moves a little fast for an eleven-year-old. Like, *fast* with the girls in the grade."

Sela hadn't known what to do or say. The idea that her baby sister, who was still so young, might be involved with a boy hadn't ever crossed her mind.

"Hey, I didn't mean to upset you," Maria said, putting an arm around her. "Look, we can work a spell later, maybe get her to calm down a little."

"She's my sister. I don't want to do spells on her; I just don't know what to do."

What she had done was confront Natalie about it, and that had not gone well at all.

"Sela, it's none of your business!" her sister had shrieked when she'd brought up the boy on their walk home from school that day.

"Really? Because you're my little sister, and I think it's totally my business." She shook her head. "Why are you doing this, Nat? Is this about what those girls have been saying? Because you know, they're just mean and jealous—you're prettier than any of them."

She'd been speaking from the heart, too. Sela had always thought that her little sister had won all of the genetic prizes to be had in their family. Unlike Sela's own unruly auburn hair, Natalie's strawberry-blonde silk fell easily to her waist. She had a dazzling smile, glittering green eyes, a melodically sweet voice, and she'd somehow been spared the freckles that dusted Sela's own nose and cheeks.

But this wasn't what Natalie saw in the mirror, apparently. "You don't know anything, Sela! Look at you! You have, what, zero percent body fat? You don't know what it's like to be short and fat and…disgusting!"

Bursting into tears, Natalie ran ahead, and Sela didn't have the heart to run after her. She saw that her sister was beautiful, but had no clue how to get Natalie to believe it. If anything, she'd just made things worse.

Now, Sable said, "Well, I can't comment on your sister since I have yet to meet her. But just what about being a really gifted artist makes you the mediocre one in your family?"

She smiled, tearing up a bit at his words. "I would've thought that you'd say being a witch is what makes me special."

Sable shrugged. "I can't speak to that, either. You haven't come into your powers yet. For all I know, you're going to be a terrible witch."

Moment over. She could've slapped him. "Wow. Thanks."

"Hey, I'm here because you're getting powers. There's nothing in the rule book that says you're going to be any good at using them."

Her phone buzzed her bedtime reminder alarm, and Sela said, "I think that's pretty much all of this conversation I need for now." She started gathering dishes and putting out food for Pluto.

"So, where am I sleeping?" Sable asked.

"I didn't think of that. Did you want to take the couch?"

He let out a short bark of a laugh. "I'm pretty sure that will further antagonize your pet demon. And despite the fact that he's my evolutionary inferior, I can respect his territory—his scent is all over that sofa."

"Okay…"

"Could I maybe take the room you don't currently use?"

Sela regarded him for a long moment. "You really liked the triptych, I guess."

"Not only that, although as I said: you're quite talented. The room also has a lot of your lingering generative energy from when you were using it for creative purposes. Hanging out in there will help me get more in touch with you on a magickal level as we get closer to the Nascent Eve."

Sela shrugged. "Well, do you need anything? A blanket? Pillow? I don't have much in my closet, but I'm sure I can find something."

"I wouldn't say no to a folded blanket to make that table more comfortable."

Sela found a plush throw and set it on the table in the second bedroom. "I'm going to leave the doors between rooms open to make it easier for you to get to the bathroom. You…do use the toilet, right?"

He glowered at her, gritting his teeth. "Not. A. Cat."

"Of course." She rolled her eyes, not bothering to hide her fatigue. She liked her familiar well enough, but Sable's prickliness was too much for Sela this late in the day. "So, it'll be there if you need it, and I'm going to bed."

"Sela?" he called after her as she left the room for her own. "Yeah?"

"Could you maybe leave the seat up for me?"

Five

Before climbing into bed, Sela opened her window as she usually did to let the warm late summer breezes help her relax. And, as usual, the combination of the August night air and her exhaustion after another day of running from job to job led her right to sleep.

On this night, however, Sela began to dream.

In the dream, she was walking down a vaguely familiar alley. It took a moment or two for her to recognize it as the passageway around the corner from a shop where she bought many of the ingredients for her handcrafted soaps and candles.

The dream alley was impossibly long and the atmosphere above it hazy, illuminated in a shade somewhere between lavender and slate grey. Sela stumbled a little on a crack in the pavement, and when she glanced down to find her footing, she saw clothes the likes of which she had never owned.

A midnight blue skirt flowed from her hips to the ground, and she was surprised to find the lower part of her midriff bare. Dream or no dream, Sela was about to judge herself for sporting such a throwback style, but then she noticed the gauzy chiffon white blouse she wore above the skirt, with split sleeves slit so that her arms emerged from soft fabric that fell like giant petals someone had fashioned as wings.

Sela.

She turned at the sound of her name, but found nothing beyond endless alley behind her. Facing forward again, she saw Sable—but he was more than Sable. Sela seemed to see him as a cat, the only form in which she knew him, but at the same time, he was much larger than a cat. The shadow he cast was as long as her own and there was nothing feline about it.

"Was that you?" she asked him.

He shook his head, concern filling his face.

Sela.

The voice sounded again, obviously not coming from Sable. Sela started down the alley, her familiar at her side.

She felt a round weight in her left palm. It had the dimensions of a handball, but was much heavier. When she lifted the object, she found a dark blue sphere glittering in her hand.

"Blue goldstone?" she murmured, and Sable glanced at her with suspicion in his eyes. She felt an inexplicable guilt, as though she had deceived him in some way without even realizing it.

Sela.

She once again turned to look into the distance behind her, seeking the source of the voice. Deep in the haze, she could just make out the silhouette of a man. Sela knew she'd seen him before, but she couldn't think of where or when. She felt oddly cold under his gaze, as though there were something very wrong with how he regarded her.

When she turned to face forward once more, she found the path she and Sable had been walking was no longer empty but filled with people; people, and what seemed to be an assortment of animals. They were also somewhat hazy, but closer than the man who had been watching her.

Three of the humans seemed to be men, and the other two, women. The animal forms belonged to a rat, a panther, two tall and slender dogs, and a huge bird that was crowned and blue like a peacock but without the signature tail. Sela knew that, like Sable, the animals both were and weren't what they appeared.

Sable put a paw on her leg to get her attention. He gestured to the right-hand wall of the alley, where a great slab of mirror emerged from the brick.

Sela barely recognized herself. In addition to the fluid skirt and ethereal blouse, her hair was shorter than she'd ever dared to wear it, cropped and feathered in a bold, stylish manner. Her makeup was flawless and she wore a confident smile she had never before seen on her own face. She was barefoot, and a serpentine rose gold anklet made its way in a loose spiral up to the middle of her calf.

The sphere was still in her left hand, but the reflected orb within the mirror pulsed with the light of stars and moons, as though she were holding galaxies. Sela's right arm was pointing straight out to the side, dramatically aimed at the figure of the man who followed in her wake. Draped over the fingers of that hand was a sparkling tangle of the thinnest chains she'd ever seen, forming a delicate web.

Forcing her gaze from the spectacle in the mirror, she found nothing in her right hand but a thin journal. As she brought it closer, she recognized the grey leather tome she had received as a birthday gift many years before, the volume that would be her adolescent book of spells, potions, and charms. Its pages fluttered against her grasp as a strong wind tore down the alley.

Sela.

Back in the mirror, a young man stood on Sela's left who she somehow recognized as Sable. He looked afraid, his gaze cast at the alley behind them as it was reflected in the glass.

The haze around them was thickest where Sable's eyes rested, but all Sela could see were the reflections of the people and animals gathered to their left and the lone man silently staring at her from their right. There was something further in the distance that she could not make out. It shouldn't have been so far away; the alley was narrow and its bricks should have lay close behind them.

Sela scrutinized the mirror, trying to glean what it was that called her name over and over again…

But by the time she'd recovered from the early morning alarm shattering her deep sleep, the visions from the alley mirror were fading, and her memory of all she'd witnessed fell into the obscurity of her retreating dream.

Six

After getting up at the crack of dawn to walk Porter (who Sela was certain had no clue that his jacket and leash matched her own clothes), she went across town to baby-sit Ashton, a little boy who was being homeschooled until he recovered from a series of invasive surgeries. While she wasn't big on babies, Sela liked kids, and Ashton was fun even by six-year-old standards.

"Hey, buddy," she greeted him when she arrived.

For his part, Ashton responded with a pretty epic monster face and accompanying roar.

Sela tugged at her own cheeks. "I've got to stretch for a bit before I take you on, but I'm definitely going to win today's monster contest."

"I don't think so," Ashton replied in a growly voice.

Angela, Ashton's mother, gave Sela a quick hug followed by her usual volley of apologies. "You're a lifesaver, Sela! I can't believe my boss switched my shifts at the last minute again. I'm so sorry I didn't give you more notice."

"Really, it's not a problem," Sela assured her. "You called me Monday. That's more notice than I usually give myself for …life."

Angela gave a laugh as she adjusted her scrubs. "Okay, I've got to run." She gestured to a small stack on the kitchen table. "All the work for today's math lesson is here. There's a snack on the top shelf of the fridge if he gets hungry, you can eat whatever you'd like, and Kris will be home to relieve you in two hours. You guys going to be okay?"

"I'm going to win monster face!" Ashton declared.

His mother kissed him on the head. "Lessons first, then monster faces. You do everything Sela says—if I hear about one problem from you, no shows after dinner tonight."

"We'll do great," Sela promised. "Thanks, Angela."

"Thank *you*! You're the best!" And she was out the door.

They started on Ashton's math assignment. Sela had to give the kid credit; she figured if she'd had to stay home from school at his age, she wouldn't have handled it nearly as well.

There had been a couple of weeks during which Maria had disappeared from classes when they were in the ninth grade, Sela recalled. Her friend hadn't said much other than to claim she wasn't feeling well, and whenever Sela had gone to drop off homework, it was Maria's mother who answered the door.

"Hey, Mrs. Gonzalez," Sela had greeted her the first day, forgetting Maria's mother had changed her name when she'd remarried.

"It's Mrs. Sullivan, remember, Sela?" She'd offered a tight smile and glanced nervously over her shoulder, which told Sela that Maria's stepfather was probably somewhere in the house.

"Right—sorry, Mrs. Sullivan."

"Not a problem, sweetie. Are those Maria's notes?" She reached out a shaky hand to take them from Sela, and some of the papers slipped to the ground between them. "Oh, I'm sorry. I'm so sorry."

"Don't worry, Mrs. Sullivan."

Sela immediately bent to gather the papers. She knew she should make the interaction quick; whenever Maria's stepfather was around, her mother became a different person. Her cheeks lost their rosy glow, and her bright blue eyes, nothing like Maria's dark-brown gaze, almost seemed to fade. She wouldn't use any of the Spanish words Sela had learned simply by spending time at their house, either. It was as though something would temporarily leave the woman, taking both the language and her laughter with it.

"Thank you for bringing her work, Sela." There was gratitude and something else in Mrs. Sullivan's hushed tones, an apology that went beyond regret over a few dropped papers.

"Is she coming back to school soon?"

In response, Sela received something that was part head shake, part shrug. "Thanks again, honey." And the door closed in Sela's face.

When Maria had finally come back to school, she was almost as tight-lipped as her mother had been about her absence.

"You feeling better?" Sela had asked a little warily when they met up during lunch.

Her friend wasn't wearing her signature dramatic black eyeliner and mascara, and her thick, dark-brown curls were pulled back into a bun instead of styled. Her curves were hidden under a baggy sweatshirt and long black jeans.

"I've got something for you. Come on."

Maria led her out of the cafeteria and into an empty classroom, careful not to attract the attention of any passing teachers or administrators. Once they'd sat down, she'd pulled a thin grey book from her backpack and handed it to Sela.

"What's this?"

"I've been saving it for your birthday, and I think you should hold off on blessing it until then. It can be your Book of Shadows." Maria's grin reached her eyes, and a ghost of her usual self warmed her demeanor back to what Sela was used to from her best friend.

Sela had carefully looked over the journal that rested in her hands. It was soft leather and an unusual shape: a perfect square, twelve inches by twelve inches, not too thick, filled with beautiful artist's paper. It seemed almost like a sketchbook, given the dimensions and how it lay flat when Sela opened it. But her friend was right: it was the perfect size and shape for a witch's Book of Shadows.

Overwhelmed, she began, "You didn't have to—"

"No, Sel," Maria cut her off. "*You* didn't have to stop by my house every day when I was too shitty to come downstairs and say hi. It meant a lot."

Sela shrugged. "You would've done the same if I was sick."

Maria nodded, not saying anything for a minute. Then she smiled again. "You like it, don't you?"

"I love it! I've always wanted a Book of Shadows, but nothing ever felt right." She held the tome to her heart. "I'll put it away until August so we can bless it together."

They hugged tightly, and Maria whispered in Sela's ear, "Happy four-months-early birthday, sister witch."

"GROOOAARRRR!" Ashton bellowed mightily now, baring his teeth and turning his hands into claws as he crossed his eyes in one of his most impressive monster faces.

"Welp, that's a way to get my attention," Sela laughed, shaking memories of the past away as she tried to muster up an equally silly face.

As much as hustling a gazillion different jobs at once was more of a challenge than she'd ever wanted, she could think of worse ways to spend a Thursday morning than with Ashton. Even her midday walk with Porter was pleasant enough. He wasn't such a bad dog—he hadn't peed on her since the day before, so Sela decided to give him the benefit of the doubt and attribute that act to a bit of stranger-danger. And she loved being outside this time of the year: late summer was delicious, with its long, hot days and warmth that blew through the night, promising fall was just around the corner.

Although she had two more tutoring jobs scheduled for later that evening, as well as another stop over at Porter's, Sela managed to squeeze in a quick trip to the store so she could make a decent dinner for herself and Sable.

"I'm back!" she called as she came into the apartment with her grocery haul.

"Welcome home." Sable waved to her from the dining nook in the kitchen.

Pluto came out to greet her, remembered his nemesis, and started to hiss and growl.

Sable barked at him, "Fucking really?" in response to which the cat once again resumed his place under the sofa.

"We probably need to figure that out," Sela sighed.

"You could always find a nice home for him somewhere that isn't here," Sable suggested. His nose twitched. "Is that food? Because all I've had today was some of that cheese you had in the fridge, and it was...questionable."

"I hope you like sweet potato casserole," she replied. "It's going to last us into the weekend."

She was sure her familiar would complain about having to eat the same thing for several days, but instead, she learned that sweet potato was actually one of Sable's favorite foods. Apparently, they had more in common than she'd thought.

They talked about their respective days. While she'd been at work, Sable had apparently read one of the novels that had been gathering dust on her bedside table for months. In the midst of him spoiling half the plot, Sela's phone rang.

"Hey!" Natalie's cheerful voice rang out against a chaotic background clamor that Sela guessed was a rave of some kind.

"Hey, what's up?" Sela tried not to shout into the phone, though the noise made her want to raise her voice against it.

"Sela, I am beyond excited to see you next week! I miss you so much!"

Sela, who from the time she'd answered the phone had been trying to think of a believable excuse to get her sister to cancel her visit, smiled in spite of herself. "I really miss you, too."

"I can't wait to catch up!"

"Yeah, um, about that…"

Natalie immediately asked, "What's wrong?"

Sela felt her stomach drop. She knew Natalie would be more than disappointed if she cancelled now.

"No, nothing," she tried to backtrack, cursing herself and wondering how the hell she was going to hide a talking cat from her baby sister.

"It didn't sound like nothing." Natalie might be many things, but oblivious wasn't one of them. "Did you not want me there?"

"No!" Sela yelped, worried as she always was about the emotional state of her sister. "I…it's just that I'm having trouble getting out of work on Thursday. You know, so I can pick you up from the airport."

Relieved laughter filled her ear. "God, Sela! You're always so fucking serious! I thought you were canceling on me. Don't even worry about it—I'll get a cab."

"Thanks." Sela shook her head, annoyed at her own lack of resolve, but also happy that her sister who she loved so much would soon be bouncing around her typically lonely apartment. "That would be a huge help."

"Listen," Natalie went on above the ever-increasing din in the background, "I'm with some people now, so I've got to go. But I'm so psyched! Can't wait to see you!"

"Same here."

"I love you, Sela!"

"Love you too, Nat."

After the line was dead, Sela stared down at the phone. How was she going to handle next week? Should she bring up the whole witch thing? Was she even allowed to tell anyone about it? And how badly would Natalie freak out when she found out her big sister was going to sprout magickal powers at any moment?

Sable, who had been obviously and unabashedly eavesdropping on the entire conversation, casually remarked, "You know, you could always tell her you've gotten a second cat."

Sela blinked at him. "A second cat?"

"It would probably be easier than trying to explain me. I mean, you're not going to tell her you're a witch and then not be able to prove it because you've got no powers yet. Although, who knows? By then, you might."

"We need to talk more about this Nascent Eve thing," Sela told him. "But thank you."

"For what?"

"For giving me the perfect excuse to tell Natalie. She'll just assume I'm turning into a sad cat lady. And that makes sense."

He sighed. "You know, after you get your powers, we should work on your confidence. You need to be a little kinder to yourself."

"This from someone whose first words to me were about how shitty my car is."

"Um, excuse me: my first words to you were to correct your assumption that I was a filthy, garbage-eating raccoon."

"So, what's going to happen on my Nascent Eve, exactly?" Sela asked innocently, pretending she hadn't heard him and passing over some mashed sweet potato to stave off any further bickering.

Sable seemed content to accept the peace offering. "You and I will perform three rituals," he said between bites. "The first is your acceptance of your powers, the second secures our bond as witch and familiar, and the third allows you to begin spellcraft."

"Hmm." Sela thought this over as she started blending herbs into the softened butter for the casserole. "I have to accept my powers? I don't just...I don't know, poof?"

"It's always 'poof' and 'boom' with you," he complained. "Witchcraft isn't compulsory; you have to choose to take it up."

"What about the second thing you mentioned? Our bonding moment, or whatever?"

"As I said, the emphasis throughout the Nascent Eve rituals is pretty consistently on choice. So, just as you have to accept your powers, you also have to accept me as your familiar. And in turn, I accept you as my witch."

"I wonder if that's ever a problem," she said teasingly, but Sable grew serious at her words.

"You'd be amazed."

"What do you mean?"

"A witch and a familiar are fated for one another. There's no audition process—if a witch rejects a familiar, she doesn't get another one. It would be akin to rejecting a soulmate."

"Is that also true if a familiar rejects a witch?"

He nodded. "We don't really have other options, though there are those who try to seek them out..." His expression turned dark as he drifted into thought.

Sela furrowed her brow in confusion. "What does that mean?"

Sable took another bite of sweet potato and said brusquely, "I don't want to talk about it."

What's up with that? she wondered, making a mental note to bug Sable about the topic at a later time. *Maybe he's less prickly when he's drunk.*

"Can I ask what happens if a witch just rejects her familiar and leaves it at that? Hypothetical question," she added quickly, pushing some more sweet potato at him.

"It's a good question," he told her. "A complicated one, actually. See, the witch would have to reject her familiar during the Nascent Eve for her to remain a witch. Your powers are latent, but the familiar's arrival signals that it's time for them to wake. If you decided you didn't want anything to do with your familiar before your Nascent Eve, any potential for magick would eventually fade and you'd just continue your life as an ordinary human."

"No thanks."

"Once our bond is sealed during the second ritual, we can't reject one another. So, the only way it's possible for a witch to reject her familiar is for her to do so immediately after she accepts her powers, but before the third ritual, her passage into spellcraft."

"Well, what does that mean?" asked Sela. "That she just can't do spells?"

"First, it's an incredible betrayal." Sable's eyes were somber now. "There is no worse experience for our kind than to be rejected by our fated witch. The humiliation and the grief would be incomparable to anything I can think of."

"Dude, don't worry about me," she told him. "I've already come to terms with the fact that I'm stuck with your snarky ass."

He smiled at her affectionately, his tail flicking the air in a manner she'd come to recognize as contented. "Well, in this hypothetical, there's also great risk to the witch. Any who would choose to reject her familiar condemns herself to an ineffective and downright dangerous magickal existence."

"Because she isn't able to engage in spellcraft?"

"She can try," he snorted derisively. "But the spells won't work, at least not in the way she intends. It's a lot like those folktales where trickster figures grant wishes, and the wishes always turn out to be some kind of a nasty trick."

"So, all of this emphasis on choice," Sela reflected, "is kind of a crock of shit."

"It's not." Sable shook his head. "To choose to be a witch grants you a life that you would never have otherwise. It's a choice like none you've ever been given and none you'll likely receive again." That same dark cloud seemed to roll across his eyes, and he muttered, "After all, none of us ever ask to be born."

Before Sela could pester him further, a timer went off telling her to put the casserole in the oven. She let herself forget their conversation for the moment, making sure everything had gone into the baking pan before hauling it onto the top rack.

As she shut the oven door, she reflected on all she'd just learned from her familiar. *This should work out. We're already a good team, and how different are spells from casseroles, at the end of the day?*

Seven

With Sable for company and plenty of odd jobs to keep her occupied, the weekend flew by, as did the start of the following week. Sela got so invested in balancing work and having a friend at home that she almost forgot she was about to become a witch—until, of course, she remembered that "friend" was a not-cat familiar. But a strange normalcy took hold of her days, and cleaning the apartment in preparation for Natalie's visit seemed to be the most exciting thing on the horizon for the time being.

That was until Thursday morning, when Sela groggily blinked awake while it was still dark outside. Her clock read 4:53 a.m., and it took her a second to realize that what had woken her was the overwhelming smell of flowers. She sat up grumpily, too sleep-dazed to understand much beyond the fact that she was up more than two hours before she actually needed to be.

Then, in the faint light of very early morning, she found she could make out just enough of her bedroom to realize that something was different.

"What the fuck…Sable! Fuck! Sable, get in here!"

He ran into her room, cussing up a storm himself (apparently, another thing they had in common was that neither of them were morning people). "Sela, what the actual—oh, okay. I see why you shouted."

Sable jumped onto the bed as Sela was climbing off of it, switching on the lamp that sat on her bedside table. A sharp gasp escaped her as she surveyed her room.

It was filled with flowers, blossoming from twisted vines that seemed to extend everywhere. Sela recognized a rich variety of plants, some of which she'd used to make soaps and aromatherapy blends, and others she'd never known to grow in her part of the world: burgundy passion flowers, purple wisteria, delicate blue pea blossoms, clematis in every color imaginable, and giant climbing roses. They'd wrapped themselves around the legs of the furniture, thrown their blooms and leaves along the windowsills, and were even climbing haphazardly up the walls.

And, as Sela's brain woke up more, she realized that the source of the vines was apparently the space underneath her bed.

"Sable, *what* is happening?"

"Breathe, Sela," he told her. "I mentioned that there would be signs of your latent magick as your Nascent Eve drew closer."

"Signs?" She gaped at him. "*Signs*, Sable?"

He smoothed his fur at her sarcastic echoes of the word, saying snippily, "Yes, signs—indicators that your powers are going to wake from their dormant state."

"A sign is a dove," she said, her voice growing increasingly shrill. "A sign is a full moon, or a flower—*one* flower—that falls at your feet when you're walking down the sidewalk. This...this...little shop of horrors is not a sign, it's a fucking downpour!"

"Well, if it makes you feel any better, it's not a *bad* sign."

"I can't even begin to deal with this." She rubbed both hands over her face, still exhausted from the catering job that had brought her home just a few hours before.

NASCENT WITCH
51

"This room is full of magickal life," Sable went on. "These are strong, healthy flowers and vines. It suggests that you're going to exhibit very generative and creative magick. You may end up having some talent with plants."

She slumped back onto the bed next to him, glaring at the generative and creative flowers that were all over the fucking place. "Do you know that I could have slept for another two hours?"

Sable was ignoring her to study the plants with what seemed to be genuine fascination. "Or you know, this could mean you're a healer. I mean, healers usually have sweeter dispositions than you do, but plants do often have an affectionate spot for them. Or maybe—"

"Sable!"

"What?" His fur puffed out a bit. "Why are you shouting at me? You already shouted to wake me up, and now I'm up and I'm looking at what you woke me up for. What do you want from me?"

"I'm sorry," she moaned miserably, falling forward into her rumpled comforter. "I've only had three hours of sleep."

"I'll remind you that I wait up for you each night and we went to bed at the same time," he huffed. "I'm not exactly running at full capacity, either."

"I know, I know." She pouted at the mess of vegetation in her room. "Why are they coming from under my bed? That's super-fucking creepy."

"Um, because up until a few moments ago, *you* were in your bed. They're not coming from the bed. They're coming from you."

She sat back up in alarm. "Is this going to happen while I'm at work?"

"Doubtful. At night when you sleep, you're uninhibited. The flowers probably came forth because you were in a relaxed state."

"Probably?"

He rolled his eyes at her. "You can go to work. Just, you know: don't be surprised if there are a few more signs as we get closer to your birthday."

"Really? There's a fucking garden in my bedroom that I apparently conjured while I was unconscious, and you want me to contain my surprise if more of this shit happens?"

He curled up at the foot of her bed. "Listen, I thought you had two or so hours left to sleep. If I keep you company, will you shut up so we can rest a little longer?"

Switching off the bedside lamp, Sela climbed back under the covers, silently grateful for Sable's presence. "As long as these plants don't try to kill me in my sleep."

"Get some rest, chickenshit."

"You too, fake cat."

Eight

Sela spent the better part of an hour trying to make her bedroom look less like the garden department of a Lowe's superstore. She'd ended up getting out of bed early, anyway; shockingly, it was really difficult to sleep amidst a bunch of magickal flora one had unintentionally summoned during the night.

"At least somebody around here is getting a little rest," she grumbled loudly at the door to the second bedroom. At some point, Sable must have gone back into his room because he was nowhere to be seen when she woke up.

As she was downing coffee in the kitchen, Sela started writing herself a list of things to pick up in preparation for Natalie, who would be arriving that evening. "Peanut butter…extra towels…back-up toothbrush…plenty of wine, so I can knock myself out hard enough to not make more magickal flowers…"

Pluto, who had taken advantage of Sable's momentary absence to leisurely traipse across a coffee table, pulled a typical cat move and knocked over a small bowl of beads in his path. As Sela looked up from her list to tell Pluto off for making a mess and proving Sable right about the feline species, she found that what had been ordinary beads were now small chunks of crystal quartz scattered all across the wooden floorboards.

And every piece of quartz was glowing.

"*Sable!*"

Despite Sela having bellowed loudly enough that Pluto returned to his sanctuary beneath the sofa, Sable did not respond. Sela tore through her room and burst into the second bedroom, shouting, "What is wrong with you?! I need help, the living room—"

She froze and stared. Stretched out on the table, his head resting on the blanket she'd given Sable to sleep on, was a completely naked man. His skin was deep russet and he was leanly muscular, though not very tall. His head was a mess of thick, golden-brown curls, adorned with many silver strands that were clearly not indicators of age, since he seemed to be Sela's peer. Upon her arrival, he blinked, revealing large eyes of two different colors under a thick set of lashes: one amber and one slate grey.

"Oh," he said with Sable's voice as he sat up, looking down at himself with surprise on his face.

Sela took a step back, about to bolt from the room and the apartment, if necessary.

"No, Sela, wait! It's me!" He held his hands up in a calming gesture. "I would've warned you, I just…didn't think this would happen so soon."

"Sable?" she managed, disbelief in her voice.

He nodded and shrugged, smirking a little, so that any lingering doubt as to who he was quickly evaporated from Sela's mind.

"Sable! What the actual fuck? I come in here because there is glowing quartz all over the living room, and you're—"

"Quartz?" He jumped down off the table and made as if to go investigate the living room. Sela spun around, feeling her face turn bright red. "Sela?" he asked, sounding puzzled.

"Dude, you are like super-naked right now."

"Oh, right," came his reply, and she knew that if she'd been facing him, she would have seen his heterochromatic eyes rolling at her. "Humans and bodies—always such a big deal. Never mind that you and I slept in the same bed last night. Is this better?"

Sela peeked over her shoulder and saw that the blanket was now wrapped around Sable's waist like a towel. She turned to face him again and replied testily, "Yes, it's better. You know what else? You're *fucking human*, Sable, and whatever explanation you're going to give me needs to happen in under ten minutes because I have to get to work." She threw up her hands. "I mean, god! How did this even happen? Are you just a person? A person who has been pretending to be a cat so you can get out of paying half the rent?"

"First of all, let's remember that all events preceding the Nascent Eve are catalyzed by the witch and her dormant powers," he began, crossing his arms. "That includes the transformation of the familiar. So technically, the fact that I'm in human form right now is *your* fault."

"*My* fault? Are you fucking kidd—"

"On top of that," he cut her off, his agitation growing to match hers, "if you think I choose to walk around looking like a domesticated animal I loathe so that I can live in your home, eat whatever you choose to feed me, and put up with that abomination you keep in your living room, you're a lot more self-centered and a lot less intelligent than I've been thinking you are."

"But I didn't—"

"And I resent you saying I'm suddenly a person. Familiars are people; just because we spend stretches of our lives looking like more simple animals doesn't detract from us as individuals."

She stared at him for a long minute. He was definitely still Sable—no one else could get so prickly after giving her the shock of her life.

Maybe I am being selfish, she suddenly thought. If she really had caused him to transform like this, then he did have reason to be annoyed with her. If things were reversed and his magick had turned her into a cat without warning, she'd probably kill him.

"All right," she breathed deeply, trying to calm herself. "I'm sorry—really. I would never mean to imply you're not a person, and I apologize that that's the first thing that came out of my mouth."

He nodded, not uncrossing his arms or giving up his martyred stance but offering a mumbled, "Apology accepted."

"But Sable, I don't understand all that's happening, and as ridiculous as it might sound, I do have the pressing, non-magickal problem of needing to be at work on time. Do you think I could get a quick explanation?"

"We need to prioritize a little here," he told her. "I have to get a look at the crystals in the living room before anything changes them. It might surprise you, but quartz is actually a lot more significant than me taking this form."

She shrugged helplessly as she followed him to the living room. "Of course, sure. Now-human you is clearly the secondary concern, because today, that totally makes sense."

Sable's eyebrows shot up when he saw the stones.

"What?" she asked nervously.

"It's…unusual," he murmured.

"The glowing, you mean?"

"No, that's actually not unusual." Sable walked the perimeter of the room, looking at the crystals from every angle. "It's more the magnitude…How did you say they ended up like this?"

"Pluto knocked over a bowl of beads on the coffee table."

His gaze moved sharply to her. "These crystals were just beads? They weren't crystals to begin with?"

"Well, yeah," she shrugged. "I mean, you turned into a human being this morning—are beads turning into quartz that much more special?"

He sighed, running a hand through his curls. "You're stuck on this, obviously. Look, Sela, this isn't the first time I've been in this form, and it won't be the last, so you'd better get used to it."

"Get used to it? What the hell is that supposed to mean?" She couldn't help gaping at him. "What, is this like your autumn suit or something?"

"Familiars always take human form during magickal milestones in our witches' lives," he explained, pretending not to hear her snarky tone. "This is the first time I've taken this form in years, and it's because your Nascent Eve is fast approaching, as I've said."

"Wait a minute," she narrowed her eyes at him, "if you knew this would happen, why would you not tell me?"

"I didn't know, exactly." He held up a hand once again to stay her anger. "I suspected—I mean, it usually happens—but I didn't know for sure."

A nagging suspicion pulled at her. "Why not?"

Sable looked up at the ceiling. "Well, when a witch isn't very…powerful or talented, sometimes there's kind of a glitch, and the familiar doesn't make the Nascent Eve transformation. I just didn't want to assume anything."

She set her hands squarely on her hips. "You thought I would be a shit witch."

"That's not true." He shook his head. "I just didn't know

either way."

If Sela had had more time to think about it, she would've been surprised that she was so hurt by Sable's omission. But with the time crunch she was under, all she felt was the hurt, and she lost the struggle to conceal it. "So what, did I pass this little test of power or whatever? I'm not going to embarrass you in front of all the cool familiars at school?"

"Sela," Sable began, and she could have kicked him for the sincerity in his face and the way it chipped away at her anger, "despite the fact that you are both overworked and underpaid, resulting in a persistent aura of crankiness, I am already very happy to be your familiar."

"Mm-hmm."

"And regardless of how your power manifests and what your talents prove to be," he continued, "I enjoy your company. I think we'll grow to be great friends in the years to come."

Perhaps it was because the tension in the room seemed to be fading, but Pluto chose that moment to come out from his hiding place beneath the sofa. He looked up at Sable and, being a cat who was generally friendly with any human guests, he proceeded to rub against Sable's legs, purring a request for affection.

"You must be joking," Sable said in disgust.

Sela giggled, earning a small smile from her familiar in spite of his repulsion for her cat. "Okay," she told him, glancing at her microwave clock, "all of this is happening really fast, but I'm going to try to deal, for both our sakes. I really do need to get to work—maybe later we can talk about why the crystal quartz is so interesting?"

"Works for me."

Sela started shoving her feet into her shoes and throwing keys and other essentials into her purse. "Also, there are some baggy sweatpants in my closet that will probably fit you, and feel free to grab a t-shirt or whatever—I'm sure you'll find something."

"You mean for when your sister arrives? I'm comfortable without clothes, otherwise."

"Shit!" She smacked a hand to her forehead. "Natalie's coming. What am I going to tell her? That cat lady excuse is obviously out the window."

"Um, that I'm a friend who also wanted to celebrate your birthday?"

"A friend. Right. Because I have so many of those."

"You know, I've been wondering: why is that?" Sable asked, genuine curiosity on his face. "I find your company enjoyable most of the time."

"I think you just answered your own question."

"Maybe you just answered it yourself," he shot back.

"Fine! You win, snark-fest over. So, what do we say— you're an old friend from college? Or a new friend I met online?"

"Online sounds better," Sable said. "That way if she remembers your friends from college, she won't wonder where I was."

"Great," Sela nodded, not feeling great at all but absolutely needing to head to work. "Can you do me a favor and just not be naked when she gets here?"

He grinned. "I can probably manage that."

"And could you maybe hide the flowers and the quartz? I'm so sorry to be asking all these favors; I just really need it not to look magickal when Nat gets here."

"Not a problem. But can I borrow some money for food before you go? I'm starving."

She dug into her bag and handed him a twenty. "There is

stuff I made for us in the fridge, you know."

Sable's grin widened. "If you had more than a cat-sized appetite for the first time in years, you'd want more than what's in the fridge."

"Meaning?" She raised an eyebrow, never having known Sable to have a cat-sized appetite since she'd met him.

"Meaning I don't think you're stocked up on ice cream or Thai food. Or rum."

"You know, we should figure out how to get you into human form more often. It sounds like the nights leading up to our Nascent Eve are going to be a party." As she opened the front door, Sela spun around. "Oh! Can you feed Pluto? I didn't get a chance."

Sable stared at her in disbelief.

"Come on!" she begged. "I'll…I'll come home with Thai food for dinner if you do!"

He sighed, looking longingly at the twenty. "That leaves more money for fancier rum and ice cream, I guess. Why is that combination so wonderful?"

"Thanks, Sable!"

As the door shut behind her, she could hear Pluto meowing plaintively for food, and Sable responding, "You should know that you are a disgusting, stupid beast and I resent that I'm about to play a part in keeping you alive."

Nine

Given that she had just manifested magickal flowers, then also manifested glowing crystals, and then found herself with a newly human familiar, Sela figured getting to work by the skin of her teeth wasn't such a bad thing. Was she usually a few minutes early? Sure. Did she usually have to deal with a talking-cat-turned-naked-man who exhibited a weird hankering for rum?

"Definitely not," she answered aloud as she started to get settled at Evelyn's desk. Evelyn was a receptionist for a dentist, Dr. Miller, and whenever she couldn't make it to work, Sela filled in for her.

"Uh, definitely not what?"

It took all of Sela's willpower not to jump right out of her skin. She was supposed to be the only one in the office—Evelyn always got in an hour before Dr. Miller to set up, and that hadn't been Dr. Miller's voice. As Sela turned to see who had spoken, she had to resist a second jump.

Standing behind her was the most attractive guy she'd seen in months, possibly years (aside from Sable earlier that morning, of course, but he wasn't on her list of eligible anything). He was tall and broad-shouldered, with cheekbones Sela herself would have killed for, skin that glowed with a warm summer tan, and a thick head of cropped black hair. And, appropriate for a man wearing a white dentist's coat in the middle of a dentist's office, he sported a set of dazzlingly perfect teeth, gleaming out at Sela from behind an easy, irresistible smile.

"Hi," he said, offering her a hand. "I'm Peter Cheng. I'll be filling in for Dr. Miller today."

"Dr. Cheng?" Sela echoed dimly, not sure how to get her brain function back to full capacity with this man who could've been a model smiling in front of her.

"Pete, please," he laughed, waving the palm he'd extended to let Sela know she hadn't actually shaken it yet.

"Oh!" She awkwardly grabbed his hand and shook, probably a little too vigorously as she tried to stop fantasizing about what looked to be super-soft lips (though now she had the additional problem of super-strong hands to avoid thinking about). "I'm sorry, I'm a little under-caffeinated at the moment. I'm Sela. I'm not actually the receptionist here; Evelyn is. I'm filling in for Evelyn for the next few days. I usually sub for her when she's away. I think she's at her daughter's wedding or something?"

Why don't you tell him your zodiac sign and your bra size while you're at it? she thought, wanting to kick herself in the head for this bout of verbal diarrhea.

"Sela," Pete repeated, and his smile widened. He was definitely the hottest guy she'd met in years. "That's lovely. Do you have a last name to go with that? Or do you moonlight as a pop star?"

Sela giggled nervously, despite the fact that he was the one who'd just made the dad joke. She cleared her throat in an effort to stop the laughter that was pitched somewhere between cheerleader on steroids and cartoon villain. "Sela Glaser."

"Well, nice to meet you, Sela." He let go of her hand. "So, do we have a full day ahead of us?"

"Oh," she said again, and she knew that if Sable had been

there, he would've thrown those glowing crystals at her for babbling so hard. "Right. Um, I'll check as soon as Evelyn's computer boots up. It usually takes a few minutes."

"Hey, no rush. I was setting up too when I heard you moving around up here. In fact," Pete glanced over his shoulder, "I'm about to get back to it—new office and all, I like to get my bearings. But I'll let you know when the coffee's done, okay?"

She flushed. "I'm so sorry. If I'd known you were going to be here, of course I would've made some already—"

"No criticism meant," he interjected kindly, and Sela wiggled her toes to make sure she wasn't melting. "I'm used to offices where the first person to arrive sets up the caffeine, and I got here early. Besides, you're in for a treat: my mom taught me to make a mean pot of coffee."

She nodded. *You can talk to the handsome man, Sela*, she thought to herself, disturbed that her inner monologue sounded a lot more like Sable than it should have. *Use your words with the pretty man, you awkward mess.* "Thanks, I'll look forward to it."

Pete turned to head down the hallway to the exam rooms in back, then added quickly, "I thought filling in here for the next few days was going to be kind of a drag, but…well, it really is nice to meet you, Sela."

Clenching her stomach against the butterflies that were suddenly all over it, and hoping they weren't manifesting the way the flowers and crystals had that morning, she managed a smile back. "Same here."

Pete disappeared down the hall, and Sela tried to get a hold of herself. Glancing at the small mirror Evelyn kept on her desk, she winced—hair still needed a good trim, tired eyes, no makeup, and she was about a month overdue for an exfoliating mask. Even her freckles looked like they needed coffee.

"Some witch," she muttered, being careful not to speak loudly enough for Pete to hear. "Can't even manage to look human."

As the computer continued to wake itself up, Sela dug around in Evelyn's desk, hoping the woman would forgive her stealing a bit of makeup. She figured it wouldn't be a big deal; Evelyn was the kind of person who would lick a tissue and use it to rub a smudge off a stranger's cheek, which she'd done to Sela the first time they'd met.

"Thank you, Evelyn." She began applying a caffeinated under-eye roller she'd found in the desk when a chill suddenly swept up her spine.

From the corner of her eye, Sela caught sight of someone in the lobby staring through the locked glass doors of the office. As she turned to get a better look, a flash of brown leather and the shadow of a body heading out to the parking lot were all she managed to glimpse. But even that brief moment jogged something in the back of Sela's mind.

Brown leather…a brown leather jacket…

Two distinct memories from the previous week slammed together as she realized where she'd seen the jacket before. The guy who'd been creepily following her around the bookstore just before she'd met Sable, and the man who'd been staring at her outside of Courtney and Porter's house: both of them had been wearing that same dated, beat-up looking jacket.

Had it been the same man?

Not entirely sure what she was doing, Sela shot up from the desk chair and tore out the entry of Dr. Miller's office, fumbling with the lock so that she could get back in once she was done doing whatever the hell her instincts were driving her to do. But when she finally got outside, all she found was an empty parking lot, heat rising visibly from the asphalt in distorting waves that were only perceptible if your eyes were carefully seeking something, squinting into the bright morning sun.

There was no sign of a man anywhere.

Sela retreated back into the air-conditioned office, a little shaken. This might be nothing—a coincidence, a weird fashion throwback that was suddenly going to be in vogue for the fall. Why someone would want to wear leather in the heat of late summer other than to make a fashion statement was beyond Sela. As she continued setting up the desk and trying to make herself look passable, she pushed aside the nagging feeling that she was missing something, something important.

"Nothing a cup of coffee won't fix," she murmured, smiling in the direction of where she knew the handsome Dr. Pete Cheng was also setting up for his day. Weird coincidences notwithstanding, Sela had an extremely good-looking reason to want to do her best work.

Ten

"Hello, Dr. Miller's office, this is—"

"Sela! I'm in a cab almost at your place! Are you getting home soon? I can't wait to see you!"

"Natalie?" Sela anxiously glanced at the clock on Evelyn's computer. "I thought your flight wasn't getting in for another two hours."

"Well, we must have had a great pilot because I'm here! Can't you leave early?"

"I don't think so, Nat. It's just me and Pete here, and—"

"Hold up: who's Pete?"

Sela cleared her throat. "I mean, just me and Dr. Cheng."

"I thought you were working at a Dr. Miller's office," Natalie said slyly, a knowing note in her voice.

"I am." Sela silently cursed herself for giving her sister emergency contact information for the day. "But Dr. Miller is also at Evelyn's daughter's wedding, so Dr. Cheng is filling in for him."

"Uh-huh," Natalie replied, and Sela could actually hear the grin in her little sister's voice. "I'm guessing Dr. Cheng is young, single, and a lot better-looking than old Dr. Miller. Am I right?"

Sela rolled her eyes and gave in. She wasn't going to fool anyone, least of all Natalie, about how intensely she was swooning over Pete: Pete, who'd made the best coffee she'd ever tasted, and who smiled kindly at every person who came into the office; Pete, who had her practically pinching herself every few minutes to make sure she hadn't dreamt him up.

"Okay, you're not totally off the mark," she admitted to her sister.

"I guess I'll be staying in an empty apartment tonight!" Natalie said gleefully.

"Please," she snorted, "I'm not you!" But then Sela remembered her apartment was anything but empty. "Um, actually, I didn't get to tell you: I sort of have a friend staying with me at the moment."

"A friend?" Her sister's voice raised in excitement again, and Sela knew that if the cab driver had a popcorn machine, Natalie would've been downing the stuff about now.

"My friend Sable—you've never met him."

"Sela, I am actually scandalized. You're juggling a mystery hottie at home, behind the handsome Dr. Cheng's back?"

"Can you stop?"

"Are you kidding? I haven't had this much fun at your expense since you were in college!"

"Look," she told Natalie, "Sable's a little strange, so just don't get weirded out by him."

"What's that supposed to mean?"

"I don't know…" She tried to think of a way to explain her familiar without explaining him at all. "He doesn't get out much. We met online."

Natalie groaned. "Sela, if you want to meet guys, you know you don't have to pick up weirdos off the internet. I can always introduce you to someone. I know a lot of people who would love to date you."

"We're not dating," Sela said firmly. "He is a friend, and he needed a place to stay."

"Whatever you say, sis," Natalie answered in a voice that was nowhere near convinced.

At that moment, Sela became aware of Pete's presence coming up the hall. "Natalie, I've got to get back to work. I'll see you at home, okay?"

"I won't wait up," Natalie teased. "I'm sure you and the sexy Dr. Cheng have big plans to—"

Sela slammed down the phone, hoping the receiver hadn't been loud enough for her sister's voice to reach the incredibly sexy Dr. Pete Cheng, who was smiling down at her.

"So sorry about that," she told him. "My little sister's flight landed early. She's visiting me for a bit."

"Oh, so you'll be busy after work, then."

"Yeah. Well, I mean, no. Not necessarily, I mean—what?"

Sela stopped her relapse of verbal diarrhea to blink up at Pete. To her amazement, he seemed to be blushing slightly as he ran a quick hand through his short black hair.

"I was going to ask if you had dinner plans. I figure, Thursdays are usually quiet and maybe we could go somewhere nice without needing a reservation." He shook his head, and Sela realized that she was witnessing Pete's own version of nervously talking too much. "But of course, if your sister's coming, you'll want to spend time, and I'd never want to interrupt a family—"

"Are you asking me out?" she interrupted helpfully, grinning a little.

"Well, yeah." His blush deepened. "I swear I wasn't eavesdropping, but as I was coming up the hall I overheard you saying there was somebody who you definitely *aren't* dating, and I thought, maybe that meant you'd have time after work to grab an early dinner with me."

Sela knew that going to dinner with Pete was not a good

idea. Natalie was already in town, Sable was possibly rum-drunk, she wasn't sure he hadn't let Pluto starve to death, and she'd spent her morning conjuring magickal items without meaning to. She wasn't dressed particularly nicely, she was wearing minimal cosmetics that had been stolen from another woman, and she was pretty sure she needed to floss her teeth because she'd been foolish enough to get a sesame seed bagel for lunch. Dinner with Pete was in fact probably a bad idea: bad timing, bad outfit, and most likely bad decision to date a coworker, even a temporary one.

"My sister can get settled in the apartment without me for a bit," she found herself saying. "She'll probably be jet lagged, anyway."

Pete's eyebrows rose in pleased surprise. "Uh, really? I mean, so that's a yes?"

Sela laughed, and it didn't come out maniacally this time. "Yeah, that's a definite yes."

"Great!" Pete beamed at her, then cleared his throat, trying to play it cool several seconds too late, which only made Sela want to pull him towards her and see if those lips were as soft as they looked.

"Is it okay if we travel separately?" she asked, thinking: *Floss before dinner. Floss before dinner. You haven't had sex in how long?* "I need to make a stop beforehand. You know, just a quick errand."

"Yeah, of course." Pete nodded. "Do you like fusion? I know this great place that does French and Thai—"

"Oh, over on East Avenue?"

"You know it?"

"I love that place." She happily added to herself, *Thai means you get to pick up the food-bribe you promised your familiar this morning, too.*

The door to the office opened, and Pete's next appointment walked in. As he went in back to prepare, Sela quickly shot off a text to her sister: *Having dinner with Pete—won't be too late. You can rub it in my face when I get home. Love you.*

And when Natalie texted back several inappropriate fruit and vegetable emojis, she couldn't stop the grin that spread across her face. In spite of all the weird magickal shit, Sela could imagine far worse than a day that ended in dinner with a hot guy and a much-needed visit from her sister. And if Sable hadn't been a total hog about it, maybe there would be a little ice cream and rum waiting for her at home, too.

Eleven

"It's amazing that you know this place," Pete told her as they settled at their table for dinner. "I feel like whenever I mention it to people, they look at me like I've got three heads."

"I guess it's a well-kept secret, but I have no idea why," Sela laughed. "Between the rad na and that truffle thing they do for dessert, I've definitely pushed the limits of my stomach and my bank account here on several occasions."

No matter what Sable might have to say about Sela's trusty old Toyota, it had gotten her safely to the restaurant after providing her with one of her favorite lip glosses she'd thought she had lost (under the driver's seat) as well as a tube of emergency mascara (glove compartment, beneath a pile of plastic forks). She'd even had time to floss her teeth in the rearview mirror with one of the sample packs from Dr. Miller's office.

"So, tell me some more about yourself. When you're not covering for Evelyn, are you a receptionist at another office?"

Here we go, she thought.

Sela's first dates usually ended without proceeding to second dates for one of two reasons: either the guys she went out with were terrifying, or they found her lack of a conventional career path, well, terrifying. But she didn't want to bullshit Pete; there was this warmth about him that made her want to open up in ways she hadn't for a really long time. And part of opening up meant talking about how she was failing.

"I am…sometimes a receptionist elsewhere," she began, taking a sip of her Riesling as she tried to figure out how to explain her many jobs without seeming like a complete flake.

"Okay," he laughed. "And? I feel like there's a part two to that statement."

Maybe it was Pete's easy demeanor, or the wine, or the fact that she'd made lots of magick without even trying to that morning, but Sela felt suddenly and oddly less self-conscious.

"I am also sometimes a tutor, sometimes a camp counselor, sometimes a baby-sitter—also a dog-sitter, can't forget that. Um, what else? Waitress, holiday bookseller, catering staff, telemarketer—that one didn't last long, though."

"You like to keep things exciting, I guess?"

He's not running, she realized as she took in the dreamy smile that hadn't left Pete's face. *This isn't scaring him off. Huh.*

At that moment, their server came over to refill their water glasses, giving Sela a chance to think about what she wanted to say next, and she realized: she wanted to tell Pete the truth, the *real* truth. She was tired of letting happenstance write the narrative of who she was.

"Actually, I'm an artist doing what artists do to support their art until their art can support them."

"What kind of art do you do?"

"In college, it was more the kind of thing you would create for a gallery. But lately, I've been really into practical crafts. You know, soaps, candles, handmade journals—that kind of thing."

"You know how to make a candle?" He seemed genuinely amazed.

"Yeah, well, you know how to detect microscopic cavities

and eradicate them from inside people's mouths," she said, making Pete laugh again. "If anything, I should be the one who's impressed."

"Well, thank you for appreciating my special powers," Pete chuckled. "But if anyone at this table is doing something impressive that they don't teach you in school, I wouldn't say it's me."

Special powers? she thought, smiling. *If only you knew.*

Sela excused herself once their appetizers had been cleared, in part because she'd had nonstop water and wine for the past half hour, but also so she could see if her sister had ever texted in response to her message that she was leaving work. She frowned: nothing, not even a single eggplant emoji.

"That's weird," Sela muttered, putting her cell back in her pocket. "She's anatomically attached to that thing."

As she touched up her lip gloss in the bathroom mirror, Sela heard a commotion coming from the dining room.

Could that be Pete...?

She hurried back out, silently praying that her dreams of the first decent guy she'd dated possibly ever weren't about to be shattered.

The scene in the dining room was one of bizarre and recent chaos. A vase lay broken in two in the middle of the floor, water spilled and flowers scattered everywhere. A hush had come over the room as onlookers whispered at the spectacle over their meals, and Pete was off to the side speaking with their server, who was straightening her blouse, looking upset.

"What happened?" Sela asked as she approached them.

Pete was shaking his head. "This guy came in and just started flipping out! Do you—I mean, was somebody meeting you here or something?"

"What?" she asked in confusion. "No, why?"

Now their server spoke up. "The guy came in here and started asking me if I'd seen a young woman. I told him that like half the people in here are women, but you were the only one about our age, so I figured he might mean you and sent him over to your table." She cast her eyes apologetically towards Pete. "If I'd had any idea..."

He waved aside the apology. "How could you have known?"

"What did he look like?" Sela asked, thinking with concern that something catastrophic might have caused Sable to show up. But how would Sable have even known where she was? "I can't think of anyone who would've wanted to talk to me—I didn't even tell my sister where I was going."

Pete shrugged. "He was blonde, average height, about our age. I don't know, there wasn't anything remarkable about the guy, except...he was wearing this brown jacket."

A coldness slid up Sela's back. "A brown jacket?"

"Yeah, I noticed that," their server said. "It was leather— way too heavy for summer and super-beat up, too."

A beat-up, out-of-season brown leather jacket. *This must have to do with my Nascent Eve*, Sela thought. It was too strange, and the guy was showing up too often, enough for her to remember his presence even though he always seemed to appear randomly and at a distance. She wanted to tell Sable, but how could she describe a stranger who sort of seemed like he was following her? She didn't even know what the guy looked like, really.

"Sela? You okay?"

She blinked, remembering herself. "Sorry, I must be more tired than I realized. What was that?"

"I asked if you knew the guy."

Pete's eyes were apprehensive, and Sela could guess what

he was thinking, as it was a thought she'd had on many first dates herself: *Is this the part where you go from someone who seems nice to someone who's scary?*

"No." She put on her best poker face. "I was just thinking about whether he might be someone who had followed us from the office, but that doesn't sound like anyone we helped today."

"Definitely not," Pete agreed, his face full of relief as he was likely absolving her in his mind. "I'm so sorry—here we are, barraging you with questions the minute you return from the restroom. Let's sit back down."

"Thanks," she smiled, guilt eating away at her. She knew on some level that the stranger must have been seeking her out because she was a witch, and Pete shouldn't have to deal with something so frightening because of her.

"You're sure you're okay?" Pete asked their server, who was straightening up an empty table nearby that had been part of the fallout.

She nodded. "I swear, we get someone in here screaming about one thing or another at least once a week. I'll be back with your dinners in a second—they should be up about now."

Once she'd left, Sela asked Pete, "What exactly happened?"

"So the guy comes in, and when he comes over to our table, he just starts repeating...what was it? 'Hers forever,' I think."

"That was it?"

"Well, I tried telling him that my date was in the restroom, and that was when he just lost it!" Pete shook his head. "Started knocking stuff over, threw a vase...I got up to try to calm him down, but he kept repeating in this really agitated, kind of robotic way, 'Hers forever.'"

At that point, their server returned and started setting their entrees down. "That's not what he said," she corrected Pete. "It was even weirder, like he was some fantasy nerd who didn't know where he was. He kept saying, 'Hers within forever.'"

"That's right!" He nodded. "God, the poor guy—what could that even mean?"

"You know," the server said to Sela, "you should be careful. If this guy actually was looking for you, he might be a stalker or something."

Now Pete grew doubtful. "Do you think that's likely?"

"Hey, men try to follow us out to our cars when we pull late shifts all the time, and that's just working here," the woman told him. "My friend's a bartender in a more remote part of town, and she actually once had a guy sitting in her car, waiting for her to get off work. She had to call for help and everything."

This conversation was bringing to mind some of Sela's worst dates, and she really didn't want to have to think about those now. "Thanks again," she told their server. "Hopefully, he was just confused and wasn't actually looking for me."

The rest of the date went really well. Sela and Pete had a ton in common, from favorite shows to favorite foods, and she felt like she could've spent years talking with him. Still, she wasn't one hundred percent present. The guy in the brown leather jacket had her rattled, and she wouldn't feel better until she could let Sable know what had happened.

But when it came time for Pete to walk her to her car, she found herself in the moment once more. As they exited the restaurant, Pete reached out a hand into which Sela happily slipped her own.

"Well, despite some unexpected excitement," he said as they reached her car, "I had an amazing time with you tonight, Sela."

"I did, too," she told him with a grin that was impossible to suppress.

"I'm glad to hear that," he said, reaching to brush some strands of hair from her face that a troublesome wind had moved. "Because I'm going to ask to see you again this coming week."

"That's good, because I'm going to say yes."

"Really."

"Mm-hmm."

The kiss was everything Sela had hoped it would be. Pete's arms around her were strong, and she pressed her hands up against his chest as they moved closer to one another, new passion pulling them in. He smelled of warm spices from their meal and a soap that was subtle, sexy, and clean, so different from the herbal stuff she crafted at home. His lips were soft as she knew they'd be, but the kiss was anything but, and a deep longing resounded throughout her body that left her head spinning in delicious circles.

Pete pressed his lips to her cheek after their mouths had parted, and that silly grin that had been on Sela's face before the kiss spread even wider.

"Thank you for this evening," she told him, turning to open her driver's door before she decided to pull a Natalie and shove him in the backseat.

"I'll see you at work tomorrow," he told her as he held her hand, helping her down into the car. "Get home safe."

As she drove into the dark streets towards home, that last word echoed through Sela's mind: *safe.* She missed Pete's presence as she went along her way, feeling chilled in the wake of the reassuring warmth that seemed a core part of who he was. Now that she was alone, thoughts of the man who might be following her rose up in her mind, and she drove a little more quickly than she probably should have, anxious to talk with her familiar.

Walking up the stairs to her apartment, Sable's takeout in hand, Sela glanced at her phone yet again and saw that Natalie still hadn't even read her last text. The worry she was feeling expanded.

When she pushed open the apartment door, Sela was met with a dark living room. Had her sister not made it? Pluto greeted her with a sleepy chirp, and she flicked the lights on to find him curled up on Natalie's travel bags, piled in the middle of the floor.

"That's strange," she said, making her way towards her bedroom, which was also dark.

Seeing the empty room, she started to head back to the kitchen, thinking that perhaps Sable had met Natalie and the two of them had decided to go out and grab food while they waited for her to come home. But a sound from the second bedroom made her turn back, concerned for both her sister and her familiar.

Sela pushed the door open. There on the wooden table was Sable, naked again, but he wasn't alone. Natalie, also naked, lay half-covered by the throw blanket that Sela had provided her familiar on the night he'd moved into this room: the room she was only just getting used to having someone live in, the room where that same someone was now taking full advantage of Sela's baby sister.

Natalie bolted up. "Sela!" She scrambled to cover herself with the blanket.

Sela ignored her sister and told Sable in a dark voice, "You need to get the fuck out."

Twelve

"Sela."

Sable had followed her into the kitchen. He was wearing her sweatpants, not having bothered to put on a shirt before pursuing her.

"You can't possibly have anything to say to me right now." She glared at him, tears of fury blurring her vision.

"I would never have meant for you to find us like that. It's just been so long since I've—"

"Oh, that's supposed to make it better?" She was incredulous; it was taking all of her effort not to start throwing things at him. "You haven't had a good fuck since the last time you were a person—I'm sorry, since the last time you *looked* like a person, so my sister's an easy target? Is that it?"

"Sela, calm down!" Natalie's voice came muffled from the bedroom, where Sela assumed she was scrambling to get her clothes on. Natalie never could get dressed quickly.

"Look," Sable tried, "I don't expect you to—"

"That's right," she cut him off again. "You don't expect anything of me, because you're getting the hell out of my home. I don't care where you go, I don't—I told you, I *told* you how vulnerable she is!" She grabbed the takeout she'd bought for him. "Well, you've had your fuck, so here: take your food and just get out."

Natalie finally came into the room, her normally pristine

strawberry-blonde hair sticking out at all angles. "Sela, please, we were just—"

"Sable's leaving, Natalie," she said coldly. "Why don't you go to the bathroom and fix your hair?"

"I'll be going, then." Sable started for the door.

"Without a shirt? Jesus, Sela, just let me get him his shirt!" Natalie quickly ran back into the bedroom and returned with a t-shirt that Sable slipped over his head. "Where will you go? I thought you were here because you had nowhere else to stay." Concern filled Natalie's voice, and Sela could practically taste the unhealthy attachment her sister was already forming.

"Natalie, please go back into the bedroom."

She knew how she sounded, ordering her sister around as though she were a child. But everything she was doing—fretting over Sable, worrying about his clothing, his shelter—all of it was textbook Natalie. This would unfold the way it always did, with Sela picking up the pieces of her broken-hearted sister.

And that was why Sable had to go.

As he stepped into the stairwell, he turned back. Sela wouldn't look at him, centering her rage on the living room floor, afraid of what she might do if she brought her gaze anywhere else.

"I didn't mean to hurt you or your sister," she heard him say quietly. "And I realize I crossed a big line. But you need to remember that we're in this together, and things are going to happen quickly." He sighed. "I can't force you to let me stay in your life, but Sela...this our time. It's your time. Please, think about it."

He was gone a breath later.

"Sela, what just happened?" Natalie walked up to her, and Sela was finally able to remove her eyes from the floor. "I thought you said you guys weren't a thing."

She echoed Sable's sigh with one of her own. "We weren't. I mean, we aren't. But I did trust him, until tonight."

"Because of me?"

Sela pulled Natalie into a hug. "Yes, because of you. You're my baby sister." Above Natalie's murmured protests, she went on, "I know you're no baby, and I am not trying to be condescending. But from one train wreck to another, can we agree that you're about as good with relationships and sex as I am with careers?"

Natalie nodded, admitting quietly, "That's fair."

"Why don't you get settled in my room for the night?" Sela suggested, releasing her sister and going to the stove to put the kettle on. After all that had happened, they could both use a cup of tea.

"Do you have any of those fancy blends you used to make? Can I have the one you always sent to my dorm during freshman year to help me sleep?"

"Of course. I'll bring you a mug once the water's boiled."

As Sela prepared their tea on a small tray, she noticed for the first time since she'd gotten home that there were arrangements of cut flowers and crystal quartz all over the kitchen and the living room. Sable had even woven a few garlands and draped them along the windowsill above the kitchen sink.

Tears welled up as Sela tried to work through her fury and heartbreak. In the short time he'd been staying with her, Sable had become more than just a talking cat who'd announced himself as her familiar. He'd been a friend, the first she'd made in years. She reflected on his final plea as he'd left the apartment. They were supposed to do this magick stuff together, but how could she ever trust him at all if she couldn't trust him with her sister?

Then she remembered that she hadn't even had a chance to tell him about the potential stalker in the brown leather jacket.

"Shit," she muttered. "What a disastrous end to a day."

Natalie was a welcome distraction, chattering happily as they drank their tea, asking about Sela's date with Pete and telling her all about school. When they were tucked in for the night, Sela's final thoughts as she drifted off to sleep turned back to Sable. She realized she had no way of reaching him and briefly wondered where he was, whether he'd found somewhere safe to spend the night. Her dreams were full of anger, guilt, and above all, worry, but in the morning she wouldn't recall a single one.

Thirteen

"Wow, you must shop here pretty often."

Natalie had come to a stop in front a small storefront Sela had never noticed before. It was Saturday, the day before her birthday, and her little sister had decided she'd had enough of hanging around the apartment while Sela went to work. As soon as she'd come in from her pre-dawn shift at a twenty-four-hour vet's office, Natalie had shoved her back out the door, demanding that they go shopping "before I kill both of us out of sheer boredom, Sela."

Now, Sela looked at the store Natalie was referring to. It was an occult shop with candles, pentacles, and a large cauldron in the front window display. Sela smiled to herself, knowing that her sister couldn't possibly understand why this might strike her as funny.

"Actually, I've never seen it before."

"Really? You used to love shit like this."

"Yeah, I did." She noticed a bowl of quartz to the right of the display, and a pang of sadness struck her as she thought of the arrangements Sable had made before she'd thrown him out.

"Well, let's go in," Natalie suggested.

"Really?"

"What's wrong with you?" her sister demanded. "This is totally your jam, and I already said we're shopping for you this weekend. Don't you want to check it out?"

Did she want to? Sela also wondered at her own hesitation. Why should a witch avoid a shop full of tools made especially for her?

Not a witch yet, a nagging voice in her head reminded her. *You'll need Sable for that.*

Deciding she'd had enough of feeling guilty about throwing her familiar out of her apartment for perfectly legitimate reasons, she nodded. "Sure, let's go in."

The shop was new to Sela, but the experience she had stepping inside was so familiar. She thought of the first time she and Maria had entered their favorite occult shop back home: it had the same incense-infused smell, the same hush above which chimes and bells hanging in the eaves tinkled, the same feeling of reverence and possibility.

A warm summer breeze followed Sela and Natalie inside, causing some pages on a logbook at the cashier's station to flutter. The movement caught his attention, and when he glanced up, his eyes immediately settled on Sela.

"Hello," he said.

"Hi," Natalie responded, a note of flirtation in her voice.

Sela couldn't entirely blame her sister—the man was strikingly good-looking, though much too old for Natalie. He was at least in his early forties, with errant threads of silver invading an otherwise lush black beard and the smallest of worry lines creasing the brown skin of his forehead. Impending middle age didn't seem to be any threat to his hairline, however; those same worry lines were half-covered by wayward strands of thick black hair. The man's eyeglass frames glinted platinum on the bridge of his long, thin nose, and above them, his steady dark-brown eyes stopped Sela in her tracks. He didn't even seem to notice Natalie had greeted him at all.

"Hello," he repeated, unblinking, which caused Sela to feel

obliged to reply.

"Hello," she echoed, not knowing what else to say or why this man's presence should have such an effect on her. It wasn't attraction, but there was something about him that was giving her pause.

"I don't imagine you're looking for anything in particular yet."

"No," Sela answered, not sure why that was her response.

"Soon enough, though." And, relaxing the intensity with which he'd regarded her, the man went back to the ledgers he'd been working over when they had entered the shop.

Natalie nudged her sister, offering a look of, *What the hell was that?* Sela shrugged, having no explanations to offer, and turned her attention back to the shop.

She quickly realized there was something different about this store that made it distinct from those she had frequented with her friends in high school. This shop wasn't organized by its wares: stones and crystals together, books and tarot cards, and so forth. Instead, everything seemed to have been set out at random, and with redundancies everywhere: cauldrons and herbs on a table to Sela's left; an altar in one corner with a book on runes settled in its center; a nearby bowl of amazonite next to a leather journal. But as she continued examining the store, she realized with a start what its organizing principle was.

"Intent," she said to herself with a smile. "It's intent."

Tools for divining the future were in one part of the shop; those for increasing good fortune were in another. There were items for finding love, for protection, and a dozen other efforts a witch might make, all set up in the most convenient way if you came in with a plan for a particular spell.

"Of course," a quiet voice behind her confirmed. "We want our customers to find whatever it is they need."

Sela turned to find a woman standing behind her who was around the same age as the cashier, her gaze as steady as his had been, though she also offered Sela a smile. Her long, twisted black locs had been gathered into a braid that hung down her back to her hips, and the emerald chiffon dress she wore flowed elegantly to her knees. One of her dark-brown legs was graced by a twisted white gold band, and Sela's mind flickered back to the rose gold anklet she'd worn in her recent dream of the alley.

Sela felt the same pull from this woman that she had from the cashier when she'd entered the shop, and so without thinking, she said the first thing that came to her mind: "I'd gladly skip eating for a week to afford a dress like that."

Now the woman's smile grew from tentative to certain. "Thank you," she laughed, and Sela noticed she spoke with a British accent. "I made it just last week. But I don't think you're looking for clothes today, are you?"

Natalie had approached, and answered cheerfully, "We might be, especially if you've got anything like what you're wearing."

The woman in the emerald dress turned her smile on Natalie, her dark-brown eyes thoughtful. "Why don't I bring you to see our summer collection while your sister shops for what she's looking for?"

As eager to flirt with this woman as she had been with the cashier, Natalie moved to follow her, but Sela interjected quickly, "How did you know we were sisters?"

The woman seemed confused by Sela's question. "Family resemblance, of course." And she led Natalie towards the back of the store, where a variety of garments were hanging.

In their lifetime together, Sela could count on one hand the number of times strangers had believed she and Natalie were even related, never mind sisters. Between her own lanky form and Natalie's curves, her freckled skin and Natalie's porcelain complexion, and her auburn waves and her sister's smooth red hair, no one had ever claimed that they looked remotely alike. She gave her sister and the saleswoman a long look before moving on to browse the shop.

She stopped in front of a black pillar candle, but it wasn't the candle itself that had caught Sela's eye. Behind it, barely noticeable amidst all of the other objects on display, was a blue goldstone sphere identical to the one she'd dreamt about.

"Isn't it a bit soon for that?"

The cashier had come up next to Sela, and over the frames of his glasses, he seemed to be scrutinizing her for something.

But before she could respond, she saw a flash of movement pass behind him: outside the store, right in front of the display window, was the passing figure of a blonde-haired man.

And that man was wearing a brown leather jacket.

"Excuse me," she managed, pushing past the cashier as she tore through the shop's front door.

She was determined not to lose him this time, and when she emerged from the shop, she caught the man's back turning a corner.

Without thinking, she called out, "Hey!"

He froze at the sound of her voice. Suddenly, a massive blue bird flew down from seemingly out of nowhere and landed in Sela's path. Startled, she took in the sight of the creature: crowned like a peacock and around the same size, but without the long tail.

My dream, she recalled again, knowing exactly where she'd seen such a bird before. "But what—" And then Sela realized that the bird had distracted her from her target. Sure enough, when she looked up again, the man had vanished completely.

"Sela?" Natalie's voice came from the doorway of the shop. "What are you doing?"

"There was a bird…" She turned to point to the large blue bird, only to find that it, too, had disappeared.

Natalie giggled. "Okay, whatever you say. Stop being weird and come back inside."

When Sela walked back into the shop, she saw the cashier wrapping the blue goldstone sphere in a black velvet cloth at the front counter. As Sela approached, he nodded at her.

"You were right to choose this now; it appears you do need it, after all."

A thousand questions buzzed through Sela's mind, many she longed to ask but couldn't with her sister there. Did this man understand who Sela really was? Could he recognize a witch on sight? An object and an animal from her dream had appeared to her in real life within seconds of each other, and now this man was wrapping one of the two for Sela to take home with her. Why was he so sure she had wanted the sphere to begin with? And why was he now saying she needed it?

True to form, Natalie spoke before Sela could even gather her thoughts. "How much?"

Sela held out a hand to stop her. "Nat, you really don't have to—"

"—buy my sister a birthday gift?" Natalie finished the sentence, smiling sheepishly. "I didn't get a chance to before I left school, so actually, I kind of do. Do you guys take Visa?"

As they were leaving the shop, the woman in the green dress reappeared and walked them to the door.

"We'll see you soon," she told Sela. "And in the meantime: enjoy your birthday."

"Okay, that was all sorts of weird," Natalie remarked as soon as they were out of earshot. "But I guess you expect weird in stores like that."

"Listen, Natalie," Sela began, suddenly wanting to tell her sister everything—about being a witch, about Sable, about the man who might be following her everywhere. But she had no clue where to start.

"What's up?"

Sela closed her eyes for a second, willing the urge to confess away. She still didn't know the rules or consequences for telling people she was a witch. Talking to Natalie could be harmless, but it could also put her sister in real danger, especially with the guy in the brown leather jacket at large.

Until Sela could reconcile with Sable and get some answers, it was too big of a risk to take. Besides, she had no real powers yet to prove any of her claims; Natalie would probably just think that her many jobs and towering debt had finally brought her to a full mental breakdown.

"I'm really hungry," she said instead.

Her sister laughed. "Shocker."

Fourteen

Sela woke to the sound of Pete sending her a birthday message. She stumbled to the kitchen, half-asleep and making a beeline for the coffeemaker. She'd worked a catering gig the night before and was awake much earlier than she should have been after getting home at three in the morning.

Through a yawn, she smiled as she texted Pete back: *I'm really looking forward to our date this week, too.*

Pete was quickly proving not only one of the most attractive guys Sela had ever met, but also one of the easiest to talk to. He'd spent the drive to work with her the night before, her phone clipped to her dashboard and Pete's warm voice coming through on speaker.

The fact that she hadn't heard from Sable at all bugged her, though. She didn't think he had a phone. Why would he? He'd only just gotten thumbs. Still, something was bothering her about the apartment and without the help of the caffeine she was currently in the process of making, she couldn't quite put her finger on it, so she assumed it must be Sable's absence.

"Sela?"

She turned, yawning again, to see her sister standing outside her bedroom. "Hey, good morning. I'm just about to make coff—"

"What the hell happened in here, Sela?" Natalie gestured around the room, her expression twisted with anxiety.

Sela blinked a few times, forcing herself fully awake in light of her sister's panic. And then she saw what had Natalie so freaked out: on every surface he'd placed them, every arrangement Sable had made of the magickal blooms and once-glowing quartz had turned a dead, ashen grey. She reached a tentative hand towards one of the blossoms nearest her, and it crumbled into a pile of soot at her touch.

"Did Sable come back here and do this?"

Now Sela realized her sister wasn't just anxious: she was afraid. She went to Natalie's side and put an arm around her. "Sable would never do something like that," she said. "And besides, he doesn't have keys."

"Guys don't always need keys to get in," Natalie replied, her voice low.

Sela pulled away to look her sister in the face. "And how would you know that?"

Natalie just shook her head, and Sela felt an old familiar anger with herself. It had happened again: here she was, preoccupied with her own shit just like when she was in high school, and it had made her totally oblivious to whatever Natalie was dealing with. Sela was so worried that she might have a stalker who, what? Had bad taste in outerwear? Meanwhile, Natalie had been struggling with who knew what kind of bad relationships; as Sela had always maintained, her sister really knew how to pick them.

"Sela, stop staring at me like that. It's creepier than all of these dead flowers everywhere."

She let her gaze shift back to the arrangements in question, and a sinking feeling told her that the ash might indeed have something to do with Sable, but not in the way her sister suspected. Soon-to-be witch and familiar had been in the apartment together, happily anticipating their Nascent Eve when

92

the flowers had bloomed overnight. And now that their bond had been damaged, those same blossoms had, also overnight, burned away to lifeless dust.

That probably wasn't the best sign.

"Are you going to turn that coffeepot on or do I have to beg?" Natalie seemed to have recovered herself. "I'll make breakfast, once I'm caffeinated."

"You don't have to do that."

Natalie rolled her eyes. "I'm not about to let my sister go without blueberry pancakes on her twenty-eighth birthday."

"Oh, I definitely won't have the ingredients for all of that in the fridge."

Natalie gave her a sly grin. "Did you really think I spent the whole time you were at work yesterday holed up in this apartment by myself with a cat? I'm not you."

And as Natalie opened the fridge, Sela's jaw dropped at the sight of all of the food stashed inside. "Nat!"

"Call it part of your birthday gift," Natalie said over her shoulder as she started digging out ingredients for pancakes.

Now Sela peeked into cabinets and drawers, finding her little sister had stocked her up with enough pantry goods to last at least a month. She took herself to the shower without another word, overwhelmed with gratitude and worried she might start to ugly-cry if she remained in the kitchen.

Sela waited all day for something to happen. She kept glancing at her bedroom window as she got dressed, anticipating a tawny-grey cat on her fire escape. While eating with Natalie, she mentally prepared herself to explain things should the blueberry pancakes suddenly explode into flowers. But the only strange thing about breakfast was Sela's discovery that her little sister was an amazing cook, which had definitely not been the case when they'd lived back home together.

By the time evening rolled around, it was clear that Sela's birthday would not be her Nascent Eve. There wasn't anything remotely magickal happening; if anything, the day had been astoundingly calm and ordinary.

A little after seven, as Sela was changing into something comfortable to take advantage of the rare early bedtime she was about to enjoy, Natalie burst into her room.

"Oh good, you're already getting dressed." For her part, Sela's sister was wearing a shimmering holographic silver dress and strappy plum heels.

"Wow," Sela remarked, "I guess pajamas just aren't doing it for you anymore, huh?"

"No, Sela, we're going dancing."

"Um, who is we? Because I'm about to knock out."

"You absolutely are not," her sister countered, yanking open Sela's closet and starting to dig through it. "We are celebrating your second-to-last year in your twenties, and this day has been so boring I'm amazed it didn't kill both of us."

"We had a great breakfast!" Sela said defensively. "I learned you could cook. That's not boring."

"That," Natalie told her as she shook out a wrinkled pink dress from the back of the closet, "might actually define boring. Put this on and do your makeup while I find you some shoes and figure out what to do with your hair."

Somehow, an hour and much protesting later, Sela found herself in line for the only club Natalie could find that was open late on a Sunday night. And for some reason, though like with the flowers that morning she couldn't put her finger on it, Sela felt a little off, though it might have been the strain of the slicked-back bun her sister had tortured her hair into.

"Natalie," she tried, "don't you think this line is a little long? Maybe we should head back. We could watch a movie, or—"

Natalie gave her a steely look, her green eyes almost electric beneath bright pink eye shadow. "We are six people from the front of the line, and there is no way I am letting you punk out, especially not after I spent half an hour wrangling that bird's nest you've allowed your hair to turn into."

"Okay, okay," Sela relented, then added half to herself, "I just have a bad feeling about this."

Before she could say anything more, the line surged forward and the two of them were walking down wide stairs lit neon green towards a dance floor. And Sela's uneasiness was lost to an explosion of sights, smells, and sounds.

The first thing she learned about the club, Visions, was that it was deceptively enormous. On the outside, it had looked like little more than a single-story warehouse, but once they'd gotten down that first flight of stairs, it was revealed that the bulk of the club was well below street level. The owners had cleverly made use of the vertical space by building multiple bars on platforms, accessible via shining steel spiral staircases. VIP tables were tucked away in corners along the sides of the club walls, elevated to street level like the bars were. The view from above must have been like gazing down into the deep end of a massive swimming pool.

Sela had read in the reviews Natalie had pulled up that Visions was the only club in their larger region that boasted a "floating" dance floor, a narrow border that ran the full perimeter of the club, built about twenty feet above the main floor. Pulsing multichromatic lights had been installed in the floating floor's underside, providing privacy for those dancers above while they could look down and find their friends below. If someone were to look directly above them to see the floating floor, they'd be blinded by an ever-fluctuating rainbow of lights.

Twin elevated stages faced one another on either side of the club, and the reviews also spoke of two bands booked on any given evening so that musical battles were fought to the delight of dancers below and above. The floating dance floors ran above the tops of the stages, too, and the lights beneath them illuminated the performers through their sets.

The continuity of movement throughout Visions was absolute; even the bathrooms were hidden down long hallways off of the main floor, such that the most formidable line would not spill into the bulk of the dancing crowd. The designated dance floors retained an inviolability of rhythm, a spatial sanctuary where only twisting, stepping, twirling, and grinding were permitted.

The aromas that had dazzled Sela when she'd stepped into the space were apparently from the club's wide selection of custom drinks. She caught sight of elegant glasses filled with fruits and herbs, such that everywhere she turned, she breathed in the sweetness of fresh-cut strawberries, the zest of grated limes, and the overwhelmingly crisp scent of mint.

Natalie had disappeared the moment they'd entered, half-screaming over her shoulder, "I'm getting us drinks!"

Sela had nervously made her way through tangles of dancers, aiming for a less crowded space. That uneasiness she'd felt had returned, even more so now that she'd lost sight of her sister. A cold wave swept up from behind her, and just as she was about to turn and face the chill at her back—

"You have to try this!"

Natalie was thrusting a drink at her, and as Sela caught it and brought it to her face, she could taste the aromatic notes of a sweet peach before she even opened her mouth to sip at the drink.

"Whoa." The sensation of bursting sweetness bubbling on

her tongue, Sela glanced behind her, but that cold feeling of dread had vanished. "How do you think they manage to get all these drinks to smell so good?"

"Don't ask me, but they're fucking amazing! Here, try mine." She handed Sela a glass of bright green liquid smelling of coconut rum, green apples, and fresh rosemary.

Suddenly, someone knocked into Sela's left shoulder, causing the peach drink in that hand to splash out of its glass.

"Sorry, dear," a gentle voice apologized, and Sela realized with surprise that she could hear the words perfectly above the din of the club, though the stranger hadn't spoken loudly at all.

She found herself eye to eye with a beautiful, if slightly off-putting, man who was perhaps a little older than she was—in his mid-thirties, at most, though he carried himself with a gravity Sela usually associated with far older people. He was thin, his bone structure sharp to the extent that his face was almost foreboding, and his extremely pale skin revealed veins so blue that under the flashing lights of Visions, she could follow them up his neck and into his temples. In the neon atmosphere of the club, he appeared angelic; even a halo of frizz had escaped the otherwise silken white-blonde ponytail trailing down from the base of his skull.

"That's okay," she replied, wanting to break this accidental staring contest. Natalie had disappeared again, and while Sela knew instantly that it was not this man who had caused the chill she'd felt a little while ago, she wasn't thrilled to be left alone with him.

"I'm sorry, do we know each other?" He was puzzling over her, his periwinkle eyes nearly unblinking.

"I don't think so," she began, though as she said it, she had the notion that something about him seemed familiar.

"You're certain we haven't met?"

"I mean, we might have at one of my jobs…"

She trailed off as her eyes drifted intuitively towards a staircase leading to the floating dance floor. A small commotion was unfolding there, but what had drawn Sela's eye was a deep feeling of combined dread and fierce protectiveness. It was a kind of magic she'd had access to long before she'd met Sable and learned she was a witch: sister's intuition.

Natalie was struggling on the staircase above with a man who had locked his hands on both of her arms and seemed to be shaking her. He was shouting, and her face had gone sickly pale, her eyes huge with fear. The man, a good head taller than Natalie, was blonde and wore a brown leather jacket. As Sela watched them in horror, she saw him stiffen as though he'd felt her gaze at his back. Natalie managed to free one of her arms during this momentary distraction, but he still gripped the other tightly in his hand.

"That's my little sister!" Sela yelled, turning back to the man she'd been speaking with and gesturing to Natalie. She didn't know why her first instinct was to look to this stranger for help, but she saw that he'd followed her gaze and had also seen the attack occurring.

"The owner is a friend," he told her, his tone reassuring. "Go to your sister and I'll find help."

Sela nodded, shoving her way to the staircase and ignoring the grumbles of everyone she knocked into. In her desperation and panic, her thoughts turned to Sable.

This is why I need you. This is why you're supposed to be here, helping me.

It felt like an eternity before she made it to the base of the stairs where she'd seen Natalie struggling. But as she prepared to climb the steps, she heard the voice of the strange, angelic-looking man saying behind her, "There she is. There's your sister, darling—you're all right, now."

Sela whipped around and Natalie flew into her arms. She was shaking, and Sela didn't know what to do but hold her.

"It was so scary, Sel," Natalie finally said.

"I know."

"Thank god these girls on the stairs saw what was happening." Natalie pulled out of the hug, but she was still trembling. "They came and helped me."

"I would have made it to you in time," Sela tried to reassure her, but her voice didn't have any of the conviction she'd intended.

Natalie nodded, her tear-stained expression so much graver than Sela was used to. Neither of them spoke for a long moment.

"The owner is having club security search for the man who attacked you so that they can remove him," the strange man told them, breaking their shared silence. "It shouldn't take long—he only employs the best. In the meantime, all of the bartenders have been instructed to give the two of you anything you would like this evening, on the house."

"Do you work here or something?" Sela wanted to know.

The man shook his head and she frowned, trying to place what was so familiar about him.

"Don't interrogate him, Sela! They're giving us free drinks on your birthday." Natalie offered her usual bubbly, flirtatious smile. "Please thank the owner for us."

He nodded. "I'll do that." And without another word, he left them, his gaze lingering on Sela before he was gone.

"Natalie, what—"

"Sela," Natalie cut her off, shaking her head, "I really, *really* don't want to talk about it. Can we please just celebrate your birthday?"

Sela gazed worriedly at Natalie. She didn't want to drop

the subject; beyond wanting to make sure her sister was really okay, which she doubted more by the minute, she needed to know as much as she could about Brown Leather Jacket. But, remembering what used to happen when they were kids and she tried pushing a tough topic with Natalie, she knew that this wasn't the time.

"Sure. If you want to drop it, we'll drop it."

"The only part I don't want dropped is those badass girls who helped me. Let's get them some free drinks so I can say thank you." She caught Sela's hand and tugged. "Come on! Back to celebrating!"

And celebrate they did. The women who'd helped her sister were Sela's age, and they were happy to join in the birthday fun. One of them confided in Sela that a date had once beat her within an inch of her life, and since then she'd become much more protective of other women.

"So when I saw that guy with your sister, it was like an instinct, you know?"

"I do," Sela replied.

They all danced together, enjoying the dazzling array of drinks Visions had to offer. Sela tasted pretty much everything on the menu, deciding that the best way to stop worrying and enjoy her night out was to use whatever means were available. And what was available, in impressive quantities, was alcohol. Before she knew it, her birthday was over and it was time to leave.

During the cab ride home, Natalie suddenly asked, "Was Pete supposed to meet up with us tonight or something?"

A little bewildered by the question and more than a little tipsy, Sela said, "No. Why would you think that?"

Natalie shrugged. "I don't know. It's just felt like all day long, you were waiting for something."

As usual, nothing got past her little sister. *Welp, I'm not about to tell her I'm a witch with this many free drinks in me.*

"I guess I've been waiting to feel…different? More adult, maybe?" She sighed. "I know you're not that much younger than me, but Nat, I can't tell you how shitty you start to feel when thirty's around the corner and you're just drifting. It's like something, I don't know, a little more magical was supposed to have happened to you by now, but there's nothing on the horizon but more drift."

It was the truth, or at least as close to it as she could get without mentioning her impending witch status—if that even was her status anymore. Sable was gone, and what if her Nascent Eve arrived before she could find him? Her birthday had passed, her sister was leaving town in the morning, and Sela? Sela got to baby-sit a set of adorable twins the next day while their parents enjoyed a romantic ten-year anniversary. She could already feel her morning hangover.

"Sela, why haven't you set up an online shop?"

This wasn't at all the response she had expected. "Huh?" she managed, the alcohol making her think maybe she'd missed something.

"Or like, why haven't you done a Kickstarter? Etsy? I think even Amazon takes indie artisans now."

"I…I mean, I…"

Her sister continued, and Sela was amazed at the no-nonsense tone Natalie was achieving, given the fact that she'd drunk circles around her big sister that night. "Why haven't you gone back to school for like an MBA or whatever? It's not like you couldn't get your weird-ass schedule to fit around a class here or there."

Was this the superpower of being in your early twenties? Tenacity and a well-structured argument after obscene amounts of liquor?

"An MBA? What are you talking about?"

"Sela, you make cool shit. I don't really get it, like the stuff in that shop we went to yesterday, but there's totally a market for it. Hell, I bet that weird shop would buy from you!"

"Buy what?"

"Don't be dense!" Her sister rolled her eyes in agitation. "Your soaps and candles and whatever else it is you can make from like, twigs and dirt. You know you're good—my hair has smelled like an actual fucking rose since I got to your apartment and started using your homemade shampoo."

"Is that where all of it went?"

"Why the hell would you spend all that time making stuff if you didn't realize you were good at it? We both know your products would sell."

Sela was flabbergasted (and still very drunk). "I…I guess I always thought you had to have like connections or whatever."

She felt so incredibly foolish. Why hadn't she ever thought of creating an online shop? Sure, she had no idea how to market herself, but she hadn't even tried.

"Look, one of my friends built her own business." Now Natalie leaned forward to pay their driver, and Sela realized that they had arrived at her apartment. Her sister helped her out of the cab. "When I get back to school, I'm going to grab coffee with her and ask her to get in touch with you."

"She has a business?" Sela asked, finding it difficult not to stumble in the heels Natalie had chosen for her. "What does she do?"

"She sells handmade lingerie."

"Natalie!" She wasn't too drunk to be a little scandalized. Or maybe that was why she was scandalized?

"I don't want to hear your judgment," Natalie said. "She's

been making enough money to put a real dent in her student loans, and she still has time to work a day job while she's making custom orders. The line is super-cute, and I'd bet anything that in a couple years, it'll get her debt-free."

Sela looked at her sister dubiously as they reached the stairs to her apartment, though she wasn't sure whether her doubts were about Natalie's friend's business or the stairs themselves.

"Seems like a longshot," she remarked about both.

"And dog-sitting and waitressing and tutoring and whatever the fuck else you do every week," Natalie grunted as she helped pull her sister up the steps, "those are all career choices that are going build you an impressive savings account?"

As they got into the apartment, Sela slumped onto the sofa and sulkily replied, "No, they aren't."

"You have talent." Natalie picked up a floral candle Sela had made. "And talent can make money. It's time to cut the crap, Sela. You said it—you're pushing thirty."

"Twenty-eight! I just turned twenty-eight a fucking day ago!"

"Close enough." Natalie sat down next to Sela on the sofa, her face serious. "How about we make a deal?"

Sela raised a suspicious eyebrow. "What do you mean, a deal?"

"I will calm down with my usual shit for, oh, let's say six weeks, if you will spend those same six weeks trying to build your crafts into a legit business."

"Your usual shit?"

Natalie heaved a sigh. "No hookups, no dating, no sex for six weeks. But *only* if you promise to get focused on something more than rando jobs that barely pay your rent." And she extended a hand.

They hadn't turned on the lights of the apartment when they'd walked in, but the moon shone bright and huge through the kitchen window. Natalie's strawberry-blonde hair glowed an otherworldly shade of pink around her face, and Sela had the ludicrous thought that her sister had temporarily transformed into a deal-making fairy, serious and determined as she was bathed in rosy ethereal light. And even in her alcohol-edged stupor, she knew that this deal was as much something her sister desperately needed as it was the kick in the pants that had been a long time coming for Sela herself.

She clumsily took Natalie's hand. "Six weeks."

"Good. Now let's get you some aspirin and water before bed, because you look like shit."

Fifteen

Pete was mysterious about their second date, telling Sela to meet him outside of a gourmet candy shop in town and to wear comfortable shoes. It was a cool Tuesday evening, and she could almost smell the crisp scent of autumn waiting just around the corner.

She was lost in texting Natalie, who'd returned safely home the day before, when she heard, "Hey, birthday girl." Sela looked up to see Pete carrying a bouquet of orange roses in his arms, interspersed with stalks of indigo larkspur.

"Thank you!" she managed after a moment of being overwhelmed by how lovely the bouquet—and her date— looked.

"We've got a bit of walking to do before we get to our destination," he said. "But first, if it's okay with you, I'd like to find out if we're compatible in a very important department." And he opened the candy shop door for her.

Sela laughed. "You know what I'm going to say, right?"

"Hmm, let me guess: something about a dentist bringing his date to a shop full of things that rot your teeth?"

"Well, you have to admit, it is a little funny."

Pete shrugged, giving her a sheepish grin. "What can I say? This is my nephew's favorite place in the world, so I've become pretty fond of it, too—lots of good memories here."

It was an adorable little shop, with colorful displays of

candy, an old-fashioned ice cream counter, and a wall of plush toys, t-shirts, and other candy-themed merchandise.

"Besides," Pete went on as they browsed, "as long as a person brushes and flosses regularly, there's no harm in indulging a bit."

"Whatever you say, Dr. Cheng," she teased.

Sela and Pete spent the better part of half an hour walking around the shop, choosing assorted candies to fill the little bags they'd grabbed. As they were making their way out the door, she looked up at him expectantly.

"So, now what?"

"Now, we walk."

She smiled. "Still a mystery?"

"Okay, here's my thing about birthdays," he told her. "I think everyone deserves an awesome surprise for their birthday, especially if they're awesome, like you are."

"Am I?"

"Um, you're an artist who works with kids and dogs on a regular basis, you're ridiculously easy to talk to, you appreciate a great restaurant, and if all that weren't enough, you're beautiful. I think we've established that you're awesome."

Sela was relatively certain she was blushing down to her toes. "You know, you're pretty great yourself."

"You think so?"

"Trust me," she assured him. "Any guy who likes sour watermelon gummies, peanut butter cups, *and* popcorn-flavored jelly beans gets full marks from me."

"Popcorn gets such a bad rap! Sure it's a little unusual, but it tastes good!"

"No argument here."

When they finally stopped walking, having snacked on candy along the way, they were in front of the local aquarium.

"Okay," Pete said, "here we are."

Sela blinked at him, then at the dark entrance to the aquarium, which had closed an hour earlier. "Um, are we breaking and entering on this date? Because I did not wear the right shoes for that."

But Pete was busy texting someone intently, and Sela had a moment to really look at him. There was something wonderful about this man, she decided—something that she could trust, even as she stood outside of a locked tourist attraction wondering whether he was going to ask her to help him commit a felony. It didn't hurt that Pete was so hot that when she thought about him too much, she found herself needing to stick her face in the freezer for a few seconds. But it was more than that; he was open in a way that most people weren't, and what she couldn't glean of him from that, her instincts seemed to fill in.

Suddenly, a light shone inside the entryway and a tall, good-looking man about their age in an aquarium staff shirt unlocked the door and pushed it open for them. "Pete Cheng, my man! I was wondering when you'd get here."

The two gave each other a quick guy hug, Pete saying, "Clarence! You're the best," as they embraced.

Clarence, who was a head taller than Pete, chuckled, "Hey, I still owe you for those free check-ups. No way I could've gotten them without insurance anywhere else." Now Clarence turned to Sela, pushing up his large plastic-framed glasses and smiling. "It's nice to see someone other than Joey coming with you for a visit."

"Joey?" Sela echoed. "Is that someone who's also helping us break into the aquarium?"

Both men laughed. "Sela Glaser, this is Clarence Wilson. Clarence, Sela's my date."

Sela nodded. "And Joey is…"

"My nephew," Pete explained. "Usually, he's the one Clarence lets me sneak in here after hours."

Sela was almost disappointed that they weren't actually going to break into the aquarium, but she wasn't going to complain about a private tour. If Pete hadn't already been the most amazing guy she'd ever dated, an evening this thoughtful and creative certainly would have earned him that title.

"If you guys will follow me inside, I just need to lock up these doors as quickly as possible," Clarence told them. "My boss is actually pretty decent about me bringing folks in when we're closed, but she'll flip out if anyone sees it and starts demanding late-night access to the place."

"So, how do you two know each other?" Sela asked as Clarence led them past tanks of shimmering, brightly-colored sea life.

"College," Pete explained. "Clarence was the best roommate. We used to have cram sessions for exams when everyone else was out partying. I would've been crying alone in the dorm room if not for this guy."

"Hey, the feeling was mutual. Fellow science major roomie with connections to get into Comic-Con every year and a generous enough soul to bring me along?" Clarence put his hand over his heart. "What more could this humble Blerd ask for?"

The two of them laughed, and Sela thought with a smile to herself, *Comic-Con, huh?* She wondered, not for the first time, about how Pete might feel if he found out he was dating a witch.

They'd come to a stop in front of double glass doors under a sign that read: Predators of the Deep. Clarence rifled through a large ring of keys. "Just give me a sec, here. I'm not the one who locks up usually, so I had to borrow keys from custodial."

"What do you do around here?" Sela asked, curious to know what jobs one could have at an aquarium. It was one of few places she'd never worked.

"That's slightly complicated," Clarence told her, trying a few keys. "Technically, I'm a researcher under one of the lead veterinarians. We spend certain parts of the year out at sea, studying cetaceans—marine mammals. When we're not on the road, so to speak, we work for the aquarium and apply for more funding for our research. I'm also working on my PhD, so I teach for the university outside town, too."

"Sounds like you have almost as many jobs as I do," Sela remarked, and Clarence and Pete both broke into laughter again.

"Success!" Clarence had found the right key. "Okay, I'll leave you to it. Glad to meet you, Sela." He shook her hand, then looked at Pete. "Keep this one around, Cheng. She's good people."

They walked through the glass doors and Clarence went back to what Sela imagined must be a lab of some kind. She hoped they'd come back and visit again someday; she figured a lab might be a sciency version of her own second bedroom, and wanted to know what it looked like. She felt a pang as she thought again of Sable and how they'd been apart for nearly a week, now. With effort, she turned her focus away from that regret and back into the present moment.

"So, Predators of the Deep?" she said to Pete as they passed a tank of iridescent, slow-moving jellyfish. "Should I be worried?"

He laughed. "I'm a dentist, remember? Sharks have like more rows of teeth than any other animal. How could I not love them?"

"You've got to follow what you love," she agreed, and now her mind flashed to her conversation with Natalie on the night of her birthday. Sure, it was only two days later, but Sela had done nothing yet to hold up her end of their deal.

"Hey, where'd you just go?" Pete asked, looking at her with concern.

"Oh, it's nothing. Just a talk I had with my sister this weekend."

"Everything okay?"

"Yeah, it's just...she kind of called me on my shit." She briefly told Pete about the deal. "And I mean, I know she's right," Sela went on as they slowly made their way through the maze of tanks, an octopus coiled in a corner here, bright anemones waving their toxic tentacles there. "I won't ever get out of this cycle of never-ending side jobs if I don't take myself and what I can do seriously. But it's scary, I guess. I mean, I'm going to be judged on products that I believe in, but who knows if anyone else will?"

"Do you have anything on you?" Pete stopped walking for a moment, looking down at her seriously.

She tilted her head, puzzled. "Um, you mean something that I made?"

"Yeah."

"I think I've got a tube of hand cream in my purse somewhere."

"Could I see it?"

Baffled, Sela dug into her bag and pulled out the cream, a blend of chamomile, rose, and orange blossom. Pete opened the tube, put a dab of cream on his hand, rubbed it in and took a whiff. His eyebrows went up. "I can see why your sister was annoyed with you. This is quality stuff, Sela."

"And how would you know that?" she asked, chuckling a little. "Are you moonlighting as a hand cream connoisseur?"

"You're not the only one with a sister who has strong opinions," he replied. "I know a certain Caroline Cheng who was extremely fussy about her cosmetics when we were growing up and still is to this day. In fact, do you think I could hold onto this?"

Sela shrugged. "Sure, if you like it that much."

"Not for myself, though there's nothing wrong with a man who takes skincare seriously. But I'd like to give it to Caroline, if that's okay? She may want to place some orders once you have a shop site up and running, and she has a ton of friends who are into these kinds of products, too."

A warmth spread over Sela. "Pete, I don't know what to say. Thank you."

He took her hand, and she gave his a squeeze. But after a few more steps around the next curve of the path, Sela was too dazzled to think about anything but the sight before her.

She'd been to the aquarium before and had even seen the shark exhibit. But without the hordes of kids on field trips and shouting parents and camp counselors, Sela could suddenly appreciate the simple majesty of giant predatory fish gliding above a huge archway, illuminated by ethereal lights on the edges of the tank. Silver fish darted by in small schools, sting rays flapped their large cartilage wings, and Sela felt she'd entered a new world, one with its own special kind of magic.

It wasn't until a moment later that she noticed the small round table beneath the peak of the archway, set for two with another orange rose in a vase, on either side of which little tealight candles brightened up silverware and gold-edged dinner plates. She turned to Pete, speechless.

He smiled, saying, "Happy Birthday." And he leaned in and they shared another impossibly perfect kiss.

As they got settled in their seats beneath the archway, Sela took in everything—the gorgeous tank, her gorgeous date, the dinner that Pete had somehow arranged for smelling delectable on the plates before them. The candles suddenly started to spark and dance, like small sparklers instead of normal tealights.

"All right!" Pete laughed. "I'll have to tell Clarence that his buddies who brought this in went above and beyond."

But Sela knew there were no such tealights available for sale in all the world, and that it was her dormant powers awakening that had caused the sparking. Her powers, and the way Pete had managed to make the evening seem enchanted, regardless of her status as a soon-to-be witch.

Sixteen

The walk back from the aquarium to their respective cars took about three times as long as it should have, and that was because Sela could not seem to remove her lips from Pete's. Their kisses were long and lingering, their hands drifting up and down each other's bodies, and from the somersaults Sela's insides were doing and how light her head felt, she knew that soon enough, they would end up at one of their respective apartments. Remembering the sparking candles at dinner, she made a mental note to go to Pete's place first, since it was the less magickal location and hopefully would dampen the effects of her awakening powers. Who knew what havoc she might inadvertently cause if articles of clothing started coming off?

"So, what are you doing Friday?" he asked with a smile as they came up for air by her car.

She resisted the urge to shout, *You, I hope!* and instead said coyly, "Why? Are you free?"

"Not anymore. Pick you up at eight?"

She nodded, leaning in for one more kiss before unlocking her car. "Perfect."

As they parted and Sela put the roses and the remainder of her candy onto the passenger seat, Pete told her, "And be ready for an order."

What kind of kink is this man into? she wondered, a little put-off by those words and the matter-of-fact way in which he'd said them. "Hmm?"

"From my sister," Pete elaborated. "She moves fast when she finds something she likes, and I know she's going to love the sample you gave me."

That same feeling of warmth spread through her once more. "Thanks again, Pete."

"Thank you for another magical evening," he replied. "Can't wait to see you Friday."

On the drive home, her mind turned to what they'd discussed over dinner. Pete had spoken about dental school and the residencies he was doing (focused in pediatric practice, of course, because he wasn't already too good to be true). Then he'd asked her how art school had prepared her for a career.

Sela's first instinct had been to snort and ask, "Preparation? What's that?" But she realized that there had been one class in which she'd learned something that would be valuable to her now. She'd taken a sculpture course with a visiting professor, Araceli Castillo. She'd only been at the school for a semester, which had upset any plans Sela might've had for developing a connection with the woman. She was the one teacher who didn't shame Sela for her interest in natural materials, instead encouraging it.

And now as she thought back, Sela could remember clearly when Araceli told them how to succeed as artists. "If this is what you truly want to do," she'd said, "then the only way to do it is to produce as much as you possibly can, and then when you think you've exhausted all your efforts: you do twice as much. Do constant work. Breathe your art, let it haunt every night of sleep; in fact, let it disrupt your ability to sleep at all. It's only after you've pushed yourself to do more work than you ever believed you could that you'll start to really see what you're capable of."

How did I forget about her until now? Sela asked herself. How had she only remembered the bad, and forgotten about those sparks of light in her past that she should have held onto all these years?

She realized with a start that she'd missed an important turn a few miles back and was apparently lost. "Dammit," Sela muttered, looking for a place to pull over and set up her GPS.

Then, she caught sight of a house she recognized. Grateful for the late-setting sun, which had coated the streets in red-orange light and allowed her to see where she was driving, Sela realized that this was an area through which she'd walked Porter.

She headed now for Courtney's massive home, knowing she could find her way back from there. But as Sela turned up Courtney and Porter's street and caught sight of the house, she noticed several people were standing outside on the lawn. Courtney was there, holding Porter in her arms, and as Sela slowed her car, she saw that the woman looked unusually anxious as she stared up at her home. A generically good-looking man stood next to Courtney, rubbing her back in a comforting way that said he was probably her husband. The other people present were workmen in uniforms.

They were all staring at a vein-like pattern of black lines that seemed to have been painted across the front of the house. Curious as to why someone would choose such an odd form of vandalism, Sela rolled down her window and squinted to get a better look.

Then, her heart jumped to her throat as she realized: those weren't lines, but cracks that had spread from the foundation up the facade of the house. A chill ran down Sela's back, and her own words echoed through her mind: *What you've said and done this eve will break apart this lovely home...*

She rolled up her window and drove faster down the street now, wanting to get away from the house. "It's ridiculous," she said aloud. "I'm not even a witch yet. I haven't had my Nascent Eve, and there's no way I could cause something like that to happen."

But without Sable there to confirm this was true, she couldn't shake the sick feeling the sight of Courtney looking fearfully up at her home had caused, those eerie cracks like the roots of some upside-down, monstrous tree invading the structure above.

Seventeen

Early Wednesday morning before the faintest glow of light hit the sky, Sela woke to find herself tied to her bed.

"Holy shit!" she yelped, then instantly regretted the exclamation. What if the psycho who had done this was in the next room, just waiting for her to wake up so he could come back in and kill her?

She took a deep breath and recognized a familiar fragrance: flowers. Sela blinked down and realized that atop her comforter was a mass of huge pink blossoms resting comfortably on their own bed of leafy vines.

"Climbing tea roses," she said, stunned.

There was no psycho in the next room; the only thing responsible for her current situation was her own magick. But as Sela struggled to sit up, she felt sharp pricks through the comforter and understood that the magickal tea roses that had appeared out of nowhere were apparently not magickally de-thorned.

"Well, this sucks. You have one great date, and the next morning, your witchy powers are a total killjoy."

She tried wriggling, but the vines held tight. After some trial and much painful, thorny error, Sela began using her hands and feet to push the weight of her body into the mattress, which allowed her to inch upwards towards her pillow. It took a good twenty minutes of struggle, but she was finally able to squeeze herself out from beneath the roses.

She turned to look at the clock on her bedside table and was for a moment dazzled by a pulsing glow. The blue goldstone sphere Natalie had bought her for her birthday was glittering brightly, not with reflected sunlight but from what seemed to be the inside out.

"Okay, that's new." Behind the sphere, the clock read half-past four in the morning. "Can these pre-Nascent Eve occurrences ever happen at like a normal hour?" she grumbled, sticking a foot down to get out of bed.

But her toes didn't meet with the floor.

As she stood, Sela found herself immersed in wildflowers. The wooden floorboards that should have been beneath her feet had turned to soil and blossoms grazed the tops of her knees.

"You have got to be fucking kidding me."

Now concerned about the extent of the mess she was going to have to clean up, and without Sable's help this time, she switched on a lamp.

The entire room was a field of flora. From wall to wall and all around her bed were nothing but blossoming flowers extending out of a thick layer of dirt. Sela quickly flicked the lamp off again. If there was even the slightest chance a nearby neighbor might look in and see all of that through her windows, there was a zero percent chance she would have an explanation.

Stumbling through the field in the low light of early morning to yank her curtains shut, she tried to calm herself. "All right, Sela, you've got this. All you have to do is get to work in one piece."

But as she headed for the bathroom, she discovered that the flowers had sealed her bedroom shut. The door would not budge against the rich earth piled five inches high, and Sela could hear poor Pluto plaintively crying on the other side.

*You're due at work in an hour and you'd need at least half
of that time to shower because you're literally covered in dirt,*
she told herself. *There is no way you are making it in time.*

So Sela did something she had not done with so many jobs
over the course of so many years: she called out sick.

"You poor thing!" Aimee, the vet tech who answered
Sela's call, was all sympathy. "You must be feeling awful if
you're staying home. I remember that time you came in with the
flu. You just focus on getting well, and we'll look forward to
seeing you in a couple of weeks."

What Aimee said was true: Sela had worked through many
a cold, flu, fever, and atrociously painful period. She'd once
even managed a week of running from job to job without
realizing she had a fracture in her foot, until it turned such funny
colors that she had to go to a doctor. Leave it to her magick to
be the one obstacle that made it literally impossible for her to
get to work.

But now that she wasn't worried about being late, a new
thought occurred to her: there was a door she hadn't tried yet.
She looked to see if the second bedroom was also barricaded by
flowers and found that while the field did indeed span the full
width of her bedroom, the door to the second room had been ajar
when she'd gone to sleep and thus wasn't sealed shut. She had
to squeeze to get through the opening, but when she finally
emerged on the other side, a gasp overtook her.

If Sela had thought nature had invaded her bedroom, it had
performed a complete takeover of this space. Along the bare
wall to her left, a waterfall was cascading from the ceiling, its
rapids never reaching the ground but instead dispersing into a
foggy vapor that played across the floor of the whole room. Sela
could feel the cool mist as it made its way around her bare feet
and ankles. Beneath tendrils of fog, she saw white water lilies

resting on the floor.

Delicate green vines had wrapped themselves up the height of both the breakfront to her right and the table before her. Lavender wisteria formed a curtain across the top of the breakfront, blooms glowing cool electric indigo in the light of early morning. The table was covered in a thick layer of periwinkle creeping myrtle, and rising from the flora were so many gleaming points of crystal quartz and amethyst.

But the most breathtaking aspect of the room was Sela's triptych, still mounted on the far-most wall but exploding with life. The shells she'd applied to the panels shone as though they still lay beneath the cover of a glimmering sea. The sands were vibrant, their shades of amber, red, and eggshell gloriously amplified such that they nearly glowed with color. And the wood of the panels themselves looked healthy, seeming to pulse with vitality as sparkling moss spread beneath them across the entirety of the wall.

Sela swallowed hard, tears filling her eyes at the sight of this room that felt so overwhelmingly like the parts of herself she had ignored for so long. "I guess we're officially at Nascent Eve."

But with that realization, Sela felt panic rise in her. Where was Sable? How would she find him in time? She didn't want to be an uninitiated witch, and pissed as she'd been when she'd found him with Natalie, she still wanted Sable as her familiar. Beyond being her magickal soulmate or whatever, he was the best friend she'd made since Maria.

If Sela was going to find her familiar in time, one thing was certain: she needed to figure out how to leave her apartment. An idea struck her, and she went to the breakfront and tried a few of the small drawers in its base until she uncovered a gardening spade. Squeezing back into her bedroom and hoping that the bright light of day might keep her neighbors from being able to see into the magickal rainforest that was now her apartment, Sela attacked the dirt at her door with renewed energy, knowing there was a clock on her finding Sable, wherever he might be.

When the door was finally clear enough for her to open it, she threw on some clothes and a pair of sandals and made her way into the living room. But once there, she figured out why Pluto had been crying.

"It's freezing!" she said in horror, her body immediately starting to shiver. "And why is it so dark?"

Her eyes adjusted and she realized that the window above her kitchen sink was obscured by a sheet of solid ice, thick enough that it dimmed the passage of daylight into the apartment.

Probably not a good sign, she thought to herself.

All of the taps in the kitchen and bathroom had frozen over; they were impossible to turn. The light switches didn't work, either. Sela only hoped that the pipes hadn't frozen, as well. She'd have a hell of a time explaining all of this to her landlord.

"Now what?" she asked Pluto, who was unhappily meowing by her feet.

Where could she go? Sable was the only person she knew who could make sense of what was happening, and she didn't know where or how to find him. And it wasn't like there was a hub around town especially for magickal people.

But that wasn't completely true, Sela realized: the shop she'd gone to with Natalie. Hadn't the people who worked there seemed a little bit...well, magickal? They knew how to accommodate witches and spells, that was for sure from the layout of their shop. And the man who'd worked there had said she must need the goldstone orb after all—the same goldstone that she'd dreamt about, the one that was now glowing like a galaxy in the middle of her bedroom.

Half-determined, half-desperate, Sela yanked open the door to her coat closet, ignoring the pain of the icy knob in her hands, and retrieved Pluto's carrier from the back. For once, the poor thing was happy to go inside of it, perhaps figuring anything would be better than the arctic room he'd been stuck inside all morning. Sela locked the door to the natural world of wonders that was apparently her home and hurried with her cat to her car. The shop might be a long shot, but it was the only one she had.

Eighteen

From the moment Sela began driving, a steady rain fell despite the bright and cloudless summer sky above. In fact, the morning was exceptionally beautiful, but the rain didn't let up until Sela arrived outside the shop at around six, at which point it stopped all at once. She noted for the first time the sign above the front store windows, which read: Essential Elements.

"We'll have to wait here for a bit," she murmured apologetically to Pluto, putting her tired face in her hands. "There's no way they'll be open for another—"

A light tapping sounded on the passenger-side window of the car, and Sela found herself looking up at the woman who'd been wearing the green dress on the day she and Natalie had been in the shop. Sela rolled down the window.

"How was your birthday?" the woman asked brightly.

"It was good," Sela replied simply, a little stunned.

"Why don't you unlock the door on this side so I can help with your cat?"

Still shocked at how much easier help had been to find than she'd thought it would be back in the cold hell of her enchanted living room, Sela nodded, getting out of the car and following the woman, who for her part was cooing affectionately at Pluto.

Once inside the shop, though, Sela's surprise melted away as her eyes caught sight of Sable, standing at the counter next to the bearded man who'd sold her the goldstone sphere. Without a second thought, Sela ran and threw her arms around him, relieved when he immediately hugged her back.

"I'm so glad you knew to come here," he greeted her warmly over her shoulder.

"Same!" she cried, stepping back out of the hug. She gave him a stern look. "You're still a piece of shit for what you did, you know, even if I am deliriously happy to see you."

"I'm still sorry for being a piece of shit," he replied. "And hoping I'll be able to make it up to you."

The owners of Essential Elements chuckled at this exchange, and now Sela turned to regard them. "Aren't you going to introduce me?" she asked Sable.

"This is Alexander Hadid," Sable gestured towards the man with the glasses, who nodded in greeting. Then Sable turned to the woman, who tilted her head at Sela. "And this is Lyla, his familiar. Lyla and Alexander, this is Sela Glaser, who I'm hoping is about to become my witch."

"We're just like the pair of you," Lyla told her warmly as Sela realized in amazement that she and Sable weren't the only witch and familiar in town. "Though it's been some time since our Nascent Eve."

"Not *just* like them," Alexander corrected. "We never caused spontaneous rain showers."

"That was my fault?" Sela asked.

"Yes," Alexander and Sable said at once, smirking at one another.

Lyla gave her witch a pointed eye roll. "It was your *doing*," she told Sela. "I wouldn't call it your fault, so to speak."

"Technicalities later I think, Lyla," Alexander suggested. "These two have a day ahead of them."

At this point, Pluto, who'd been forgotten amidst the introductions, began crying to be let out of his carrier.

"The poor creature," Lyla said, bending to open the carrier door. "Go on, stretch your legs a bit."

Pluto trotted out, ducked his head a little at the new surroundings, then was overtaken by typical feline curiosity and started tentatively exploring each new nook and corner.

"Did you have to bring that with you?" Sable asked disdainfully.

"The apartment was freezing!"

"That's weird. Why didn't you just put on the heat?"

"No, Sable, it was *freezing*. I mean, it was completely frozen over. I couldn't turn the water or the lights on."

Alexander and Lyla exchanged a concerned glance, and Sable looked guiltily at the floor.

"That's our fault," he told her. "Well, it's my fault. Tension between witch and familiar before the Nascent Eve can be... problematic."

Sela snorted. "No fucking kidding. I'm guessing that's also why I woke up tied to my bed this morning?"

"What?" Sable cried in alarm.

"Well," Lyla interjected, speaking to all of them but looking to her witch, "I think that at this point, it's clear we might be of some help."

Alexander threw his hands up, looking annoyed but resolved to do whatever it was Lyla was talking about. "I'll gather supplies," he grumbled, turning towards the shop shelves.

Now Lyla put an arm around Sela's shoulder. "Would you like to use my shower upstairs? That mess must be irritating the skin of your legs and feet."

Sela blushed, knowing that in the shorts, t-shirt, and flip-flops she'd pulled on, there had been no hiding the dirt and wildflower debris stuck all over her lower body. "There's a second floor?"

"Our apartments are above the shop," Lyla explained as she led Sela to a closed door off to one side.

They climbed a set of stairs and reached a short, narrow hall with two doors that faced one another. "Alexander lives there, and this is my place."

"You guys don't share an apartment?"

"We've had a bit more time to become established than the two of you, remember," Lyla said kindly as she pushed open her front door. "Alexander and I have been together a good fifteen years. Since then, we've grown our respective businesses, and we've been able to afford more spacious lodgings. You'll get there, too, once you're settled in your powers."

There was something about the other woman's openness—and the fact that she was encouraging Sela, despite not knowing much about her at all—that made Sela love Lyla, at least as much as one could love a person she'd only met twice.

The apartment was full of natural light. There was a thin grey carpet on the floor, a royal blue velvet chaise lounge, and a low glass coffee table furnishing the living area. And all around the room were sewing machines, dress forms, and bolts of vibrant fabric.

"My sister would love this place," Sela remarked.

Lyla nodded proudly. "It took some time, but my label is thriving, both within and beyond Essential Elements."

"That's what you meant by businesses," Sela realized. "The shop and your clothing line."

"It was easier to start with just the shop, given we provided a service to our kind. The magickal community only has so many places that cater to it, so we were lucky to have a customer base already carved out. But as the business grew, I was able to start making clothes at a faster rate, and Alexander used his professional networks to help me."

Sela hesitated, not wanting to ask too much of someone who was already offering her help, but then she saw Natalie's face in her mind, glowering at her tentativeness. "If it would be okay with you, once things get a little less crazy, could I ask you about starting a business?"

"Of course," Lyla assured her. "But now, we must hurry to get you ready. Your Nascent Eve only comes once, and you don't want to miss it."

Lyla's bathroom was tiled and painted in shades of periwinkle, mint, and black, with rose gold accents throughout. "Here are some towels, and you can take your pick of whatever soaps I have in the shower." She pointed to a small hamper and added, "Feel free to leave your dirty things there, and I'll find you something to wear for the day."

"But what if we're not the same size?" Sela asked, noting that Lyla was both more petite and curvier than she was.

Lyla laughed in response. "Remember, I do make clothes for a living!"

The shower was everything Sela hadn't even realized she needed, the water hot and the pressure strong. And Lyla had a collection of lavender-mint botanical soaps that Sela wished she'd created herself. But when she pulled back the curtain to grab one of the plush towels Lyla had left for her, Sela found that the formerly tiled floor was now blanketed in aromatic Corsican mint.

"Crap—more of this?" She wrapped the towel around herself, then called for Lyla.

"Sela? Is everything all right?"

"Not exactly."

Lyla pushed the door open and took in her new, mint-covered floor. "I see." She smiled reassuringly at Sela. "Not to worry—Alexander and I can take care of this later. In fact, it might dry nicely to be sold in the shop. And I think you can walk through. There doesn't seem to be soil underneath."

Sure enough, as Sela put a tentative foot down into the mint leaves, she found they were cool and clean, the overwhelming scent of them invigorating as she made her way out of the bathroom.

"Sorry about the mess."

Lyla chuckled. "That's nothing compared to what Alexander's Nascent Eve caused."

"Really?" Sela couldn't help but be curious. Alexander was the only other witch she'd met thus far, at least that she knew of, and she was interested to know more about him even if he did seem a little grumbly.

"A story for another time," Lyla said as she handed Sela a folded garment. "Now, this is from last year's line but it was too formal to sell out completely. Lucky thing, too—I'd say it's just about perfect for a Nascent Eve."

Sela held up a simple, stunning slip dress, light and creamy with twisted straps that resembled the many vines that had overtaken her apartment that morning.

"This is beautiful," she breathed. "Lyla, I don't know how to thank you for everything you've done."

"Although Alexander hasn't said as much, we received a good deal of help when it was our time, as well." She seemed to reflect fondly on her memories. "Like you, I was gifted a special dress for our rituals by someone who is a dear friend to this day."

"You were?"

"We're both happy to help," Lyla went on, "and I'm proud it's one of my creations you're wearing on such an important day. Witchcraft might feel solitary at first, but there's community, and more of it than the two of you might realize. You'll see, in time."

Now Lyla went to a closet and came back with a light, long trench jacket. "You can borrow this to wear over the dress as we head back to yours, just to prevent your neighbors from thinking anything nuptial might be happening."

A sudden thought occurred to Sela. "It's not, is it?"

"Sorry?"

"I mean, this isn't some kind of weird magickal marriage, right?"

Lyla's expression was now tinged with concern. "You do realize that witch and familiar bond for life, Sela?"

"Well, yeah, I figured that. But we're not like supposed to…be together or anything? I mean, you and Alexander aren't…?"

"Us? No, never," Lyla shook her head, offering a small smile of reassurance but clearly troubled that Sela was asking these questions. "I suppose Sable hasn't had a chance to tell you everything about our world, but you should know that within our community, such relations between witch and familiar are absolutely discouraged. In fact, they are considered by some to be as dangerous as uninitiated witches and familiars who do not share a mark practicing together. I assume he's spoken to you about that?"

"Not much," Sela shrugged. "I thought it wasn't possible."

"Many things are possible," Lyla replied thoughtfully. "But such pairings as the ones we're discussing can be similar, as far as emotions go. The latter, of course, often result in far graver consequences."

"Sable didn't go into that much detail with me," Sela said, confused now.

"I see," Lyla nodded. "Well, most familiars don't like to discuss these matters. In the minds of many of our kind, they're shameful. On the other hand, they're also inevitable, and to an extent, necessary."

"Necessary?" How could romance between a witch and a familiar be necessary? Or witches and familiars who didn't belong together practicing with each other, for that matter? What had Sable been keeping from her?

Lyla gave Sela's hand a gentle squeeze. "We must get moving. You can always come by after your Nascent Eve has passed. I'm happy to talk about anything Sable is too uncomfortable to discuss."

Sela breathed a sigh of relief. "That would be a huge help. I have lots of questions, and he doesn't always want to answer them."

Lyla laughed, leaving Sela by her bedroom so she could get dressed. "I'm a good deal older and I've had time to adjust to my role as familiar. Besides, you need to come by so we can chat over your mysterious business plans!"

As glad as Sela was to have Sable, her best friend of the moment and probably for the rest of her life, there was something comforting about spending time with Lyla and talking about witchcraft with her. It brought back fond memories of her other best friend, and she thought wistfully of how Maria would have loved to see all of the magick that was coming Sela's way now.

I should look her up, once things settle down, Sela thought. *It would be good to have a chance to catch up.*

She pulled the dress carefully over her head and turned to gaze at herself in Lyla's full-length mirror.

"Soon to be a witch," she said, and smiled hopefully at her reflection.

Nineteen

After Sela followed Lyla back into the shop, Alexander gave her and Sable a serious look. "Time to go, young ones. You're late."

"Late?" Sela echoed, looking to Lyla.

"Much as this party won't begin until the two of you have shown up, now that you are together, it's crucial we return you to your magickal sanctum."

"My *what?*"

"Have you taught her nothing?" Alexander asked Sable sharply.

"We did have a pretty intense fight," Sela reminded Alexander, noting her familiar's sheepish look. If he had the decency to feel guilty over what he'd done, she didn't mind defending him.

"Your magickal sanctum is the place you are most connected to within your home," Alexander told her. "It's where you can most effectively cast spells, and where your Nascent Eve rituals are to take place."

"Oh. That might explain the waterfall and the fog forest in the second bedroom."

Sable raised his eyebrows at her, saying, "You just didn't waste any time, did you?"

"Let's go." Alexander headed for the door.

"Wait," Sela called, "I have to get Pluto back in the

carrier."

"Why don't you let him stay here for the time being?" Lyla suggested. "The Nascent Eve rituals can be challenging and the magick is bound to frighten him. Besides, I've already set out food and water."

"You had cat food?" Sela looked at the bowls on the floor with surprise, earning a knowing smile from Lyla and an eye roll from her witch.

"We tend to be prepared," Alexander said brusquely. "Now, can we move?"

As they drove to the apartment, Sela tried to explain the state of it.

"It seems intense," Sable commented, then looked into the backseat to confer with Alexander and Lyla. "Am I right?"

"Green witch tricks are common enough early on," Lyla remarked in a way she seemed to mean as reassuring. But in the rearview mirror, Sela caught her exchanging a troubled glance with Alexander.

"Green witch?" Sela repeated. "Is that what I am? A green witch?"

Alexander sighed. "Sable, you've really neglected your duties here. No, Sela—there aren't any categories or tribes among us. Magick isn't so restrictive in the real world as it is in fiction."

"But I thought Lyla said—"

"All I meant, love, is that it isn't unusual for a new witch to demonstrate a bit of a green thumb," Lyla clarified, not unkindly.

"But why is what's happening with my Nascent Eve so intense, then?"

Sable hesitated. "From what I know, Nascent Eve magick is as surprising to the familiar as it is to the witch, since we're as new to your powers as we are to each other. But you're demonstrating kind of a wide range, and it all seems like a lot to me." He cast another uncertain glance at the backseat, but Alexander and Lyla remained silent.

When they got to Sela's front door, she reached out to unlock it and received a shock from a visible spark for her troubles. "Ow!"

"As I said," Alexander remarked, "you're late."

When they entered the apartment, Sela was amazed to find she could switch the lights on. "I can't believe this all thawed out already."

"The effects haven't completely gone," Lyla observed, pointing to the icicles dripping along the top of the kitchen window. "But it appears you two have begun to resolve things."

"Now what?" Sela asked, turning to Sable.

"Now, I help Lyla and Alexander unpack the tools while you go begin the first ritual."

"Already?"

"Sela, if we don't start soon, this Nascent Eve will pass us by and we'll never become active."

"I hear that, but I legit had to crawl out of my bedroom before."

Now Sable turned to Alexander. "Do you think you could help?"

"Is the room her sanctum?"

Sable shook his head. "Adjacent to it."

"I'll see what I can do."

While Sable and Alexander went to examine the door to Sela's room, Lyla dug through the bag Alexander had packed. "The onyx?" she called to him.

He was examining the door, muttering things and pushing against it in vain. At one point, he glanced over his platinum spectacles at Sela as if he had no idea where she'd come from.

"Better make it the tiger iron," he told Lyla. "These two are difficult."

"I feel like I'd resent that if I understood what it meant," Sela commented.

Lyla chuckled as she handed Alexander a stone sphere smaller than Sela's goldstone orb, but vibrant in its own right. Its swirls of red, brown, and gold seemed to warm within Alexander's palm from the moment he took hold of it.

Sela realized with a start that she was witnessing Alexander's magick at work. It was a little difficult to discern—there was no obvious glow, as with the goldstone that morning. But she could actually see a kind of heated power radiating around the stone as Alexander held it, shut his eyes, and whispered in tones too low to hear.

A moment later, the bedroom door swung open. The plants were still visible inside, but a path had been cleared so that both doors in the room were accessible.

"What kind of stone did you say that was?" Sela asked, amazement filling her voice.

"Tiger iron," Lyla replied.

Sela searched her memory for the names of crystals she and Maria would hoard their allowances in order to purchase. "Is that the same as tiger's eye?"

"It includes tiger's eye, but also incorporates hematite and red jasper."

Sela shook her head, marveling at how easily the door had opened. "It must be really powerful."

"It does aid in magicks that require stamina," Lyla acknowledged. "But the power you're observing is Alexander's."

"Really?"

"Try not to sound so surprised," Alexander said dryly as he returned to the living room and sat down on the sofa.

"Alexander works especially well with stones and crystals," Lyla added, pride in her witch filling her voice.

"Speaking of which," he interjected, "do you have any idea as to why the blue goldstone I sold you is lit up like a galaxy-themed Christmas tree?"

"It's *what?*" Sable stopped looking through the bag of tools and stalked over to Sela's room.

Sela shrugged. "I don't know. It was like that when I woke up. I just figured it's part of the general weirdness that is today?"

"It isn't," Sable said as he reemerged from her room, holding the brilliantly glowing sphere. "Sela, this is a warning. Blue goldstone is protective; the fact that it's lit up like this on your Nascent Eve means we've got trouble of some kind. Did you do anything magickal while I was away?"

She blinked at him. "How could I do anything magickal before you tell me how to be a witch?"

Sable glanced at Lyla. "What do you think?"

She shook her head. "You can't stop the rituals, even if the stone is signaling danger. That could mean anything, and you haven't the time to figure it out now."

"She's right, of course," Alexander added. "Wait any longer, and the two of you will never have to worry about anything magickal ever again."

"Okay, okay!" Sela yelped, louder than she'd meant to, but she figured it was this witch's party and she could cry if she wanted to. She hurriedly slipped out of the jacket Lyla had loaned her. "I'm all fairy-princessed up over here, so let's get this shit done!"

They all looked at her expectantly.

"Oh. Right. So...I'm gonna go do the thing!"

She started to march towards her bedroom, then paused, looking at the blue goldstone in Sable's hands, an inexplicable instinct tugging at her. "Can I bring that with me?"

He gave her a long look before handing it over. "Don't forget that I'm here, okay?"

"I won't do the ritual without you," she assured him. "I know we fought, but I do want you as my familiar."

"That's not what I meant." He shrugged, perhaps to reassure himself as much as her. "You'll be fine. Just, if you get scared or anything, know that I'm here. I'll join you once you get through the first ritual."

Sela nodded, glowing sphere in her right hand, and made for the second bedroom.

Twenty

As Sela entered her magickal sanctum, as Alexander had called it, she noted that nothing had changed since she'd found it that morning. The waterfall, the crystals, and the flowers were all there, with the early afternoon sun sharpening the lush, brilliant colors throughout the room. She hesitantly set the goldstone sphere on the table amidst the amethyst and quartz points.

"Now what?" she said aloud, half-expecting a voice to boom, *I am Oz!* and offer some magickal instruction. But she received no such assistance.

A little fatigued from her rough morning, Sela decided to plop down on the floor in front of the table, facing her triptych on the wall. "Might as well admire the changes while I wait."

And though it was strange to marvel at her own artwork, the life that had been breathed into the three panels by the magick of her Nascent Eve dazzled Sela, drew her eyes across a piece of self-expression that was at once familiar and dramatically new.

Eventually, she found herself slipping into a relaxed state that felt almost like meditation—or at least, what she remembered of it from before she was temping too much to meditate. It was like she was dreaming, even though she wasn't asleep: the swirls of sand on the panels before her seemed to ripple within her steady gaze, and the sound of the waterfall

faded into a murmur like the churning of a quiet sea. The water lilies perfumed the air, and the fog curling around Sela in fragrant whispers brought her more completely into this state somewhere between rest and waking.

I'm not dreaming, she thought, a strange twinge of desperation sounding in her mind as the instinct to withdraw from this new experience arose. *I'm awake. I'm still here.*

And are you a witch? a voice within her asked.

Sela knew that the voice hadn't come from her, exactly. She inhaled flowers and fog deeply, her eyelids closing as she sought out the source of the question. The warm, earthen tones of the triptych seemed to swirl behind her eyes, and now, she began to recognize something deep inside herself: a sign, a name, a power.

My magickal seal, she realized as she tried to understand its shape, the feeling of it as she found where it had always been, hidden within her. *My mark, the one that Sable and I share.*

Are you a witch? the voice repeated, almost coyly.

The seal was so difficult to catch hold of. Every time Sela would think she'd finally grasped it, that she could know it in its entirely, she lost it again, her mind drifting across those vibrant swirls of sand and earth once more.

A sense of challenge rose in her heart. Sable had said uncovering the seal would take time, practice, and hard work. She remembered her teacher Araceli's words, that it was only possible to produce something worthwhile after you'd pushed past the limits of what you thought you could do. And if Sela was used to anything, if there was one thing she knew she could truly do, it was constant, determined work.

And this time, she realized with a thrill, it wouldn't be meaningless hustle to get her through the most basic aspects of her life. This time, the work and its yields would be hers: *her* magick, *her* power.

I am a witch, she said within herself. *I am a witch and I accept this magick as my own. It's in me already, and I claim it as mine.*

No sooner had the words been formed than Sela heard the sound of someone moving behind her, and her eyes flew open. The sun had mostly set. It was late in the evening, almost night.

"Sable?" she called as she got to her feet again, anxious at having lost so much time without realizing it.

She turned to find her familiar smiling proudly at her, his arms full of white pillar candles. He was shirtless, wearing only the sweatpants he'd borrowed from her, and she saw that a thin chain hung around his neck, threaded through a small blue goldstone pendant that was glittering as brightly as the orb on the table.

"I'm so happy to see you with your powers," he told her, and she could hear the joy in his voice.

"But how is it night already?"

"It's easy to lose track of time during the rituals. We still have to keep moving. Help me with these?"

He had started setting the pillar candles around the table in the creeping myrtle, careful not to place them too close to any of the crystal points. Sela took a few and set them down along the windowsills.

"Do you happen to have any matches in here?" he asked.

Nodding, Sela started towards the breakfront to dig matches out of one of its many drawers, but then a new, mischievous part of her thought, *Why not?* And she shut her eyes and thought of fire.

"Sela!" Sable cried.

Her eyes blinked open to find the crystal points on the table overtaken with blue flames. Sable gave her a look of combined awe and alarm, then quickly lit one of the candles from the nearest crystal. The flames died a moment later.

"Try not to do anything experimental until we've finished *all* of the rituals, okay?" he chided her, but he couldn't hide his proud smirk as he used the one candle to light the others.

Now that her initial shock at setting the wrong objects on fire had passed, Sela felt an absolute thrill. *I'm a fucking witch!* she thought gleefully. Of course, she'd been meaning to light the candles and was a little worried about her aim, but it was hard to dim her excitement over her new powers.

"Why do we need candles?" she asked. "Aside from the fact that they're fun and witchy, I mean."

"Lyla and I noticed that your powers have been manifesting as mostly earth and water, but we haven't really seen you exhibit any inclination towards fire. It helps to have all major elements included during the Nascent Eve rituals; this way, should you need to use any of them later, it'll be a little easier." He paused. "Of course, I didn't expect you to set those crystal points on fire. We'll have to talk about your aim at some point."

"So, now what?"

Sable gestured for her to face him in front of the triptych. "Now, we acknowledge each other as two halves of a magickal set by activating our shared magickal seal."

"I thought I just did that."

Sable shook his head. "You found the seal within yourself, but now you and I have to tap into it together, at the same time. This way, both iterations of the seal speak to one another. Only after they've communicated can we accept each other as witch and familiar."

"Do we hold hands or something?"

"We don't have to have a physical connection," he

explained. "The idea is, once the second ritual is complete, we'll always be in contact no matter how far our bodies might be from one another."

This gave Sela a moment's pause. She'd be linked to Sable for the rest of her life, and as she thought on this, Pete's warm smile entered her mind. It had occurred to her that morning that neither Alexander nor Lyla seemed to have a partner, and she knew they weren't involved with each other. Did that mean they had to remain alone? Would this bond with Sable mean giving up Pete, or the dream of someone like him down the road? Sela had long ago relinquished hope for a stable career, but she hadn't stopped wanting someone to share her life with. Would becoming a witch mean giving up a future that included love?

The blue goldstone sphere seemed to sparkle in her direction just then, and she thought, *What a beautiful thing.* And then she realized: so was magick. Rare, beautiful, and something she would certainly never find again.

She smiled at Sable. He definitely knew how to piss her off, but there was something in him that surpassed friendship and perhaps even romance. Sable would always be there, no matter what else happened in their lives. And Sela realized she understood the nature of this relationship: Sable was family.

"Ready?" he asked, and she heard a twinge of nerves in his voice, the sign of a small doubt he must be holding that she might reject him and leave him without family of his own.

She grinned broadly back at him. "Let's do this."

They faced one another, Sela's brown eyes locked onto Sable's heterochromatic gaze, his amber iris reminding her of his feline form, his grey eye striking against the brown of his skin. And as she fell into another trance-like state, something outside of her struck her as so familiar, she was immediately drawn to it.

Sela realized she no longer knew whether her eyes were open or shut. All she could see and feel was her mark, calling to her, reaching out for its reflection inside her. It was taking tremendous effort not to be overwhelmed by Sable's own iteration of the mark. Just as Sela was sure she was going to lose control and spin out into chaos, a warm energy overtook the room. There was light everywhere, so bright she could see nothing but instead felt everything. She started to shake, the world spun, and again, she thought that she was going to lose herself completely until Sable's voice sounded in her heart.

Sela, I'm here.

Sable! She was sure she must be screaming, but heard nothing in the incredible brightness.

Don't be scared, he told her, though she could feel him straining, too. *We're within the seal. We're almost done with this part.*

Okay. It was taking all of her fortitude to keep communicating clearly. *What now?*

Now I ask: do you accept me as your familiar?

Those seven words echoed within the light, bearing more gravity than anything else the two of them had yet said. Sela reflected on her thoughts before they'd begun this ritual: Sable would be family, always.

Yes, I accept you as my familiar.

Within the brightness, joyful sparks began shooting everywhere.

She heard Sable reply: *I come willingly and will remain so.* Warmth filled her as she recognized a broad smile in his voice; if only she could feel her own face, she was sure it was smiling, too.

Always.

They'd said the final word in unison, as if of one mind.

Suddenly, the brightness was gone and Sable sat before her in a crumpled pile of sweatpants, the goldstone pendant now trailing on the ground as it hung loosely from his slender, feline shoulders.

"You're a cat," she said, surprised.

"*Not* a cat," he reminded her sternly, though even in feline form, she could see he was smiling in spite of himself. "But one hundred percent your familiar, Sela."

"We did it!"

Sable's gaze grew worried and he pointed with one paw. "When did you pick that up?"

Sela looked down to find the blue goldstone orb cupped in her hands, still sparkling brilliantly.

"I didn't," she answered, shaking her head. "Or, I don't know—could it have happened during our ritual?"

"We should keep going," Sable told her. His voice was steady, but Sela was overwhelmed by the sensation of his concern. It was a new sense, almost as though she could taste or smell what Sable was feeling.

"Why are you so worried?"

He sighed. "I'm sorry. Now that we're linked, it's going to be some time before either of us has any emotional privacy again. I'm not trying to frighten you."

"Well, whether you meant to tell me so or not, you're worried and it's scary."

Sable gazed at the sphere. "It seems like blue goldstone is going to be your main power stone. That's why Lyla gave me this." He held up the pendant.

"Here, let me help with that." She bent to tie the chain so that it fit Sable but was careful to keep the loop loose, that way if he shifted back into human form, it would release to its full length rather than strangling him.

NASCENT WITCH   143

He nodded his thanks. "The fact that your magick has chosen blue goldstone isn't a bad thing per se. It's a very good stone for protection and will also help you summon your energy when you need it."

"But?"

"But it's a stone that means unseen forces are at work, and some of them may mean you harm. You wouldn't need a protective stone if you didn't need protection, and blue goldstone in particular suggests that whatever poses a threat is likely to stay a mystery for some time."

"So that means…"

"It means we've got trouble," he concluded. "And we won't necessarily know what that trouble is before it hits us."

She remembered suddenly Brown Leather Jacket and the fact that she still hadn't had a chance to tell Sable about him. "That reminds me—"

"Sela, we'll have to talk later. You still need to complete the third ritual, otherwise you'll lose your window and won't be able to begin spellcraft."

She held up the goldstone. "What do I do with this?"

"Hold onto it for now."

Nodding, Sela held the orb in both hands, propping it up in front of her heart for good measure, and prepared herself for another meditative state. She took a deep breath and closed her eyes.

"Um, Sela? What are you doing?"

She peeked one eye open to look down at Sable. "Waiting for the ritual to start?"

"This one's a little less introspective," he chuckled. "You can keep your eyes open."

Feeling silly, she relaxed. "Well, what do I do?"

"You begin the hunt for your Book of Shadows."

"A hunt?"

"Yup. Once you find the book, you can begin spellcraft."

"So instead of meditating like a hippie, I'm now on a magickal scavenger hunt?"

"Try to focus," he told her. "The book won't be found at random. It will emerge from somewhere within the magickal sanctum as the conclusion to the witch's Nascent Eve."

Sela started looking for anything book-like that might be hiding in the room. "Any ideas as to where it could be?"

"You're the one to answer that, not me. It's a reflection of you: your magick, your potential. If anything, it'll be where you would most want it to be."

She continued to look around the room. Already, the candles were half-gone and the mist and water lilies had disappeared. Dawn would be arriving soon, and she felt a sense of urgency.

Where would I hide my Book of Shadows?

The moment the question formed in her mind, she realized that though the magick of the room had become subdued, the waterfall was still rushing steadily along the side wall. She walked over to it, staring into its rapids.

"What are you waiting for?" Sable asked, his voice warm with anticipation. "Reach in."

She held the goldstone in her left hand and tentatively reached into the waterfall with her right. At the touch of something cold against her hand, she gasped and drew her arm back.

The silver chain web she had dreamt of was draped over her fingers, just as she had seen it weeks ago in her sleep. It felt like fine silk thread and was faintly luminescent. She looked over at Sable, whose mouth had comically dropped open beneath his whiskers, and she uncertainly held the webbing out to show him more clearly.

After another moment of gaping at her, her familiar finally managed to speak: "Fuck."

Twenty-One

A sudden flash of light came from Sela's bedroom, visible beneath the closed door. Lyla and Alexander's voices were audible, and they both sounded upset.

Sela turned to Sable, unsure of what to do. Her hands were full of magickal objects and there was no Book of Shadows to be seen.

"Put *that*—" Sable pointed to the chain web "—very carefully on one of the amethyst points. *Not* on a crystal quartz point, you understand?"

She did as she was told, feeling via their emotional link dread and panic coursing through her familiar. It was strong enough to keep her from asking questions for the moment.

"Now, let's find out what's going on." He led the way to her bedroom.

The field of wildflowers was gone. If not for the mass of roses still lying on the bed, it would have been impossible to tell that Sela's Nascent Eve morning had even happened. Alexander and Lyla were standing by the windows, their faces grave.

"What's going on?" Sela asked.

"Sela," Alexander said seriously, "we need to know what kind of magick you were involved with before your initiation."

"What?" Sela was taken aback, both by the question and by her new friends' serious demeanor. "I wasn't involved with magick before my initiation. I mean, lots of magickal stuff happened, but I thought that's normal right before the Nascent Eve, isn't it?"

"I need you to be honest with us," Alexander pressed, clearly struggling to stay patient.

"She is," Sable told him. "She's not lying. I can feel that she's as confused as I am right now."

"I don't understand," Sela said. "What was that light we saw?"

"We were tidying your room," Lyla spoke now, her voice gentler than Alexander's but also distressed. "We thought you two would want rest after your big night. But then an intruder tried to enter through the fire escape window, and Alexander had to fight him off. That was the light you saw."

"An intruder?" Sable echoed. "What kind of intruder?"

Sela felt a cold, familiar worry move at the base of her spine.

"He was about your age," Alexander recalled. "Blonde hair, average build, and he was wearing a kind of—"

"Brown leather jacket," Sela finished quietly. The chill had moved throughout her body, and she saw Sable turning to scrutinize her and knew he'd felt it, too.

Alexander nodded. "Lyla has seen him before."

"Outside the shop, on the day you first came to see us."

"You kept me safe," Sela realized with some amazement, recalling the beautiful blue bird that had flown into her path when she'd tried to follow her pursuer. "You stopped me from going after him."

Lyla offered her a hand, giving Sela a comforting squeeze. "I didn't know what was happening, exactly. But I could tell you were being magickally tracked and that you were frightened. Perhaps you can tell us more."

"I think you'd better," Sable added, and Sela felt his rising agitation.

"I wanted to ask you about it," she told him earnestly. "I was coming home to do exactly that on the night we fought, and then I lost my chance, and with everything today..."

"You have a chance now." Sela was surprised to hear a kindness in Alexander's voice that she associated more with his familiar. "Lyla had the foresight to put tea up for the four of us in the kitchen. Let's have a seat and hear the full story; it seems you two are going to need *much* more help than we'd thought."

In the living room, Sela recounted every encounter she'd had with Brown Leather Jacket: the club, the restaurant, even outside of Essential Elements on the day Lyla had intervened.

"My guess is that he's spelled," Alexander said once she'd finished. "And since he's following you, there's a good chance that you're the one who spelled him."

"How could I spell him?" Sela asked. "I didn't even finish my third ritual."

"You *what?*" Alexander sputtered on a mouthful of tea, starting to get to his feet, but Sable held out a paw to stop him.

"Oh, she finished the ritual, all right. Instead of the book, she withdrew a gossamer chain."

Not for the first time since they'd met, Alexander stared at Sela like he didn't know what sort of creature she was. "A gossamer chain? Are you sure?"

"It's in the second bedroom resting safely on an amethyst point," Sable went on, swallowing a mouthful of tea. "See for yourself if you like."

"I don't understand." Sela put her face in her hands, starting to feel the lack of sleep that was exacerbating her state of general confusion. "If I finished the ritual, where is my Book of Shadows? What's happening?"

Lyla, who had been listening thoughtfully to the whole

exchange, held up her hands. "If we all keep our heads, I think we might figure this thing out. Sela, when Alexander took the tiger iron to open your bedroom door, how did you know to ask me if he was using tiger's eye?"

Sela shrugged. "I mean, they sound similar, I guess?"

"They do and they are," Lyla acknowledged patiently. "But what I want to know is how *you* know that."

If Sela hadn't wanted to admit to her days of pop witchcraft with her friends during high school in front of Sable, she was mortified at the prospect of talking about them in front of a well-established witch and familiar pair.

Can I just go to bed and deal with memory lane some other time? she thought.

But Sable sensed her emotions and looked at her sternly. "You are humiliated over something, and whatever it is, you need to suck it up because we need to know about it."

Sela sighed. "It's a little cringe, but when I was in high school, my friends and I...we used to mess around with witch stuff."

"You used to 'mess around with witch stuff'?" Sable's voice was incredulous. "Are you telling me you used to practice witchcraft?"

"Sort of?"

"Sela!" her familiar exploded. "The day we met, I specifically asked if you'd ever been a witch before!"

"I wasn't!" she cried defensively. "We were just kids playing around! That can't possibly count for anything!"

"Oh, it counts," Alexander told her, his fingers massaging his temples, causing his glasses to comically bounce in front of his brown eyes.

"Consider how few true witches patronize our shop," Lyla added. "If magick were meaningless when practiced by those who aren't part of our community, our business would be dishonest."

"That's the reason the third ritual didn't give you a Book of Shadows," Sable went on, his voice growing louder with each word. "You already *have* a Book of Shadows! You don't need to enter into spellcraft because you already *practice* spellcraft! This is a fucking disaster!"

"But I thought all of the spells of uninitiated witches end up going wrong." Sela was starting to panic now. "Am I never going to be able to cast a proper spell?"

"No," Lyla told Sela firmly. "You completed the ritual as you were meant to. In lieu of a Book of Shadows, you received a gossamer chain; it's a tool that helps a witch right wrongs, and it came to you so you can begin to fix everything you did while uninitiated." She smiled encouragingly. "But you did make it through the third ritual, and you are a true initiated witch."

Sela felt some small relief at that, until she considered something Lyla had just said. "Wait, what do you mean I have to fix everything from when I was uninitiated?"

"She means," Sable's agitation was coming off him in almost visible waves now, "that you need to undo all of the crazy fucking spells you did as a crazy fucking teenager, because from the moment we completed the rituals, they started to wreak what I'm sure is fucking havoc on everyone and everything involved!"

Sela covered her mouth with her hands. "Holy shit! Are you telling me that the spells I cast a decade ago are all suddenly alive and kicking?"

Sable threw up his paws. "Yes! Anything you cast, any curses or charms—as soon as you came into your powers, all of that became relevant."

"*Relevant?* What the hell does that mean?"

"It means that we have a big fucking mess to clean up, Sela." Sable was shaking his head. "I don't know how you didn't tell me about this. A magickal past doesn't just go away because you think you're adulting now!"

She looked helplessly to Lyla and Alexander. "So, I'm screwed because of things I did before I even knew how to drive?"

Alexander gave a shrug. "Well, you're not necessarily screwed. You can reverse the spells, in theory, if you can revisit the original incantations. Are they handy?"

Despite the fact that they all already knew she'd practiced witchcraft in high school, Sela didn't want to admit that she'd held onto her old spellbooks and journals for nostalgia's sake. "I mean, that was a while ago. Would there be a different way to fix things?"

"Aw, cute, she's trying to save face again," Sable said mockingly. "Don't bullshit us, Sela. Every one of you Wicca-dabbling, *Practical Magic*-watching, Loreena McKennitt-listening wannabe teen witches threw together adorable little homemade spellbooks that are probably still in your parents' basement."

Sela didn't need a mirror to know she had turned completely red. "Fine!" She threw her hands up, mimicking the gesture Sable had made just moments before. "We'll take a road trip to my family's place. And it's the attic, not the basement," she added huffily.

"This doesn't solve the immediate problem," Lyla reminded them. "Sela, you must know the young man who was trying to break in tonight."

Sela shook her head. "Only lately, from all the times I've caught him following me."

"No," Alexander countered. "Lyla's right—he has to be

from your past. You're a brand-new witch and your ties to the community don't extend beyond this room. It's way too soon for someone to want to curse you."

"Is that a thing?"

"You must figure out who he is," Lyla insisted. "We can't be with you all the time, and it took Alexander considerable effort to send him away."

"The spell on him is strong," Alexander agreed. "It's had time to cement, too. The sooner you undo it, the better."

"Well, I can't get out of work until maybe the weekend…" Sela began, then groaned and let her face fall into her arms.

"Now what?" Sable asked, clearly terrified at the prospect of what else his witch might have done.

"Work! What am I going to do about work? It's already dawn and my whole body feels like I just lost a bar fight with a rhino."

"You're calling out sick," Sable told her. "Nascent Eve rituals are very draining and we need rest. Besides, we've got to get our empathetic connection under control."

"Does that mean I'm not always going to automatically know when you're annoyed at me?"

"It means we get some privacy back. I'll always tell you when you're annoying."

"Oh, good," Alexander commented. "They're snarking back and forth again. Now we can go home and sleep."

Sela turned to him. "Thank you," she said, trying to fill her voice with as much gratitude as she felt. "You and Lyla spent your whole night here, you made my room into a room again, and you kept us safe. I don't know what we would've done without you."

Alexander cleared his throat and adjusted his glasses. "It's no trouble."

"Oh, I almost forgot! I left Pluto at your place."

"Let us care for him through the weekend," Lyla told her with a smile. "Then come by the shop when you can. We've much to discuss."

After they saw the witch and familiar pair out, Sela and Sable went into her room to deal with the roses, the only remaining part of the mess.

"Is there, you know, a simpler way to do this?" Sela suggested coyly.

"Don't even think about it, witch. You're exhausted, and we already saw your aim with those candles. Just get some gloves and I'll do the best I can with the dustpan."

As Sela gathered up the thorny vines and started stripping linens from the bed, she saw Sable working hard to sweep errant leaves and rose petals into the dustpan using his paws.

"Hey, why did you change back into a cat?"

Sable swept in silence, but Sela could almost taste his reluctance to breach the subject. Finally, he said quietly, "I don't control when I change."

"But Lyla transformed into a bird to help me the first day I met her."

Sable sighed. "Lyla and Alexander have been initiated for years."

"So? What does that have to do with it?"

Sable stopped sweeping. "Familiars can't control their forms until their witches gain some magickal experience. Our powers grow with yours. Until you develop some control, magickal energies can shift me to human form and back, but I never know when it'll happen or for how long."

Now Sela also stopped what she was doing. "Wait a minute, are you saying you have absolutely no say in the form your own body takes?"

Sable shrugged and went back to sweeping, but Sela felt a deep bitterness in his heart. Their emotional connection was too strong for him to hide it from her.

She went to grab fresh linens. When she came back into the room, she told Sable, "Just so you know, I plan to work my ass off to grow my powers as quickly as I can."

Neither of them said anything else, but as they jumped onto the fresh sheets and blankets to rest, Sela felt Sable's pride at all they had achieved so far, and she fell asleep with a smile on her face.

Twenty-Two

Sela woke to an early alarm and called all of her jobs to cancel for the day. Her eyelids were heavy with exhaustion and she could barely move, never mind get up and go to work. Though she was afraid she might lose some of the hustles she relied on most, pretty much everyone responded with kindness, telling her to feel better and not to worry about it.

"You seem surprised," Sable remarked from the lower corner of her bed after she settled back under the comforter.

"Well," she yawned, "everyone's being so nice about me cancelling."

"It's almost like you're a hard worker and they appreciate you or something."

They slept the rest of the day away until evening, when Sela's audibly growling stomach woke her.

"I'm ordering food," she announced.

"Fish, please," Sable said, rubbing his eye with a paw as he stretched awake.

"Sushi?"

"Ooo, yes. I'd kill for a rainbow roll."

"Murder won't be necessary," Sela said brightly as she opened a restaurant app. "This place delivers in under half an hour."

Twenty minutes later as the two of them were gobbling up the food on the sofa in the living room, Sela asked through a lump of sweet potato roll, "Is it normal to be this hungry after a Nascent Eve?"

Sable nodded as he swallowed a huge piece of tuna. "Magick is always a little draining, but we basically just ran a marathon without any preparation. Plus, we're probably feeding off each other's exhaustion because of the new emotional link between us."

This brought her mind back to Pete. "Speaking of emotional links," Sela began casually, "how do witches and familiars handle having relationships?"

"What do you mean?" Sable's eyes were crossing as he tried to slurp a particularly long udon noodle, which Sela might have found cute if she didn't feel so damn guilty about the fact that he was only a cat at the moment because of her.

"Well, I'm seeing this guy from one of my jobs and we're about to hit date number three, so I'm pretty sure that sex is going to happen soon. Will that be affected by our magickal bond?"

Sable blinked at her, the noodle hanging comically from his mouth. "Is this a trick question?"

"What do you mean?"

"Because of your sister? Sela, I really can't tell you how sorry—"

"Let's not always associate Natalie with sex, despite the alarming number of people who seem to do just that. Anyway, I've pretty much forgiven you." She paused, her thoughts drifting back to Pete. "I met someone, Sable. I really like him."

Having abandoned the noodles, he was studying her intently. "Yeah, I can sense that. When did this happen?"

"Our first date was the night you and I fought, actually, which is why I haven't had a chance to tell you about him."

"Things have been good so far?"

"They've been mind-blowingly great. I might actually be able to resurrect my sex life from the crypt where I've been keeping it for...too long."

"I know that feeling."

She shot him a look. "Dude, again with my sister—I don't forgive you *that* much."

"Sorry."

Sela went on, "But does that mean you'll, you know... sense things? During?"

"Huh." Sable thought this over. "How soon are you going to be having sex?"

She threw up her hands. "I feel like I'd know better if I could get past date number three without my magickal stalker showing up."

"Well, we should be able to get our emotions back under control pretty soon," he told her as he started in on a piece of salmon. "Your stalker, on the other hand, might take a bit longer."

"What's 'pretty soon'?"

"I figure our psychic link should calm down in about a week or so. Until then, maybe don't have sex?"

She rolled her eyes. "A week. Great. That's long enough for Pete to find some other temp to lust after."

"Tell me more about Pete," Sable said. From the way he was digging into the sushi, Sela felt like she was narrating her familiar's favorite soap opera by the time she was halfway through catching him up on her romantic adventures.

"Shit," she realized as they were talking, "I already cancelled work tomorrow, but Pete and I were supposed to have a date. I'm still a little zonked from the Nascent Eve."

"Don't cancel," Sable advised. "Just stay local in case you get tired."

"Really?"

He nodded. "He sounds like he's definitely not an asshole, and that's a rare thing in the dating world."

"Don't even get me started."

"Welp," Sable hiccup-burped, "there's nothing I love more than a post-sushi Netflix binge. Set me up with your laptop?"

She snorted. "Seriously?" Before she could stop the image from filling her mind, she pictured Sable in cat form gnawing on a bowl of popcorn while streaming movies. The thought was much more amusing than she'd meant it to be.

Sable gave her a glare. "I was suggesting we watch together, but since you're mocking me, you can just stay in the living room."

She gaped at him. "Hey! That was inside my head!"

"Still mocking."

"Well, what am I supposed to do while you hog my computer?"

"Why don't you call hot Pete and confirm your date?" Sable suggested as he trailed into the bedroom.

"How are you going to watch anything without my password?" she called after him. "I thought you needed me to log you in!"

He poked his head back out of the room to briefly smirk at her. "I was just being polite. You're not the only magickal creature in this apartment, you know."

And a minute later, she heard the familiar opening theme of one of her favorite shows.

"Ridiculous," she muttered, heading to her kitchen nook to put up water for tea. Then she grabbed her phone and threw herself back on the sofa, calling Pete's number.

"Hello?"

"Hey," she said with a smile, hoping he could hear it

through the phone.

"Um, hi."

Not exactly the enthusiastic response she'd been expecting. "Is everything okay?"

Pete let out a quiet sigh. "Sela, that first night when I said I wasn't into games, I was serious."

"Okay," she responded slowly. "I'm not into them, either."

"Are you sure about that?"

Still too exhausted from her Nascent Eve to mince words, she bluntly told him, "Pete, it would really help if you would just say what you mean."

"All right, then," he replied, agitation in his voice. "I drove to your place last night because my sister really loved the samples you gave me, and I was about to order more products from you. I thought I'd swing by and surprise you."

Well, that was nice.

"And I wasn't snooping," he went on, "but as I pulled up to park, I happened to catch sight of you through a window."

Oh, for fuck's sake. Sela immediately had an idea of what he might have seen, and though she knew she was about to lie to him, a low growl of indignation rose up inside her. "Okay. Why didn't you call and ask to come up?"

Pete let a long pause pass.

"Pete?" Sela pressed him. Normally, she wasn't this assertive, but she also normally wasn't a witch, either. Or this was her new normal, and apparently witch-Sela didn't like passive-aggressive accusations.

"I saw you with some shirtless guy, Sela."

"Sable," she corrected him. "You saw me with Sable."

"Does that matter?" His voice was rife with incredulity.

"Yeah, it matters," she responded steadily. It was awful, but the lie had organically formed in her mind and she was sticking to it. "That's my friend and occasional roommate, Sable."

"Who you were naked with last night."

"No one was naked," Sela argued sharply. "By any chance, during your not-snooping into windows, did you happen to notice a shit-ton of candles and crystals around?"

"Yeah, I saw candlelight, Sela." Now he sounded angry. "Are you serious right now?"

"If you had bothered to pick up the phone and call me," she continued, "you would've learned that Sable is a New Age fanatic and he had me doing meditation and hot yoga last night. He's working on getting certified to teach soon. He might even open up a studio if he can get the money for it."

For a minute, Sela was confused as to why the false words had flowed so easily off her tongue, but then she realized: she might be lying about being a witch, but what Pete thought he'd seen the night before had definitely not been the truth. She might not be able to tell him about her Nascent Eve, but she damn well could hold him accountable for accusing her of sleeping with somebody else when she wasn't.

"I…" His voice trailed off, but Sela didn't wait for him to recover.

"Pete, you need to understand something," she said calmly. "I get that you've probably dated some scary people. I've dated a number of those, as well. But you don't get to just call me up and accuse me of sleeping with a friend who, by the way, I'm currently still a little pissed at for recently fucking my sister."

"Oh, Jesus."

"Sable and I are not involved, but he is a friend and he is crashing here, so I did him a favor. I let my friend use me as a yoga student guinea pig for the night." She took a chance, not knowing how long Pete had been outside the apartment. "If you had stuck around, you would've seen our friends Lyla and Alexander come and join us later on."

"Sela, I'm so sorry. Unbelievably sorry. I just saw he was shirtless, and you weren't wearing much either—not that I'm judging! I sometimes toss my shirt when I work out, too, and I—"

"Look," she cut him off, her anger ebbing as she heard the distress in his voice, "we had space heaters running, plus the candles, so I could see how a hot yoga class might look like more from the outside. But Pete, please—just ask me next time before jumping to your own conclusions."

And now came the guilt. Sela might not be sleeping with anyone else, but she also couldn't simply come out and tell him she was a witch. There was still a lie happening; it just wasn't the one Pete had imagined.

"Of course," he replied, almost to himself. "Of course, I'm such an ass."

"You're not," she told him, then added flirtatiously, "and you could always make it up to me."

"How's that?"

"Well, I wouldn't be opposed to taking a break from driving tomorrow night," she said. "Instead of us meeting somewhere as usual, why don't you come pick me up? You can even inspect the apartment, if you like."

It was a little mean, but that last dig had its intended effect. "I deserved that," he answered. "And yes. I'd love to come pick you up at your place, no inspections necessary."

They were about to say their goodbyes for the night, Sela knew. "One more thing, Pete."

"Yeah?"

"I really don't like games, so I mean this in the least conniving way possible: it's nice to know that you like me enough to be mad about seeing a guy—who again, is just a friend—shirtless in my apartment."

Now Pete laughed, and a pleasant flutter moved deep in her abdomen at the sound. "Sela, you're one of the most incredible people I've ever met. You know that, right?"

Did she know it? She was a witch, and that was awesome. But the rest of her?

"Self-doubt is endlessly unattractive," she heard Sable shout from her bedroom.

Making a mental note to get their witch-familiar emotional connection under control as soon as magickally possibly, she said into the phone, "I'm glad I'll see you tomorrow."

"Me too."

Sela shut her eyes as she lay back on the sofa, basking in the afterglow of talking to Pete. Despite the fact that the conversation had been rocky, it had ended on a good note. She didn't like that she couldn't tell him about the witch thing yet, but she needed to get a handle on her powers before introducing the world of magick to anyone else in her life. Besides, she wanted to talk to Sable—and, for that matter, Lyla—so that she could learn what risks might come with revealing her new self to someone she cared about.

Fantasies about the night to come with Pete and anxieties about keeping her witchy nature a secret from him blurred together, and Sela didn't even notice as she drifted into a doze.

She was back in the alley, the unknown voice calling her name. The man who had followed her the first time she had the dream still watched her, and she now recognized a brown leather jacket on his back, though she still couldn't quite make out his face.

Several feet behind him, someone new began to walk forward from the haze. She was incredibly familiar, though the dream wouldn't reveal her face to Sela, either. She remained in silhouette, a small lizard perched on her left shoulder.

"I know you," Sela said. Even in shadow, she sensed the woman smiling in mutual recognition.

Sable touched her shoulder gently. He was at her side, flickering between human and feline form, and she turned to see who he was gesturing to.

The same ten figures that had been in the alley during the last version of this dream remained; now, though, the animals flickered in the same way Sable was doing, and Sela could make out their human forms much more clearly. She recognized one of them, a large blue bird with a crown like a peacock who was, at the same time, a petite dark-skinned woman with long dreadlocks and a kind smile.

Lyla, Sela thought.

Alexander stepped forward beside his familiar, eyeglasses glinting sharply through the haze of the alley. The other pairs around them were unfamiliar still; except, Sela realized with a start, the man with long white-blonde hair who stood beside the panther. His washed-out blue eyes observed her not unkindly, though the expression on his pale face was unreadable.

Where had she met him? The fog of the dream made it hard for her to recall. The panther beside him flickered such that she caught glimpses of a tall, muscular man with eyes and hair dark as his panther's fur coat. His gaze was unflinching, like that of his witch.

They're all witches, she understood as she gazed across the array of people, studying those she didn't know in particular, just to be sure: the two flickering dogs next to a tall man and woman, all four seeming to know one another intimately from how close they stood; the two smaller women, one of whom flickered in and out of the form of a rat.

Despite the fact that they were strangers to her, there was no question in Sela's mind: *Witches and familiars, just like us.*

Sable smiled at her, but when the voice called her name again, the expression faded and left in its wake one of worry and fear. The goldstone pendant that hung from his neck glittered brightly, signaling danger not far from them.

"Sela!"

Her eyes flew open, and she ungracefully fell from the sofa to the living room floor, where she was suddenly eye to eye with her familiar.

"Huh?" she managed dazedly, confused as the details of her dream slipped away.

"I repeat: I am having an ice cream crisis."

"What kind of crisis?"

"The ice cream: it's in the freezer."

"So?"

"It's in the freezer and not in front of me."

"For fuck's sake, Sable," she grumbled, getting up and stumbling to the freezer. "How can you possibly eat after all that sushi?"

"Fat-shame me when you can cast a decent spell without setting the whole apartment on fire," he retorted. "Until then: I would like the Phish Food, please."

Rolling her eyes, she handed him a pint of Ben & Jerry's and stumbled off to bed, into a dreamless sleep.

Twenty-Three

"You can't seriously be thinking of wearing that."

As Sela dug through her closet for an outfit that would work for a Friday night date, Sable sat on her bed, happily eating spaghetti. He had resumed human form at four in the morning, scaring the hell out of Sela as he fell to the floor in a loudly cussing heap. Sela could tell he was feeling extremely pleased with himself, no emotional link necessary—the smug look on his face said it all.

"This is the fifth outfit you've vetoed," she snapped at him. "I'd rather have you figure out what we're going to tell Pete with you hanging around like this."

Sable shrugged. "Aren't I your slightly eccentric, very charming, yoga-loving sometimes-roommate?"

"Okay, roomie," Sela put her hand on her hip. "Where's your stuff? Where do you sleep? And where the hell am I supposed to entertain Pete?"

He thoughtfully chewed a mouthful of spaghetti. "Can't you fool around in the living room?"

She glared at him before yanking outfit number six from the closet. "This one."

Sable shook his head vehemently, his mouth still full. His thick curls bounced gently around his face and, thinking about having to style her own hair and do her makeup once an outfit had been settled on, she was seized with a moment of envy at

Sable's smooth brown complexion. The last time she'd checked the mirror, the usual lines and shadows under her eyes seemed to have doubled.

Choking down the pasta, Sable told her, "That's so matronly! No way is Pete going to want to take that thing off and see what's underneath. Also: why are you sending jealous vibes at me? Did you want spaghetti, too?"

She threw the dress at him. "What am I vibing now?"

"Hey, watch it! You could take out someone's eye—or their brunch." He clutched the bowl of spaghetti protectively. "What's the big deal with tonight, anyway? You never obsess this much over clothes."

"You're the one making me try on a million things," she huffed as she wiggled into a high-waisted pencil skirt. Since their Nascent Eve had come and gone, Sela was comfortable enough with Sable to not force him out of the room while she changed. It wasn't like her underwear was coming off, and his judgmental attitude towards the bulk of her wardrobe was reminiscent of growing up with Natalie, if nothing else.

"Only because your anticipation is making me jittery."

"If you must know," Sela said as she buttoned a nearly-sheer chiffon top, "Pete called me incredible last night."

"That one!" Sable sat straight up as she turned to show him the outfit. "Just unbutton that top button and it's perfect."

"Separates? Really?"

"He'll think it's super-sexy, believe me."

Sela blinked. "But I'm not having sex with him tonight."

"Could've fooled me."

"Again: where am I supposed to have the sex if my familiar is on the premises?"

Sable shrugged again. "I could always head to Lyla and Alexander's for the night. You could have the apartment to yourselves."

Sela flushed. She knew from the intensity of their last encounter that she and Pete were on the brink of a date that would extend into the next morning. And as much as she was looking forward to that, the prospect of being psychically linked to Sable during sex was putting a huge damper on her anticipation. As awesome as not always having to talk to communicate with her familiar was, the creepy factor was pretty glaring.

"Yeah," Sable winced, catching her train of thought. "I'm not exactly comfortable with the idea of us sharing empathic orgasms, either, as hot as Pete sounds."

She sighed, turning to the mirror and preparing to brush her hair. "It's way too soon. I just got my powers, plus we're road-tripping to my folks' place early tomorrow and—"

Sela shrieked as the towel around her damp hair fell to the floor.

"What happened?" Sable leapt off the bed.

"My hair!" She spun around and held up the ends of her hair: the bottom few inches had inexplicably become a rich shade of lavender.

"Oh," Sable replied, underwhelmed at the sight. "What, did you mean to go from the roots?"

"I didn't want this!" she yelped. "I thought all these magickal freak accidents were supposed to go away after we were initiated!"

"That's not an accident," Sable told her. "You made your hair purple."

Sela didn't know whether to cry or strangle her familiar. "Are you out of your mind? I did *not* make my hair purple!"

"As frightening as it is to insist while you're fantasizing about murdering me, I promise: you either dyed it or you spelled it. Either way, that's not a random act of magick."

"Spelled it?" A memory was jogged from the depths of Sela's mind, and she groaned, slapping a hand over her eyes. "Oh my god. Oh, we've got to get that Book of Shadows back and undo all my crazy shit."

A grin of realization spread across Sable's face. "So, this is a spell from Sela's teen witch days."

"I wanted purple tips so badly and my mom wouldn't let me. But I don't want them now! What about my date?" Then, Sela remembered she was an initiated witch. "Okay, if magick got me into this mess, I'll just use magick to get out of it, right? We can think of a spell to get my hair back to normal, and—"

"Sela," Sable interrupted, "are you forgetting that you have yet to cast any spells at all?"

"So what?"

"So, if your aim hasn't improved since you set all those crystals on fire during our Nascent Eve, you could try to remove the purple and end up removing your own head."

The man with the beautiful hair had a point. "Well, what am I supposed to do? I can't cancel on Pete at the last minute."

Sable evaluated her. "It's been a few years, but I'm not half-bad with a pair of scissors."

"Hang on: you mean to tell me that you won't let me try a spell because of the risk that I'll decapitate myself, but you expect me to let you near my head with sharp and pointy objects?"

"By 'not half-bad,' I mean I'm actually good," he retorted defensively. "Maybe it's lucky I'm in this form."

"On that subject," Sela said, wanting to get her familiar's mind off chopping up her hair, "wasn't it kind of soon for you to transform again? We haven't even gotten any practice in."

"I don't think it's going to last very long," he replied

glumly. "Sometimes, excess magickal energy from the Nascent Eve changes the familiar back to human form for a few more days. I'll probably be on all fours again within a week."

Feeling his frustration at not being able to control the change and desperate to make him less morose, Sela found words leaving her mouth that she never thought she'd say: "What choice do I have? It's not like I can afford a salon. I'll go get the scissors and then you can do your worst."

Her efforts worked, at least. Sable lit up, smiling at her. "Really? I promise, I won't fuck it up. I'm really good."

"You'd better be," she told him as she went to find the scissors.

Sable draped a towel over the bathroom mirror and absolutely refused to let Sela have even a peek at what he was doing. It was the longest and most terrifying haircut she'd ever experienced, with Sable positioning her head meticulously before each snip. Then he insisted that she let him do her makeup, too.

"It won't be a finished look if I don't at least do your eyes."

"How did you even learn how to cut hair and do makeup?" she asked, curiosity overwhelming her apprehension for the moment.

A warmth entered Sable's voice as he brushed shadow onto her closed eyelids. "There was another familiar I knew back when I was about eleven or twelve. Her name was Diana, and she was like the big sister I never got to have. She taught me how to cope with the unexpected changes between forms; they tend to get a little worse during puberty."

"How old was she?"

"Nineteen. She still had years before she'd meet her witch, but she was already preparing to uproot herself and move when the time came."

"Move?" Sela tried not to flinch as Sable applied liner and mascara to her eyes.

"It's pretty rare for a witch and familiar to grow up near one another. We sense you before you're even aware of what you are, so we have to be ready to drop everything and find you in time for the Nascent Eve. Usually, that means leaving home quickly."

The more Sela learned about how a familiar's existence revolved around his witch, the more guilty she felt, like she'd been doing Sable this huge disservice for his entire life without even realizing it. She pushed hard at the feeling: guilt was never of use to anyone, and she wanted to help Sable gain control of his body. She'd practice her magick diligently until that happened.

"Anyway, Diana was the most stable person in my life when I was growing up. We spent a lot of time together, and when we happened to both be in human form, she insisted on teaching me to help her with her makeup. She said it was a skill that might come in handy more often than I realized. We used to trim each other's hair, too."

"You do have great hair," Sela said enviously.

"Thanks—so do you, as of a few minutes ago. Okay, we're about ready."

She opened her eyes to find Sable removing the towel from the mirror, the smug look he'd been wearing earlier back on his face. She got up slowly, steeling herself for the worst.

The shoulder-length auburn tangle that Sela had gotten used to was gone, as were any traces of her magickally purple ends. A familiar though before unrealized version of herself stared back at her from the mirror: she was sporting the haircut she'd glimpsed in the alley of her dreams. It was a variation on a pixie cut, but Sable had used the waves in her hair to create a feathered, fearless look that showed off her long neck and gently dusted her forehead. And Sela's eyes looked huge: her familiar had somehow achieved that impossibly fine balance between natural makeup and an evening look, making her brown eyes seem to smolder. A nude lip brought the whole look together, accentuating the angles of her face.

"Well?" Sable asked impatiently.

She burst into a broad grin. "I look hot."

"You do," he confirmed.

"I never look hot!"

"You're a witch now," Sable reminded her. "You'll look however you want."

"However *you* want, you mean. I'm never making my own style choices again if this is what you're capable of."

"Take me shopping with you and you'll see some real magic."

She laughed as they made their way back into her room. "So, what are you going to do while I'm out?"

Sable shrugged. "I'll probably walk around town a bit. Alexander left me clothes the other night so I could wear more than just your old sweats, and Lyla spotted me some cash."

That same frustrated feeling that overwhelmed her whenever Sela thought about her familiar's dependence on her magickal growth flared up once more. What the hell were familiars supposed to do, just exist in financial and bodily limbo until their witches weren't train wrecks?

Hesitating because she knew it was likely to piss him off, Sela said, "I can always give you money, you know."

"I don't need to be given anything," he replied sharply, which she'd expected. "I fully intend on paying Lyla back once I've got control of my form and can work."

"I can always *loan* you money, then." Sela ignored his

agitation; it was her fault he was in this mess, after all. "Sable, you've uprooted your entire life just to come teach me how not to suck at witchcraft. The least I can do is take you on that shopping trip this weekend. There are a lot of great stores in my hometown. We can make it part of our road trip."

He didn't say anything, but she felt the irritation he'd been emitting a moment before relax into what she knew was a real and growing affection for her. She went into the kitchen and dug around in a drawer.

"Here," she said, handing him a folded cartoon map of town that was bordered with ads and coupons. "I got this when I first moved in. I circled all the best cheap places to eat within walking distance."

"Awesome." Sable happily took the map, his excitement at the prospect of more food pushing aside any other emotions he might be feeling.

"The one thing I ask is if you happen to pass by wherever Pete's planning to take me, try to avoid us. I'd like to sleep with him before I introduce him to everyone important in my life."

"Those priorities are slightly different than most people's, I think," he teased.

"Exclusivity first, sex second, and family third," Sela replied firmly. Then she added as an afterthought, "And revelation of witchy status last, I suppose."

"That's a conversation we are going to have to sit down and have one day," Sable told her gently.

She nodded, not trusting herself to articulate the mess of emotions she felt over lying about this most important aspect of her life to Pete. Sable knew how she felt without her saying anything, anyway, and Sela was grateful for that.

Twenty-Four

"For fuck's sake, Sela, what are you doing? The buzzer rang twice already!"

Sela jumped, yanking out noise-cancelling earbuds as Sable stood shouting in front of her. She'd been trying to meditate while she waited for Pete, to go over her magick in her mind and start retracing her seal so that she could prepare herself to learn as quickly as possible, for Sable's sake as much as her own.

Of course, it would have been a good idea to set a timer before starting to meditate, but why would she have done a smart thing like that?

"Shit! I totally lost track of time," she cried, running out to the living room and slamming her hand on the buzzer to let Pete in. As she heard his steps coming up the stairs, she stage-whispered at Sable, "Go hide in the room!"

"Okay, okay, just gimme one sec." Sable leaned forward, fussed with her hair, then turned her around and before Sela could do anything but squeak in surprise, he shoved his hands up the back of her top, unhooked her bra and then re-hooked it on a tighter setting.

She spun back at him and hissed, "Are you kidding me?"

Ignoring her, he smoothed the sides of the top, snapped her bra straps up at the shoulder, and adjusted her hair once more. Then he smiled broadly at his masterpiece. "Perfect. You'll thank me when you have sex again." And he ran to her room and shut the door behind him.

What is my life? Sela thought as Pete knocked at the door.

"Hey," she greeted her date, relaxing into a grin as she saw him take in her new look.

"Sela...wow," he finally managed. "You look amazing! I mean, you always look beautiful, but the haircut, and you just...." He took a breath and gave a sheepish laugh. "I'm going to take this opportunity to stop babbling."

She laughed in return. "Babbling is always appreciated. Did you want to come in for a glass of water or anything before we leave?"

Pete's voice grew ever so slightly deeper as he met her eyes. "Would you like me to come in?"

Sela's toes practically curled at the question. Pete also looked particularly hot tonight, with his hair combed back to bring out his gorgeous smile, wearing a sexy black button-down shirt and jean combo that Sela guessed would not be altogether difficult to remove.

Then she remembered: Sable was still in the apartment. There was absolutely no way she was going to have sex with Pete while her familiar was in the next room.

"Hmm. Maybe we can come back for tea after dinner?"

Pete smiled. "Sounds perfect."

He took her to a fancy pizzeria that wasn't on the map she'd given Sable, Sela was relieved to note. They decided on a pie for two covered in fresh ricotta, arugula, and yellow peppers. Pete also ordered them a bottle of champagne.

"What are we celebrating?" she asked him, flirtatiously lifting her glass.

"Well," Pete cleared his throat, raising his own champagne in turn, "I am on my third date with an incredibly bright and beautiful woman. And, in addition to celebrating the two of us, I'd like to toast to the fact that as of tonight, I believe you can start calling yourself a small business owner."

Sela's eyes widened. "What does that mean?"

Pete laughed, setting his glass down for the moment and digging into the back pocket of his jeans. "I was going to show you this after the toast, but now is as good a time as any." He handed her a folded piece of paper.

"Pete...this looks like an order form."

"It is an order form. Caroline flipped for your hand cream, and so did all of her friends. They all want tubes for themselves, and if I'm not mistaken, they might have demanded a bunch of other random products that I'm not even sure you make?"

Pete wasn't mistaken. Sela saw on the order form requests for foot lotion, body butter, even one for an exfoliating scrub.

She shook her head. "This is amazing!"

"I'm sorry if they went too far. Like I said, my sister is a force to be reckoned with."

"No apologies necessary," Sela told him, already envisioning how she could bundle the orders in beautiful tissue paper and devising to include handmade candles as a free gift for her first customers. "I can make all of this stuff and more. Give me a couple of weeks to get it to you?"

"Of course!" he replied. "I will say, I suspected that cream was good, but the way my sister responded, it's apparently better than that—almost magical."

She nearly dropped the order form at that remark, but recovered by reclaiming her champagne glass and raising it to touch Pete's. "To my third date with an amazing guy who is more supportive than I ever could have asked for. Thank you."

Sela meant it, too. She had her sister and Sable, and that was something she didn't take for granted, but they were family—family was supposed to be supportive. To have Pete believing in her to this extent filled her with something that felt a lot like hope.

He reached for her hand across the table. "Well, aside from knowing better than to ever question my sister's taste in cosmetics, I think it's important to support the person you're with."

This was taking a turn. Sela tensed, seeing how serious Pete had grown. Was this going to be a fucked-up goodbye? The old up-the-romance-right-before-the-end routine? He wouldn't be the first guy she'd encountered to pull such a move.

"Sela," Pete went on, "I'm wondering if we could… well…"

Not a bad sign, she realized, relaxing. This wasn't a break-up: he wanted to have sex and didn't know how to ask without being an asshole! And since she also wanted to have sex and Sable had just given her a confidence-haircut, she blurted, "If we could sleep together?"

Pete's jaw dropped but he recovered quickly, though Sela was shocked to see that he was blushing. "Um, what I was going to ask was if we could see each other exclusively. You know, make this a relationship."

Pete might be blushing slightly, but Sela was pretty positive that every ounce of blood in her body had just rushed to her face. She was *mortified*. Here Pete was, trying to have a romantic moment and respectfully ask her if they could be a couple, and she just took her libido and stampeded right through it!

Wherever Sable was at the moment, it clearly wasn't far away enough for their emotional connection to weaken, because she suddenly felt him responding to her own mortification with extreme annoyance. She could almost hear him asking: *Now what the hell have you done?*

Pete cleared his throat. "I should say that, in addition to being in a relationship, sex would be very nice."

She let out a huge breath of relief. "Well, thank fuck for that."

Pete laughed again. "I really do have the best time with you, Sela."

"That's good," she said, regaining her composure, "because I do want to be exclusive. And, you know, have sex at some point."

He raised her hand to his lips. "Thrilled to hear it."

By the time they made it back to her apartment, it was near midnight. Now, they were struggling up the stairs—Sela wouldn't exactly call stopping to kiss breathlessly every two or three seconds "walking."

Her body felt like it was on fire. Pete's arms were strong, his mouth solid against hers, and if they pressed into each other any closer, they'd be committing public indecencies.

Coming up for air and to open the apartment door, Sela found it unlocked. "Oh no," she groaned.

It was late enough that Sable must have come back for the night. Sure enough, now that she had something to focus on beyond Pete and the prospect of ripping his clothes off, she realized she could feel her familiar's presence nearby.

"What's wrong?" Pete murmured into her neck, apparently still preoccupied with his own thoughts of getting naked.

Sela winced. "I think my friend who's been crashing may have come back for the night."

That effectively killed the moment. "He has keys?" Pete asked quietly, and Sela could see him visibly struggling to keep a calm expression.

She shrugged apologetically. "Look, he's a little weird and

the thing with my sister was fucked up. But he's a good friend and he really does need my help. Do you think we can just try to have some tea and you can get to know him a little?"

Pete sighed, nodding. "He's your friend, so I guess I'll be meeting him eventually."

Sela kissed him once more. "Thank you. Next time, maybe we can go to your place?"

"Count on it," he said sternly, but his good-natured smile had returned.

Upon stepping into the apartment, though, Sela was almost ready to turn back outside to check if she had the right address. Chant music sounded loudly from her laptop, sitars and bells playing out into a living room hazy with smoke. There was so much incense in the air that Sela's eyes actually teared up a little, candles flickered on every available surface, and all of the furniture had been pushed back against the walls so that the living room floor was a huge open space.

There sat Sable, wearing a white t-shirt and pajama pants, eyes shut and legs in a perfect lotus position. If Sela hadn't known better, she would have legitimately believed that he was a yoga teacher and meditation expert.

After she'd flicked on the living room lights, Sable opened his eyes and smiled. "Hi Sela," he greeted her, and although his serene expression looked sincere, she felt waves of snark radiating off of him.

He thinks I'm not going to kill him for this later, she thought to herself, sending her own vibes out that she was sure her familiar was picking up on. *Now Pete's never going to have sex with me!*

As though he'd heard her exact thoughts, Sable added, "You must be Pete."

"And you're Sable, right?" Apparently unfazed by the yoga

studio that used to be Sela's living room, Pete went to offer Sable his hand, and Sela watched her familiar carefully evaluating her now-boyfriend as he returned the handshake.

"I like you," Sable said to Pete. Then he turned to Sela and repeated, "I like him. He's honest."

True to form, Pete started laughing. "I think I like you, too."

She'd found the world's most good-natured man, and he wanted to be in a relationship with her. As much as she wasn't thrilled with Sable at the moment, she couldn't help but smile gratefully at her boyfriend for being so incredibly sweet.

"I hope you guys don't mind," Sable said, shooting Sela a quick but pointed look. "I needed somewhere to sleep."

"We were about to have tea," Pete told him. "You want to join us?"

"I'll do you one better," he said, smiling. "I'll make the tea for all of us."

Sela was happily surprised to sense that Sable was truly fond of Pete already, and that he would offer to make tea.

Then he added, "Sela's okay in the kitchen, but if you want to eat or drink anything good, you'll want me to be the one to make it."

I'm absolutely going to kill him.

As the next half hour passed, it seemed increasingly to Sela like Pete and Sable were the ones on the date. They had each other laughing nonstop about who knew what, and all she could do was drink her tea in silent amazement at the fact that her familiar had managed to hijack one of the most romantic evenings she'd possibly ever had.

Pete's phone sounded a series of bells, and he glanced down at it apologetically. "I would love to stay, but this is my final bedtime alarm. If I don't get some rest now, I'll be pretty useless during all the work I've got for residency tomorrow."

"See you soon, Pete," Sable called after him as Sela walked Pete out to the top of the stairs. "I'll cook next time!"

"Wow, no wonder you're letting him crash!" Pete told Sela after she'd pulled the door shut behind her. "I feel like I was such an ass—he's a totally great guy."

Sela tried to laugh without sounding agitated. "I didn't realize how well you two would hit it off."

Pete shrugged. "Some people just give off really good vibes, you know?"

He bent to kiss her again and that deep longing she'd felt on their way up to the apartment sparked once more as she leaned into his chest.

"But nice guy or not, I want you all to myself next time," he murmured into her ear, sending pleasant shivers up and down Sela's spine.

That's more like it, she thought in satisfaction. "Just us next time," she promised as she pulled away.

As she came back into the apartment, Sable called over his shoulder, "I really meant it, you know." He was in the kitchen, washing the teacups. "I like him a lot."

Sela considered her familiar. Even though she had temporarily wanted to murder Sable for bromancing her date away from her, here he was, her new best friend and magickal confidant, washing dishes she and Pete had dirtied after brewing them what Sela had to admit was a damn good pot of tea. He'd uprooted his life and without complaint had moved from who knew where into an apartment with little space for himself. And now, despite what she knew was a deep and persistent inclination towards snark, he was doing his best to be genuinely nice about Sela's boyfriend.

She went over and gave him a hug. "I'm really glad you

do," she said into his shoulder. "Because I'm definitely starting to fall for the guy."

"Good," Sable replied. He'd been surprised by the hug, but now gave her a gentle squeeze back. "I would greatly object to you dating an asshole, and so many of them seem to be single and on the prowl at our age."

"Yup," she agreed, releasing him. Then a thought occurred to her. "Our age? Sable, when is your birthday?"

The question made him uncomfortable, and he hesitated. "Familiars...don't really celebrate birthdays."

"Why not?"

He shrugged. "Well, we're only born because of you."

That response took her aback. "What do you mean?"

"A familiar is born at the exact moment his witch is," Sable replied. "We come into the world together because a magickal seal is unique and can only come into existence once. A witch's seal is upon her at birth, so the two births have to match up precisely."

This whole magick deal sucked for familiars, the more she learned about it. But rather than keep Sable on a topic that clearly bothered him—and Sela was certainly beginning to understand why—she impulsively said, "Listen, I want to bring some furniture back my from folks' place tomorrow."

Sable shrugged. "I don't mind lifting stuff, but why? This place seems to have everything you need."

"I think we should convert some part of the apartment into a room for you—maybe the second bedroom, or even the living room, if you want. It's shitty for you to have to sleep on a table, especially if you're not in cat form. And besides, you'll need a place to put the clothes Alexander gave you because we both know my closet's a hot mess."

Sable's face had brightened. If Sela didn't know his snarky

self better, she'd have thought he was touched. "Well, we can't mess too much with the magickal sanctum—it has energies that shouldn't be disrupted and they're tied to the furniture that's already in there. But I'll be fine with the table if we could grab a couple of extra pillows and maybe a light blanket for when it's cold."

"Just one blanket? I don't know, the heat isn't great in there and we're getting into fall now." If he was trying not to be a bother, she was going to want to kill him again. "I want you to feel at home, you know."

"I do," he assured her. "Little known fact about feline-form familiars: our body temperature runs a little high, even when we're in human form. But I'll take you up on the offer for somewhere to put my clothes."

Sela nodded. "Now that the giant waterfall is gone, there's a big space where we could put a wardrobe or a chest of drawers. My parents are bound to have something in the house."

Sable sat at the dining nook table and looked at her expectantly. "So, are you going to tell me about the date?"

She broke into a grin and was about to join him at the table when her eyes caught sight of a newspaper on the kitchen counter. "What's that?"

"Hmm?" Sable turned to look. "Oh, I figured it would be good to start getting to know the neighborhood, so I grabbed a local paper."

Sela shakily made her way over to the counter, her whole body washed over with cold dread. There, on the lower portion of the cover page, was a picture of what had once been a house. It looked as though an earthquake had made the entire structure cave in on itself. And Sela recognized the properties that bordered the wreck that had once been someone's home.

"Sela, what's wrong?"

"Sable...I did this."

"You did what?"

She pointed to the picture. "That's the house where Porter, the dog that I sit, lives." Tears rolled down her face, her voice cracking. "I said a spell...It was before I was initiated, I didn't know what I was doing, but I...I destroyed their home."

In shock, Sable looked between the photo and Sela's tearful face. He glanced through the article, then put the paper back down and pulled her into another hug.

"No one got hurt, Sela," he said soothingly into the top of her head. "The article says everyone—even the dog—was out of the house when it happened."

"But I wrecked it!" It didn't matter that no one was injured, Sela thought; she'd gotten envious and mean, and because she was a witch, those feelings had ruined a family's home. Courtney was an awful person to work for, but no one deserved to literally have their life come crashing down. She kept crying, hating herself for what she'd done.

"We're going to get this under control," Sable promised as he held her, though she sensed a deep uneasiness in his heart. "First thing tomorrow, we're going to start setting everything right."

Twenty-Five

The drive to her parents' place was the most fun Sela and Sable had had together yet. Their shared love of 80s glam rock, which had been a surprise, made for some pretty incredible sing-alongs. But when they finally turned down her old street, Sable grew strangely quiet.

"Are you okay?" she asked him.

He nodded, but she could tell from their emotional link that he really wasn't. And as they started up the path to the house, he began visibly sweating.

"All right," Sela said, stopping in her tracks and putting her hands on her hips. "What's wrong with you? You look frazzled, and your vibes are all...wonky."

Sable ran his hands through his curls in frustration, then sighed. "I don't really *do* family."

"What does that mean?"

"I told you, I never had much of a stable home life. And I don't know, I guess houses like this—suburban homes where the family inside leads a perfect life?" He shrugged. "They make me uncomfortable."

"Why didn't you mention this on the drive here?" she asked gently. In addition to discomfort and frustration, Sable was projecting a wistfulness that hurt her heart.

"What good would that have done? I didn't want to be the downer on the road trip."

"Well, for one thing, I could've reminded you that we're family now." She took one of his hands and squeezed.

"Ow," he complained, but a small smile played on his lips and he let her resume leading them up the path.

"And for another," Sela went on, "I would have just told you about the two years my dad spent on his sister's couch because my mother found out he had gambled away their retirement savings. Any more debt and we would've lost the house."

He looked at her in surprise. "Seriously?"

She nodded. "I'm not saying that we didn't live the kind of life you're talking about. I grew up in a beautiful home in a safe area, and my sister and I got to go to good schools. But we also had debt collectors waking us up all hours of the night, and I was sure my dad was going to end up in jail. Natalie was afraid whenever the phone rang for a long time."

"Then what happened?"

"My folks didn't speak again until my father could prove he'd been getting professional help." It was a hard memory as Sela thought on it, but Sable deserved to know as much about her life as she could tell him. She knew most of his secrets just by virtue of being his witch, after all. "Then they both had to work multiple jobs for years to reverse some of the damage, although I still don't think their finances have totally recovered. And they really didn't like each other for a while."

"What about you and your sister?"

"We spent a lot of time alone together. At first, it was annoying because I thought I'd be stuck with her tagging along after me forever. But we ended up super-close, as you know."

Sable looked apprehensively at the front door as Sela dug around for her keys. "Knowing all of that doesn't make this easy."

"I know." She thought back on Courtney's house, which dwarfed her family home two or three times over—or it had, until her spell destroyed it. "But I guess I just want you to know that perfect families can be fucked up, too."

"So, you're saying this is a house of fuck-ups?"

"Uh-huh."

"Okay, that's at least a little relatable. Let's go inside."

But as Sela was about to turn her key, the lock suddenly moved of its own accord. She stepped back nervously, thinking it was her magick acting strangely again. Then the door swung open to reveal not her mother or father, but Natalie.

"Oh my god, Sela—your hair! It's amazing!"

Of course she would notice that first, Sela thought through her shock at seeing her sister.

Then Natalie turned to Sable, her eyebrows raised in surprise. "So, does this mean you guys made up? You know, after…everything?"

"And I thought it was the fucking suburbs that would make this awkward," Sable muttered.

"Natalie, why aren't you at school?" Sela asked anxiously. "Are you okay?"

"That's kind of a long story." Natalie waved them inside. "Mom and Dad went out to run some errands, but I've been making lunch for everyone. Mom didn't say anything about you bringing company, but I think there should be enough."

"You've been making lunch voluntarily and not just for yourself?" Sela grabbed her sister's face in both hands. "What's wrong with you? Are you sick?"

"I'm *fine*, Sela," Natalie said, rolling her eyes and pushing Sela's hands aside. "They're just sandwiches."

"This visit is getting stranger by the minute," Sela replied. "I never thought I'd see the day you'd prepare a meal for company."

"How do you think I feel?" Natalie shot back, eyeing Sable where he stood behind Sela. "That last thing I expected was to see you coming in the front d—" Natalie's words dissolved as her mouth fell open and she started screaming.

"Natalie, what in the fucking hell?" Sela spun around to see what kind of spider or insect had made her sister suddenly start acting like she was possessed, and there she found Sable, sitting in a heap of the clothes he'd been wearing a moment ago.

That is, right before he'd transformed back into a cat.

"Wonderful," Sable remarked, inciting Natalie to actually fall on the floor.

"Sela! What the fuck is it? What the *fuck*?"

"Wow," Sable shouted to Sela over the din of her sister's screams. "And I thought you overreacted when we first met."

"Natalie! Please calm down!" Sela begged her sister, kneeling to put soothing arms around her. "It's still Sable. He's just a cat right now, that's all. It's okay!"

Natalie turned to face Sela, her green eyes practically bulging out of her head. "It's okay? It's *okay*? Sela, what the fuck are you saying, *it's okay*?!"

"I will tell you everything," Sela promised, "I swear, but I really need you to stop screaming. All right? I will make this make sense, but you need to calm down."

Natalie was crying a little at this point, but she relaxed ever so slightly into her sister's arms. "I'll calm down," she sniffed, still looking at Sable in terror.

"Good," Sela replied as she plopped down on the floor next to her sister. "I really don't know how to go about explaining this."

"I'd go with: just fucking say it," Sable offered.

Sela glared at him as Natalie whimpered more. "That really

isn't helping."

"What?"

"You talking so much. It's obviously freaking her out."

"So what do you suggest?" he asked indignantly. "Am I supposed to act as though I walk around meowing all the time?"

"Sela," Natalie whispered. "You guys are talking to each other, right? I'm not hallucinating right now? You're talking to that cat?"

"I am *not* a ca—"

"Yes," Sela cut Sable off, shooting him another withering look. "I'm talking to Sable, who now happens to *look* like a cat."

"Why does he look like a cat?" Natalie had finally stopped crying and was looking at Sela in confusion.

"Well, the thing is: Sable is a familiar. A witch's familiar."

"I don't know what that means."

"It means," Sela continued hesitantly, "that I'm a witch, Natalie. I am a witch, and Sable is my familiar."

Natalie blinked at her in disbelief. "So, he really just turned into a cat?"

"For fuck's sake," Sable huffed.

"Yeah, Nat. He's magickal, so sometimes he looks human like us, and at other times, he looks like a cat."

Natalie started to rise to her feet. "What do you mean, you're a witch?"

Sela shrugged as she also stood up. "Just that, I guess. I'm newly initiated, so I can't do much yet."

"Do much?"

"Magick," Sela clarified. "Spells and stuff."

Now Natalie crossed her arms and demanded, "Show me."

"That's not a great idea," Sable said.

Natalie turned to face him, and Sela hoped her familiar caught the same thing she was sensing: now that her tears had mostly dried up, Natalie was responding to all of this information by growing increasingly agitated. "You're still Sable?"

"That's right."

"You're the same Sable I met when I visited for Sela's birthday?"

"The one and only."

Realization dawned on Natalie's face. "Wait a minute: were you...when we..." She turned back to Sela, agitation having yielded to full-on anger. "Did you let me fuck a cat, Sela?"

"No!" Sela cried. "In fact, if you remember, I was pretty pissed that the two of you had sex in the first place."

"Oh my god!" Now anger was turning to panic, and Sela wondered briefly how many stages of shock her sister was going to go through. "Did I commit bestiality?"

"You most certainly did not," Sable told her icily. "I am *not* a cat."

"Well, you really fucking look like one!" Natalie shouted at him.

"That's because I've changed my form."

"Why don't you change back?"

At this point, Sable had apparently had enough. "Because I can't. And if you can't get yourself under control, I think we should leave. Sela?"

"Natalie, please." Sela took her sister's hands imploringly. "Remember that guy when you were in eleventh grade? I covered for you with Mom and Dad, even though I wanted to kill you at the time."

"What does that have to do with me fucking a cat, Sela?"

"I've always had your back is what," Sela replied, "even when I've been upset with you. Now I need you to have mine. I had no clue I was a witch until a month ago." Sela gestured to Sable. "Sable's been the only one I've had to help me get through it all. I've been scared and overwhelmed, and honestly, really frustrated with myself. And now that you know, I just... I really need my sister."

Natalie stared at them for what felt like an age. Then she finally said, "Okay. Let's go have sandwiches."

Although Sable's indignation was extending out in angry waves, Sela was grateful that he followed them into the kitchen without complaint. He sprang up to sit at the table, waiting for his food, and Sela was glad she'd ended up with such a hungry familiar. It made him bribable at the worst times.

"Um..." Natalie began, but Sela grabbed a ham sandwich from the pile her sister had been assembling and threw it on a plate for Sable before the question of what he was able to eat could even be raised. As for Sable, his table manners were even more human than most humans'. Sela swore that if he'd had pinkies, they would have been sticking primly out.

"If you're a witch," Natalie asked Sela, keeping a wary eye on Sable, "then does that mean I'm going to be one, too?"

The question took Sela totally by surprise, and she felt more than a little foolish for never having thought of it before. "Oh my god, is that a thing?" she asked, turning to Sable.

Still peeved about having been referred to as a cat so many times in a row, Sable reluctantly answered the question. "No. It's extremely unusual for witch siblings to exist, unless you're from a witch family."

"A what now?" Sela realized that Natalie's sudden discovery of her magick had opened the door for a new opportunity to ask Sable more questions about witches and familiars, a subject on which he was still pretty tight-lipped.

Sable sighed, giving in to the inevitable third degree.

"Witch families are exactly what they sound like: families of witches who try to ensure that their children marry other witches, so as to guarantee that most members of the family will ultimately be witches."

"Why would anyone do that?" This all sounded bizarre and vaguely cult-like to Sela.

"In some ways, it's practical," Sable said through a mouthful of ham. He'd apparently forfeited his impeccable manners for the moment. "It's easier to be raised by someone who has gone through what you'll go through in the future. But for the most part, witch families are invested in accumulating magickal power."

"That's creepy," Natalie echoed Sela's own thoughts, wrinkling her nose in distaste.

"Totally," Sable agreed. "And it's often dangerous. The younger witches in the families usually consent to arranged marriages their elders endeavor to create—they're raised to only privilege the acquisition of power, so they'll do whatever it takes to get it. But things tend to go very badly wrong in our world when witches try to force covens, which these families almost always do."

"Okay, I'm lost." Sela held up a hand. "What do you mean, they're forcing covens?"

"They try to create a coven within their family rather than allowing one to form organically, under the natural laws of magick."

"There are organic coven formations?" Sela's head was reeling with all of this new information. She had already had her mind blown by meeting Lyla and Alexander and seeing another witch and familiar in action. Now there were covens? And magickal families? "Why didn't you tell me about any of this? Are we supposed to be part of a coven or something?"

Sable shook his head. "It's actually really rare to be a member of a coven. Most witches and familiars practice independently. I very much doubt we'll be any different."

"Then what's the point of covens at all?" Natalie asked. Now that she was over her initial shock, she seemed to be adapting to the rules of the magickal world even more quickly than Sela. "Is it just like a magickal social club?"

"Covens are important to the larger witch community because they have the capacity to help witches and familiars in trouble. That help can take any number of forms, but whenever a magickal creature is in over her head, she'll receive help from the nearest coven."

"Is that what witch families try to do with their power?" Sela asked. "Go around helping people?"

Sable snorted. "That would be nice, but they're usually so preoccupied with building power that they take on a pretty selfish aspect. I mean, I've never heard of a witch family helping anyone."

Just as Sela was about to ask another question, sounds came from the front of the house.

"Hello?" Sela heard her mother call. "Sela? Natalie? Anyone home?"

"Sable!" Sela hissed. "Please, just jump on the floor and… act like a cat."

"Are you serious?" he demanded.

Natalie let out a bark of laughter. "Dude, if you think I had problems, you *really* don't want to see what'll happen if our mom encounters a talking cat."

"I'll get us pizza the minute we get back home," Sela promised him. "Any toppings you want."

He jumped to the floor. "I knew this trip would suck."

Sela's mother walked in and exclaimed, "My baby girls,

both here at the same time!" before wrapping her eldest in a strong hug.

"This is a wonderful occasion," her father agreed, kissing Sela on the head. "And who's this?"

"Oh," Sela said quickly as her parents noticed Sable, "that's a rescue I picked up so Pluto could have some company. You know, I work a lot and I figure he shouldn't be alone in the apartment."

"I wouldn't touch him, Dad," Natalie cautioned as their father was making moves to greet Sable as though he were an ordinary housecat. "He likes to strike when you least expect it."

"So, why are you home?" Sela's mother asked. "Just for a visit?"

Sela felt a twinge of guilt. She didn't visit often, largely because she hadn't really done much worth coming home to tell her folks about. It was hard to know that she'd left them with the intention of making the most of her life and still hadn't accomplished much of anything in the years since.

"Yeah, I just wanted to catch up with you guys a bit," she said. "Actually, Natalie and I were going to head up to the attic so I could grab some old stuff that I never took with me. Just some memories that I thought it might be nice to have."

"Well, you know I'm not going to stop you kids from attacking that mess up there," her father quipped.

"Speaking of which, shouldn't we head upstairs, Sel? I think we need a few hours to rifle through your old stuff before dinner, right?" Natalie gave her a pointed look before bending down to scoop up Sable, who had never appeared more furious in the time Sela had known him.

"Yep, sounds good!" Sela agreed, vibing the biggest apology of her life at her familiar.

"I'm cooking a roast chicken, so make sure to work up an

appetite!" their mother called after them as they made their way towards the second floor of the house.

"Let me follow you girls upstairs," their father said. Sela could see Sable stiffen in Natalie's arms. "I've got to run and grab a sweater—it got cold out there!"

"Yeah, I always forget how much warmer it is at school than back here," Natalie replied cheerfully, as though she had no idea the creature in her arms was having active thoughts of murder.

"Don't make a bigger mess than we've already got!" Their father winked at them as he retreated into a closet.

Natalie swung the door to the attic stairs open, and Sela remarked, "You never told me why you came home, by the way."

"I'm doing a semester online so I could move back here for a while," Natalie told her brightly as she started up the stairs. Sable peeped over her shoulder and stared at Sela threateningly.

"Why would you want to do that?" she asked, pretending not to notice the feline gaze of death.

Natalie glanced over her shoulder, above Sable's seething face. "Because I promised my big sister I'd start taking better care of myself, and I meant it."

A wave of emotion washed over Sela at those words, made up mostly of relief and gratitude but also some concern. A semester at home would be calming for Natalie, to say the least. But Sela worried about the fact that her sister had felt the need to leave campus entirely. Had the situation there been so bad that she actually needed to flee to their parents' house?

The minute they'd finished the climb to the attic, Sable leapt from Natalie's arms.

"You're welcome," she told him sassily.

"Oh, I'm sorry," he snapped back at her, smoothing his fur

furiously with his paws as though she'd wrinkled his best clothes. "Was I supposed to be honored getting toted around like a housecat by a woman I had in the throes of passion just weeks ago?"

"No more throes of anything talk, thank you very much," Sela said. "Let's just find what we came here for, okay?"

"What did you come here for, exactly?" Natalie asked.

"Witch stuff," Sela told her. "My old spellbooks and supplies."

Natalie laughed. "Wow, I totally did not think any of that weird shit you did with your friends would ever come in useful."

"Well, it has! Come on, help me look."

Twenty-Six

The attic was more cluttered than Sela had remembered. She and Natalie rummaged around for a solid half hour, getting covered in cobwebs and dust without much luck. As for Sable, he was apparently on strike.

"Can't you do something to help?" Natalie complained to him. "Like, can you sense the magickal shit that's up here or whatever?"

"My senses all seem a little dull at the moment," he replied dryly. "Maybe it's from an identity crisis, since everyone around here seems to believe I'm a common housecat."

"Ignore him," Sela told her sister. "Sable might be in danger of many things at the moment, but an identity crisis isn't one of them."

He huffed at her and stalked off to another corner of the attic, but Sela could tell through their emotional link that he wasn't as pissy as he was acting. Mostly, he was bored, and Sela couldn't blame him. How long would it take to dig through all of this junk before they actually found something useful?

But just then, Natalie called out, "Hey, I think I've got something!"

Sela turned to see her sister emerge from behind an old bookshelf, a small wicker box in her hands.

"Awesome! That's where I used to keep all of my spellbooks and journals."

"Including the one you need? The shadow-book, or whatever?"

"I hope so," Sela said, taking the box. She wiped the dust off of it to the best of her ability, then unlatched the lid.

There, so many volumes greeted her like old friends she hadn't spoken to in an age. Books by Ann Baring, D. J. Conway, and Silver Ravenwolf were interspersed with journals where she'd practiced writing out runes, sigils, and oghams. A tarot deck was nestled on top of the first few books in Cate Tiernan's *Sweep* series, and wrapped around the novels, a quartz crystal pendant glittered up at her on its black leather string. She'd bought two such necklaces and had given one to Maria; they'd both worn them religiously from junior year through graduation.

Echoes of laughter and whispers of chants filled Sela's mind as she thought of the times she and Maria had snuck up to the attic after everyone in the house was asleep. They had drawn circles and cast spells; one time, they'd even convinced themselves that a spark had run through their joined hands as they'd chanted an incantation over a dish of flame.

She recalled one night with clarity. Maria had shown up without warning; she'd even used the old throw-rocks-at-the-window routine to catch Sela's attention. When Sela had tiptoed down to the back door to ask what her friend was doing there, she saw streaks of tears gleaming down Maria's face. They'd made their way to the attic in silence, and the first thing Maria did was pour a thick circle of sea salt around them.

"What's up?" Sela had asked gently. She had a feeling she knew what, but didn't want to rush her friend.

"Did you know that Kendra wants the coven to cast a spell for revenge on those girls who wouldn't let her join the cheerleading squad?"

Sela nodded. "She told me in physics yesterday."

Maria looked down at her empty hands, a thick curtain of dark-brown curls shrouding her face so that Sela couldn't see her expression for the moment. "Revenge can be really fucked up, you know? I don't want to do it."

"We don't have to. You and I are priestesses, too. We can outvote her."

Now Maria looked up at her, frustration and something else on her face. "She always gets her way, Sela."

That was true. Kendra was sometimes so forceful that Sela found herself feeling uncomfortably grateful to be considered her friend, because at the end of the day, the girl was something of a bully. But the more Maria spoke, the less Sela thought that what she was really talking about was Kendra.

"I'm so tired of people who go around taking whatever they want," Maria whispered, pulling her hoodie more tightly around herself despite the fact that the attic was stiflingly warm.

"Are you okay?"

At the question, Maria seemed to remember that someone was in the room with her. She stared directly into Sela's eyes, a hollow echo of her typically gorgeous smile pulling at her drawn face. "No, I'm really not."

"Want to talk about it?" Sela offered, although she knew what Maria's reply would be.

"I don't. Can we just cast a spell?"

"Yeah," she said, ready to agree to whatever Maria asked. She was stronger than anyone Sela had ever known, but it was clear that she had been pushed to a limit. "What kind of spell?"

Maria reached into her sweatshirt pocket and withdrew two dandelions, both a little wilted. She handed one to Sela. "Something that will help us call each other if we ever need help, so that no matter what, we can always find one another."

"Cool. Do you have an incantation?"

"I thought of it on the walk here."

A sudden pain in her finger jolted Sela from the memory. "Ow!" She stuck her finger in her mouth and glared down at the piece of wicker that had stabbed her from inside the box.

"Careful, Sel," her sister chided. "You've probably got knives and shit in there."

"I never bought an athame," Sela said sulkily, her finger throbbing with pain. "That was Kendra's thing."

Natalie rolled her eyes. "You guys were *so* weird. And I was always so mad you would never let me up here when you were doing all your chanting or whatever."

Sela shrugged. "Well, now that the magick is actually real, you're here."

"Have you found your Book of Shadows yet?" Sable was more impatient than ever. "Or am I going to be made to sleep on a cat bed overnight in this place?"

"It's not in here," Sela sighed. Why hadn't she left her Book of Shadows in a sensible place? *I probably believed I'd never need it again.*

But that thought struck her with a vague memory.

"Natalie, is there a loose floorboard near where you're standing?"

"I don't know." Natalie started stomping around.

"Stop!" Sela cried. "Do you want Mom and Dad to come up here?"

"Well, how the hell else am I supposed to find loose floorboards?"

Sela stalked over to where Natalie was, got on her hands and knees, and started to shift her hands around the boards. Finally, one wiggled loosely; she tucked her fingertips along its edge and managed to lift it.

"Found it!" she told Sable and her sister. Then she slowly

reached down into the space below.

A worn black briefcase that her father had long ago abandoned met her fingertips. Sela angled it so that she could remove it from the snug space beneath the attic floor. The sight of it triggered a memory of the night before she left for college, when, feeling a strange mixture of relief and sadness that such a perfect hiding place existed in her own home, she'd tucked the briefcase and its contents away. At the time, it had seemed she was destined to bury this chapter of her life beneath a dusty attic floor for good. Now, Sela was grateful she'd thought to set the book aside instead of destroying it.

"This is where I hid the book before I left for school."

"So weird," Natalie remarked.

"Hey, you were ridiculously nosy," Sela reminded her. "I didn't want you finding it while I was away."

Setting the briefcase down, Sela prepared to fiddle with the locks, having long ago forgotten the combination. But as she raised her hands to touch them, they snapped open of their own accord. The briefcase lid rose slowly, revealing the book inside.

"Holy shit!" Natalie said, and Sable came forward with interest, forgetting his state of indignation for the moment.

"That's your Book of Shadows, all right," he confirmed. "It's rippling with magickal energy."

Sela lovingly took the book in her hands, its grey leather cover still soft and lush as she remembered; the briefcase had preserved it well. The cover felt cool, and she opened it to find the inscription she'd written on the front page:

Sela Glaser

May all of the words I speak from these pages
come to pass.

"You have to give me points for determination," she laughed.

"Why do you need this thing in the first place?" Natalie wanted to know. "Neither of you explained that."

"Your sister has a magickal stalker," Sable replied.

"Sela, seriously?"

Sighing, Sela nodded. "Yeah, turns out that all those times I was up here chanting and whatever, I was actually casting spells that became legit the minute I was initiated into witchcraft."

Natalie looked at her in dismay. "But you were so weird!"

"Hence the disasters we've been dealing with lately," Sable said. "Sela, can you verify that this is the book in which you wrote the spell that has this guy coming after you?"

She blushed. "I mean, I can't verify anything when I don't even remember who he is."

Now Natalie smirked. "Oh, she definitely cast a freaky love spell."

"Why would you say that?" Sela demanded, even though it was probably the truth.

"Sela, you were *terrified* to talk to guys in high school. No wonder you loved this witchcraft shit so much. It was probably the only way you ever thought you'd get a date."

"I could talk to guys!"

Natalie glanced at Sable. "Total verbal shut-down. She couldn't even say 'excuse me' if a halfway decent-looking guy was in her path."

Sable considered this. "Well, let's look through the book and see if Natalie's right—maybe there is a love spell in here."

Too irritated to defend her adolescent self further, Sela began paging through the book. Despite its slender appearance, it was filled with many pages. Sela found drawings of goddesses sketched into margins alongside elemental spells, invocations for lucid dreams and astral projection, pages of feathers and pressed flowers, all glued around the bubbly neatness of her teenaged handwriting.

One page, which she'd apparently stained pink using a floral tea, had red rose petals glued to its margins and a flat rose quartz heart on its upper right-hand corner. She began to read the untitled spell, written over ten years before:

I call thee, Jackson,
come to me:
Come and set
this longing free.

Be my love,
hold my heart,
and from you
I shall never part.

Think of me
with every step,
with every move,
with every breath.

Find me ever
in your path,
and know our love
will ever last.

I pledge my heart to you
and swear:

where you go,
you'll find me there.

All my self and soul
now thine,
and thee, within forever,
mine.

This spell I bind as destiny:
as is my will, so mote it be.

Sela's cheeks had grown pink with the melodrama of the rhyming lines she'd penned at fifteen years of age, when everything in her life seemed like it would make or break her. But then, realization dawned as she remembered: "Jackson. Oh my god, Jackson Woods. I was totally in love with him for at least half of tenth grade."

"And you're only remembering this *now*?" Sable was incredulous.

"Well, he changed schools. He left the summer before junior year, and then I just moved on to liking someone else."

"Of course," Natalie interjected, rolling her eyes.

"God, I was so into him—I can't believe I forgot! He had this whole James Dean thing going, with the combed-back hair and everything. And wherever he went, he wore what I thought was this totally sexy…" Her whole body flooded with cold as she swallowed hard, then finished her sentence: "…brown leather jacket."

Jackson Woods—a guy she hadn't seen in over a decade, someone she had never thought of again after the tenth grade— he was her stalker. He hadn't even known she was alive during that year she'd had her crush, Sela was sure, and now he was following her everywhere, frightening her, all because she had made up a page-long sequence of rhymes when she was fifteen years old.

"Oh my god, it's total stalker poetry!" Natalie's voice sounded right next to her ear, and Sela jumped, not having noticed her sister reading over her shoulder.

"I was a kid!"

"Yeah," Natalie snorted, "a kid who obviously wanted to provide material for a *Lifetime* original movie."

"Oh, I'm sorry: did we forget that you recently fucked a cat?"

Natalie shoved her indignantly. "It's not like he was a cat while we were fucking!"

"I am sitting right here." Sable had rolled his eyes up to the ceiling so dramatically that Sela would have wondered whether to stick her arms out in case he fainted, except she could feel nothing but pure agitation through their psychic link.

"Well, what do you think?" Sela asked him.

"I can't think anything if the two of you keep yammering and don't actually show me the spell so I can read it," he answered tartly.

"Oh. Oops." Sela took the journal and set it down in front of her familiar.

As he read, Sable's eyes narrowed and widened, resulting in several facial expressions that Sela found alarming. Finally, he looked up at her again.

"What was going on with you in high school, exactly? Did they love her more?" He gestured to Natalie with a paw. "Was that it?"

"Sable, what the fuck?"

"This spell, if we're calling it that," he went on, "is absolutely batshit. You're lucky he hasn't gone ahead and killed you yet!"

"That's why we're here, remember?" she said defensively. "To find some solutions, rather than picking on who I was as a teenager?"

"And what's this?" Sable demanded, pointing at the open page.

Sela squinted down at what seemed to be a thin brown thread that had been carefully taped to a corner of the spell.

"Oh god," she moaned in embarrassment, putting her face in her hands.

"Oh god *what*?" Sable asked with narrowed eyes. "Spill it, witch."

"Okay…I may have done something a little creepy."

"You mean, other than writing stalker poetry?" Natalie asked helpfully.

"So, I may have snuck into the boys' locker room while Jackson was in gym class," Sela confessed, her ears burning with humiliation as the memory came forward in her mind. "And I may have…borrowed a thread from his jacket so I could cast the spell."

Sable looked as though he was going to explode. "Of all of the witches in all of the world, I end up with the one who spent her childhood casting come-disembowel-me spells on teenage boys."

"I just wanted him to like me back!"

Now Natalie's face grew serious. "Wait a minute: Sela, you said this guy had a brown leather jacket? He's not…this isn't the guy who attacked me at the club on your birthday, is it?"

Sela looked down. "Yeah. It's the same guy."

Natalie sat with a thud on the floor, and although Sela could see her trying to keep control of herself, her little sister's hands trembled in her lap.

Sable abandoned glaring at his witch for the moment and went over to Natalie. "He was enchanted when he attacked you," he told her gently. "Once we do a reverse enchantment and break the spell, he won't hurt Sela or anyone else."

"But I thought she couldn't do spells yet."

"She's going to practice and get her magick under control." He put a reassuring paw on Natalie's knee. "I promise, I'll make sure she learns quickly. And in the meantime, you're safe here with your parents. He won't come for you again. It's us he's after."

"I don't want him coming for you guys, either!" Natalie shook her head.

"Nat, can you tell me what happened at school?" Sela asked.

Her sister remained silent, and Sable shot Sela a glance that told her to drop the subject. "Let's gather everything we need from up here, and then we can head downstairs so you two can spend some time with your parents." Then he gestured to a small chest of drawers. "And we're taking that, too, because Sela's closet back home is a hot mess."

Twenty-Seven

"There are three things you need to remember when you're going to attempt spellcraft."

Sela groaned. "Really? We just got on the road and I can't take notes when I'm driving."

"I thought you'd be happy to learn how to cast," Sable said, surprised.

He wasn't wrong. Between the stockpile of old magickal supplies in her trunk and the fact that she finally had her Book of Shadows, Sela should have been ecstatic at the prospect of learning more about her powers. But she couldn't shake the worries that had accumulated during her visit home. The idea that Natalie was walking around feeling unsafe wherever she went, and the fact that Sela had contributed to that feeling—it was all just a lot.

"It's late," she offered weakly. She knew brushing Sable off wouldn't work. They were still psychically linked, and besides, by now he knew when she was avoiding something.

"It is late," he agreed, a stern look in his eye. "And you have an enchanted stalker who'll do insane shit to you if he finds you, a little sister who's terrified for you, and a familiar who doesn't want to see you maimed or killed. So, do you think you can pull it together long enough to listen to the basics of spellcraft?"

Sable certainly had a way with pep talks. "Yes. I'm sorry,"

she said. "Pulling it together now."

"Good. As I was saying, every spell you cast will have three main components: your will, your tools, and the communication of your intent."

"A pen and paper would be super-handy right now, but: will, tools, and communication. Got it."

"Would you like explanations to go with that?"

"Yup. Would you like a croissant from a Dunkin' drive-thru?"

"This is why I don't want you dead," Sable told her. "You understand me."

As she flicked on her turn signal, Sela realized that some of her fondest memories with her familiar were probably going to be made in drive-thru lines. It occurred to her, not for the first time, that whoever decided on magickal pairings knew what they were doing when they put her and Sable together.

"Your will for a spell is somewhat simple," Sable went on. "It's your intended outcome. For example, if you'd decided not to let me make you look absolutely fabulous with that haircut and instead tried to spell your lavender hair back to its natural auburn, that would have been your will."

"You're right, that's really simple," Sela said, sticking her head out the window to shout her request for a coffee and a croissant into the drive-thru speaker.

"It's not *really* simple," Sable corrected. "You do have to carefully think over your intent and acknowledge any excess feelings you might have about it."

"What's that mean?" she asked. "Also, hide under the seat for a minute. I don't want to have to explain you to this guy at the window."

Rolling his eyes, Sable dove under the passenger seat of the car and continued talking. "Okay, let's say your purple tips had been a stylist's snafu, since that's simpler than what actually happened. Maybe you'd asked for pink hair and got purple. If you just left your intent at 'fix my hair,' that would be too vague."

"How so?"

"Well, it could mean making your hair pink or it could mean returning it to its natural state. That's not a clear intent, and that lack of specificity doesn't work for the will of a spell. But beyond that, you would have to make sure you weren't harboring any resentment for the stylist or distress that you'd wasted your money, because then your spell could result in a misdirect."

"What's a misdirect?" Sela asked as she set her coffee in its holder and put the bag with the croissant on the seat for Sable, who popped back up the moment they'd driven away from the window.

"It's when your spell acts in ways you don't mean it to. Your resentment could get the salon shut down or the stylist fired, for example."

"That would be fucked up." She took a sip of the coffee. "But I get it: my intent has to be super-clear before I do anything. So, what about the tools?"

"That's something you seem to know about already," Sable replied, munching contentedly on his croissant. "Still, you should practice with as many different spellcraft supplies as possible at first. That way, we'll get a sense of what kind of magicks you have a knack for, and we can play to your strengths."

Sela thought back to their Nascent Eve. "Didn't Lyla say something about me showing a talent for plant magicks?"

"That's not unusual for a new witch, but it doesn't mean it's what you'll definitely be most skilled at." Sable waved a dismissive paw. "We're getting off track. The point is, the tools you use should always fit the spell. If you're casting a standard protection spell for your home, you might use selenite or a black candle, but you wouldn't go for carnelian, because that's a stone that works better for other things."

"I definitely understand that. But what about the communication part?"

Sable's intensity was suddenly so strong, Sela had to fight to keep her hands steady on the wheel. "Communication of intent is how we ensure that we never, *ever* have a situation like your enchanted stalker again."

"Am I going to live this down at some point?"

"I don't know," Sable returned sharply. "We'll see how bad it gets before we fix it."

She sighed. "I don't know how to fix anything yet."

"Hence why we're discussing spellcraft basics. Now, communication of intent: the words of the spell you're going to be casting."

"So, what? I practice my rhyming?"

"You really don't have to rhyme," Sable told her, sounding as judgmental as she knew he was feeling. If she didn't need to keep her eyes on the road, she would've stuck her tongue out at him. "I mean, if that feels more comfortable for some reason, rhyme away. The important thing is that your will for the spell is written in clear, specific, and direct language. It's the thing witches struggle with most."

"Why is that?" Sela asked, curious.

"Think about it: no one's great at spelling out what they really want. If more people were, this would probably be a happier, or at least more well-adjusted, world."

When they finally arrived home, Sela opted to leave the chest of drawers in her car until the next morning. She was exhausted and couldn't wait to climb into bed. But as she was putting her keys down and slipping off her shoes, a warm breeze rushed past her, strong enough to slam the door of the apartment shut.

"Did you leave the windows open?" Sable asked, alarmed.

"I don't think so..." She hurried to the bedroom, her familiar by her side.

The room was completely trashed. The windows were shattered, along with the mirror, and her bed had been ravaged. Her lamp had been thrown violently across the room, her closet gutted, and there were clothes scattered everywhere in a mess of broken glass on the floor. Even the flowers left over from their Nascent Eve, which she and Sable had carefully set to dry the day before, had been ripped from above the windows and strewn haphazardly around the room.

"Sela." Sable was insistently tapping her leg. She realized tears had been streaming down her face and that she was shivering, despite the warmth of the early fall air.

"I'm sorry," she sniffed, wiping her face and trying to collect herself. "It's just...I mean, shit, you know?"

"Yeah, I know." Sable carefully stepped around pieces of glass, making his way to the second bedroom. He peeked inside, then said in a relieved voice, "The sanctum protected itself. He never made it inside."

Sela tried to find that as reassuring as Sable apparently did, but she couldn't stop looking in horror around her bedroom. How could Jackson grow up to be so violent? One of the reasons she'd had a crush on him, she remembered now, was because he was quiet and chill. How could he do something like this?

Then she realized: this wasn't Jackson. It was her. Her magick had taken a gentle personality and turned him dangerous. She may as well have trashed the room herself.

"How soon before we can undo the spell?"

"You need practice," Sable said, a thoughtful tone in his voice as he jumped up onto the bed. "And there's no better way for a new witch to practice than with a solid protection spell. Let's clean this up, grab the goldstone sphere, and get to work."

Twenty-Eight

After working a shift shelving books at the local library the next morning, Sela picked up Sable so they could visit Essential Elements. As they entered the shop, Sela noticed that flowers and herbs had been tied up to dry alongside the chimes and bells filling the ceiling. She breathed in the rich scent of fresh flowers and saw a large vase of Peruvian lilies next to Alexander, who was poring over a book of inventory.

Sela relaxed for the first time since the night before. Even after she and Sable had cast protection spells all over the apartment, Jackson's break-in had left her feeling unsettled and afraid. The fact that she was a brand-new witch casting spells for the first time didn't help her feel particularly safe, though Sable promised her that the protection spells would be effective. And explaining to her landlord that a freak storm had broken her windows hadn't been much fun, either.

Lyla came to greet them with Pluto snuggled cozily in her arms. While he was thrilled to see his human, it was clear that Pluto was very comfortable in the role of shop cat.

"We've grown quite fond of him," Lyla told Sela as she set Pluto down. He twined through her legs happily until he locked eyes with Sable, growled, and retreated to the back of the shop.

"How?" Sable demanded.

"Not all of us have such disdain for the creatures we resemble," Lyla told him, to which Sable replied with a sickened eye roll. "If things become too difficult while Sable is in his current form and you think it best for Pluto, we're happy to keep him here."

Sela felt a strange guilt at this offer. She'd cared for Pluto through really rough times—had always managed to bring him to the vet and feed him a healthy diet, even when it meant cutting back on the quality of her own food. And she didn't doubt that Lyla and Alexander could care for him, maybe even better than she could. But she had never thought she'd give up the one companion that had seen her through her most difficult years.

"Thanks for the offer," Sela said. "We'll think about it."

"What's to think about?" Sable cried, but Lyla nodded. "Of course. It's not easy to give up someone you love."

"You're also welcome to keep him here part-time," Alexander suggested. "We can watch him during store hours if you want him in the evenings."

Sela was surprised. "I didn't think you'd be big on pets."

"I'm not," Alexander sighed. "But there is nothing customers love more than a black cat in an occult shop, and yours is particularly friendly. I'm actually pained to think of what our sales might revert to without his charms."

"That is completely unbelievable," Sable decreed as he regarded Pluto from across the shop with open hostility. For his part, Pluto had taken refuge in a large cauldron and was hissing at Sable from within its pewter hollow, selling the role of Halloween cat perfectly.

"I can see what you mean about his marketing skills," she giggled affectionately. That sad, strange guilt panged in her heart again as she realized that Pluto would probably be happier at the shop. Being a witch might mean making sacrifices she hadn't anticipated.

"Well, I believe we have a few pressing matters to discuss,"

Lyla said. "Sable tells us you accidentally demolished someone's house?"

Sela winced. "Yeah. It belonged to one of my dog-sitting clients."

"Remind me never to hire you for anything," Alexander remarked, not looking up from his books.

Now Pluto started growling, apparently not willing to cede this new and delightful space to the intruder that Sela kept bringing into his territory. Lyla suggested, "Why don't we take Pluto up to my flat for a bit and have some tea? You can tell me more details there."

"What about me?" Sable asked, clearly insulted that he hadn't been invited.

"I'm sure Alexander could use your help."

"With what?"

Sela would have warned Alexander if she'd had the chance, but he spoke too quickly. "Like I said, shop cats bring in more money." Still bent over his work, he was completely oblivious to the indignation he'd just incited in Sela's familiar.

Lyla took Pluto from the cauldron and led Sela back towards the stairs, leaving Sable and Alexander to bicker at the front of the shop. "It'll be nice to have a chat, don't you think?"

Back inside Lyla's apartment, Sela noticed new garments that were under construction: one striking red gown in particular caught her eye, which was draped on a dress form awaiting some finishing touches from Lyla's careful hand.

Pluto curled up next to Sela on the blue sofa. The kettle was already warm, as though Lyla had known when to expect her, and she quickly brought it back to a boil while preparing a pot of blueberry-mint tea. The sweet smell of the brew filled the air, calming Sela's nerves even as she anxiously awaited the conversation they were about to have.

"Now," Lyla said, settling down next to Sela, "where would you like to begin?"

All of the fears that had been tumbling through her mind poured out of Sela before she'd even taken a sip of tea. Lyla only interrupted to ask for clarification here and there, particularly when Sela was discussing the magickal occurrences leading up to her Nascent Eve. She also seemed very interested in the spells Sela had cast before her initiation, particularly the one on Courtney and Porter's house.

Finally, Sela had questions of her own. "Lyla, why are you so interested in the spell that destroyed the house? And in all of the plants I made appear?"

Lyla sipped at her tea. "To answer your first question, I'm interested in the house because your spell was so effective."

"I don't understand. Should it not have worked because I didn't know what I was doing?"

"I think part of you very much knew what you were doing, whether you were aware of it or not at the time." Lyla paused, considering her. "But it's that lack of awareness—the fact that your magick seems determined to run its course without you even knowing how to make it so. That's what concerns me."

"Then why hasn't Sable said anything?"

"Be patient with Sable," Lyla said, a note of compassionate sadness in her voice. "It's not any easier to be a newly initiated familiar than it is to be a newly initiated witch."

"All I mean is, why do you seem to know so much about things he's unclear on? Is there some kind of magickal database somewhere that we should be accessing?"

"There are many ways to learn. You should speak to Alexander about it. He conducts a good deal of research, mainly about ancient uses of crystals and stones."

"Is that how you learned? From Alexander?"

Now, Lyla set her cup down carefully on the glass table. "Sela, I hope you don't mind me being a bit presumptuous, but from our previous conversation, I got the impression that Sable hasn't been quite forthcoming about us. About familiars, I mean."

Sela sighed. "I can't get him to tell me a thing, most of the time. He's explained about our emotional connection and how he can't control his form for now, but that's basically it."

"It's not unusual for familiars to be profoundly uncomfortable discussing ourselves."

"But why? Sable's watching me fumble through all sorts of embarrassing fuck-ups with my magick. How much worse could familiar stuff be?"

"Not worse, but different. To play on a parenting cliché, I am going to tell you where familiars come from, and hopefully that will clear things up a bit. Now, Sable told you that witches and familiars sometimes pursue relationships that are considered taboo within the magickal community, yes?"

"He said something about uninitiated witches and familiars trying to work together, although again, I couldn't really get specifics out of him."

"That's one such kind of relationship," Lyla confirmed. "In such cases, the witch and familiar in question attempt to force a magickal bond that isn't there. They may be successful in their endeavors, but usually, the consequences will outweigh any benefits. It's an extremely selfish choice to make, actually, and we can speak about why another time."

She took a moment to refill both of their teacups before continuing. "There is another taboo pairing that occurs in our world, one that's more relevant to our conversation today. And that is when a witch and her familiar become romantically involved."

Sela felt her jaw go slack. "But I thought that wasn't...you mean, that's really a thing?"

Lyla regarded her with a curious smile. "Surely, you've noticed that Sable is extremely attractive, no matter which form he takes?"

Sela rolled her eyes. "I mean, yeah, and my little sister is stunning, but I'm not about to go for her!"

"Ah," Lyla nodded. "And that is where most witches and familiars fall on the subject. We almost inevitably become family; for you, Sable is like a sibling. I'm sure he approached you in such a way that made it so. And it's much the same between Alexander and myself. But for some familiars and witches, there is an instant and incredible attraction, perhaps made even more intense because it feels forbidden."

"Shouldn't it be?" Sela was disturbed hearing all of this. Sable was her best friend; he felt like he was a part of her. Those were lines she couldn't even imagine crossing.

"If it were," Lyla responded, "then there would be no familiars."

"I'm sorry?"

"A familiar is always born of a female witch and a male familiar. While witches are conceived with their magickal seals, they're typically born of ordinary human parents and so must experience a magickal rebirth in order to come into themselves as witches. That is why the Nascent Eve exists. We, on the other hand, are literally born into magick."

The magnitude of this revelation stunned Sela into near silence for a moment. All she could think to ask was, "Why?" She knew it was a ridiculous question even as it left her mouth. Why should anybody know the reasons behind their own conception?

But Lyla apparently had an answer. "It makes sense, in a

way. A familiar must seek out a witch before the Nascent Eve and reveal to her who she truly is. We need to know more about you than you do about yourselves, at least in the beginning."

"That's why you've been able to explain all of this," Sela realized. "Your mother was a witch."

"I was fortunate." Lyla smiled, and there was a wistfulness in her eyes. "My form was easy to birth, and my mother was clever and resourceful. She knew about caring for children as the eldest of four herself, and what she didn't know about rearing a familiar she figured out as we went along. Few of us are as lucky as I was."

"Why?" Sela asked again, aware she was throwing endless questions at Lyla but desperate to know more. "And what do you mean, you were easy to birth?"

"We are not born in our human forms," Lyla explained. "And while familiars who take forms like me and Sable—cats, birds, smaller animals—are not difficult to birth, there are familiars of all kinds. Predator forms, forms with hooves, forms too large for a human woman's body to carry to term, never mind to birth."

The horror of this struck deep within Sela. "What happens then?"

"These days, we have modern medicine at our disposal. We try, if we can, to find a witch who is also a doctor or who can at least perform a caesarian section. If the familiar's animal form is large enough, we attempt to contact a coven in the hopes of sustaining it magickally after a deliberately premature C-section."

Lyla looked down at her hands. "Before modernity, the death rate of witches pregnant with familiars was staggering. We had many more challenges connecting as a community— some could travel great distances using magick, but most were restricted to the means of travel common to their time, so finding help was often impossible. Few could boast both medical and magickal skill adequate to help those witches whose pregnancies were sure to kill them. In those times, obstetrics in general was a far cry from what it is today, even for ordinary humans. And magickal help was also hard to find because it was so dangerous to seek out. You recall learning of witch trials and hunts in school?"

"Yes," Sela said, "but I thought ordinary people were the ones killed."

"For the most part, they were. But sometimes, familiars who had not yet found their witches were subject to the unexpected transformations of their bodies, which would betray them to ordinary humans. On some rare occasions, a witch who had birthed one of us would be caught, and she and her familiar offspring slaughtered. That's why there are so many depictions of witches feeding demons who had taken the forms of animals at their breasts."

Tears welled up in Sela's eyes as she listened to this horrific history, full of unbelievable consequences for women who made the mistake of falling in love with the wrong person. "They weren't demons."

"They were us. Sometimes, if familiars whose witch mothers were caught managed to escape that same fate, they were reared by brave members of your kind. It is never easy for a witch who parents a familiar; many do not have the fortitude to try."

This made Sela think back to Sable's discomfort at visiting her parents' place, and she felt a spark of agitation. "Why not? Why wouldn't you try to care for a defenseless child? These situations are horrible, but it isn't Sab—it isn't the familiar's fault."

"Sela, I know this is difficult to process," Lyla told her gently. "But you must remember, most witches spend the first three decades of their lives as ordinary women. As frightening as childbirth can be under normal circumstances, to birth a creature of another species—to have an animal emerge from the most intimate parts of one's body—it's more than some women can take, psychologically speaking. This is fortunately less common now, as there is much more sharing of information within our communities. But even today, some witches lose their minds during childbirth."

"Wait, you said all of these pairings happen between a male familiar and a female witch. Why not the other way around?"

"Such pairings exist—there are no limits to who one can love, and that holds as true within the witch community as it does outside of it. But such couplings yield no children. Female familiars are sterile, as far as we know."

"What?" *How could Sable not have told me any of this?*

"We've evolved as such, and it also makes a kind of sense," Lyla said. "As Sable informed you, until our witches reach a certain level of mastery in their magickal practice, we never know when we ourselves might transform. A pregnancy would surely result in disaster if the body changed forms in the midst of it."

"Lyla, I can't even begin to digest all of this." And she couldn't; it was overwhelming. Lyla couldn't have children, even if she wanted to. If Sela was impregnated by Sable—not that they ever would, but still—it could actually kill her.

Lyla put a hand on her shoulder. "It's a lot to take in. But it's important that you know all of this, though I understand why Sable doesn't want to talk about it. Our birthright can be a mark of shame for many of us."

"Not for you?"

Now the other woman's smile returned. "I found my witch a powerful, brilliant, kind-hearted man. He and I have acted as partners in everything: our magick, our business, all of our endeavors. Together, we are thriving, and I have a very happy life with him. And now, we have wonderful friends in you and Sable. How can I possibly be ashamed of where I come from when it's brought me all of this?"

Sela wasn't surprised by this response; she was learning that her new friend was one of the more remarkable people she'd ever known. But a new question rose as she considered Lyla's last remark. "How do you find us? Witches, I mean?"

"During the brief time before your Nascent Eve, your magickal seal begins to…I suppose the best way to put it is that it signals us. We feel a magickal pull from within, and we follow it until we find our witches."

"Just like that." The bitterness she'd felt from Sable when he'd told her about his inability to control his transformations filled Sela's mouth.

"Remember, Sela, we don't *have* to come to you. We have a choice in the matter."

"You mean remaining an animal for the rest of your lives? That's not much of a choice, is it?"

Lyla sighed. "You're quite influenced by Sable's version of things."

"Why shouldn't I be?" Sela asked, feeling defensive of Sable. "He's my familiar. I'm the one wrecking his life."

"You've wrecked nothing," Lyla countered firmly. "While the frustration he feels over the unexpected transformations seem to be influencing how he regards his animal form, Sable may one day come to be grateful for his dualistic nature. Many of us spend as much time as we possibly can in our animal forms."

"I've rarely seen you as a bird."

"Sela, you've seen me in my place of business. In cities and towns, it's more difficult for us to shift between forms as we might wish. Ordinary people tend to react poorly when cats, birds, and other creatures demonstrate proficiency in human language and mannerism. But at home, I often take this form."

And Sela found herself looking at the lovely blue bird that Lyla had transformed into to save her from Jackson outside the shop on the first day they met.

"Lyla, I don't want to be rude, but can I ask...um..."

"What is the name of my animal form?" she finished the sentence knowingly, and Sela blushed. Lyla laughed, "Don't be embarrassed! Most people don't know a Victoria crowned pigeon when they see one."

Even the way Lyla spoke and moved in her animal form was very different from how Sable behaved in his, Sela realized. Sable frequently adopted human postures and expressions, but Lyla conducted herself like a bird.

Then Sela noticed something else. "Hey! Your clothes didn't fall all around you. Where are they?"

"Oh, Sable will learn how to stop shedding his clothes once he gets control of the change. We sort of...tuck them away, magickally."

Somehow, Lyla's transformation hadn't woken Pluto, who had been snoozing between the two of them for most of their conversation. Sela figured that was probably a good thing; as bad as his reactions had been to Sable, she was relatively sure that a bird bigger than he was would lead Pluto into causing considerable ruckus.

Lyla changed back into human form. "Of course, I can't go into the shop as a bird, and I think it's probably time we check whether the lads have killed one another." She scratched Pluto affectionately between the ears, waking him just enough that he rolled over and demanded a belly rub, which made her laugh again. "Will you be bringing him home with you?"

"Not for now," Sela decided. It was bad enough that Sable was living on her terms, regardless of what he might want or need. She couldn't add someone else to the list of lives she'd recently ruined, especially not a sweet cat like Pluto. "I think he's happier here than with Sable. All he does in my apartment now is hide."

"Well, we promise to keep him spoilt and happy as long as he's with us. He's a beautiful little thing, and quite sweet. Even Alexander has taken a liking to him, and that's unusual."

As they made their way back downstairs, Sela remembered something. "Lyla, you never told me why you're so interested in my plant magicks."

"Hmm," Lyla murmured. "How to put this: it's less the plants themselves than the quantity in which they emerged."

"What do you mean?"

"Well, if I didn't know any better," Lyla chose her words carefully, "I'd say that multiple witches made those plants appear as they did."

"But aside from Alexander, I'm the only witch I know."

Lyla nodded, and continued into the shop without another word.

Twenty-Nine

There were some customers wandering around the shop when Sela and Lyla returned. Sable was sitting near Alexander on the front counter and Sela could tell he'd calmed down, though her own rattled emotions from everything Lyla had just relayed drew his attention immediately. She forced a smile, trying with effort to close her feelings off from him. Although their empathic connection was nowhere near as strong as it had been in the days after their Nascent Eve, it still wasn't under control.

While most of the customers were unremarkable, there was one who drew Sela's attention, possibly because he was staring directly at her. He was somewhere in his mid-thirties, very fit, wearing black jeans and a tight black t-shirt. His jet-black hair hung into his unusually large dark-brown eyes, and he should have been strikingly attractive, with deeply tan skin and a five-o'clock shadow that worked to his benefit over a strong jaw. But there was something Sela found unsettling about him, enough to offset his good looks and leanly muscular frame.

After she'd met and held his gaze for a few moments, he stalked directly over to her and without so much as a smile demanded, "Do we know each other?"

Sela detected more than a hint of agitation in his voice. "I don't think so," she replied, certain she'd remember if she had spoken to this man before.

He continued to stare her down. "You seem very…
familiar." And he added a slight emphasis to the last word,
enough to draw Alexander's attention from his work.

"Finding everything you need?" he asked as he approached
them.

"I'm not sure," the stranger replied, not taking his eyes
from Sela. As put off as she was by his behavior, something kept
her from being actively frightened by this man.

Lyla rang up the two remaining customers at the front with
subtle but definite haste, walking them out of the shop
graciously and then locking the door behind them. She pulled
down a blind that covered the window of the front door, and
then drew curtains Sela had never even noticed across the
display windows of the shop.

"Closing early?" the strange man remarked, not turning to
look at Lyla.

"Clearly, we're in want of some privacy." Lyla's voice
didn't waver, but Sela could tell from the look she and
Alexander shared that they were also more than a little
concerned over this man. Sable had also stood to attention and
was watching the stranger keenly.

"Yes, well, it does allow one to get more comfortable,
doesn't it?" the man said as he effortlessly transformed into a
large black panther.

Although she was almost one hundred percent certain the
shift in form meant that this was a familiar who probably didn't
mean them harm, the small part of Sela that was not accustomed
to being in rooms with giant predator animals made her jump
back.

"And here I thought we'd been getting along famously,"
the panther remarked. Sela could swear he smirked as he spoke.

"That's enough," Alexander replied sharply.

Sable had jumped down from the counter and moved to stand beside Sela. "Introduce yourself if you have something to say to us."

The panther seemed to regard Sable with some amusement, and Sela felt immediately insulted on behalf of her familiar. Who did this guy think he was?

However, despite his mocking demeanor, he answered Sable: "My name is Micah."

"What brings you to these parts, Micah?" Alexander asked, not offering his own name in return.

"That's the odd thing," Micah replied, and his gaze once again shifted to Sela. "My witch seems to think we're visiting an old friend, but I'm not so convinced that's the only reason we're in town."

"What old friend?" Lyla spoke now. "Perhaps it's someone we know."

"I'm sure, given how few of our kind reside in these parts. In fact," he added, "aside from our friend, I think you all might be the extent of us locally. Am I right?"

Sela put up her hands. "Can I just interrupt the weirdness for a second?" She looked around at all of them. "How the hell did he know it was okay to transform in front of us?"

Micah seemed surprised. "You are a baby witch, aren't you? When was your Nascent Eve—just last night? Or is your familiar sleeping on the job?"

Sable seemed about to defend himself, but Sela was speaking before either of them knew it. "Okay, asshole, let's get something straight: I may be a brand-new witch, but I'm not new to this planet, and thanks to a long hell of dating jerks, I'm pretty much over cryptic bullshit and passive-aggressive posturing. So, why don't you cut the crap and tell us what you want?"

A moment of generally shocked silence passed before Sable added, "What my witch said."

Micah sighed. "Baby witches take the fun out of everything; you take it all so seriously." Before Sela could lace into him again, he quickly continued, "We're here visiting Idris Tremblay at Visions, as far as I know. And baby witch, for the record, we can all pretty much recognize one another."

"Who can?" Sela demanded, not caring if she sounded naïve. She could feel Sable's pride in her and it kept her from backing down, even if she was sassing a full-grown panther.

"Witches, familiars—we all sort of walk around with magick-goggles permanently glued to our faces. You'll develop it soon enough." He seemed to appraise her. "In fact, I wonder if you haven't already."

"What makes you think you're here for more than Idris?" Alexander wanted to know. He still hadn't relaxed his stance, Sela noticed, and then she saw that he had a small crystal tucked into one of his hands.

At least one of us is prepared to use magick to protect everyone, she thought, frustrated by how useless a witch she was for the moment.

"Well, Idris is a good friend of my witch—who by the way is called Thackeray, should you run into him at any point. That's Thackeray Owens. But we were quite invested in our work back home, several states away, and I don't know that a sudden visit was warranted."

"That's not all that's troubling you," Lyla observed, and Micah turned to her.

"No," he agreed.

"Then what?" she asked.

He paused for a moment before saying, "A certain... *familiar* sensation."

"Of?" Alexander pressed him.

"Oh, the two of you wouldn't understand, I'm afraid." He indicated Sela and Alexander with his gaze. "But for the rest of us, it's an invitation of sorts: the kind one feels one really can't refuse."

Now Sable and Lyla shared a glance, and Sela felt herself grow uneasy. Sable's emotions had progressed from suspicion to concern and confusion. She blurted, "So, does anyone know what the fuck is going on? Or are we going to continue to speak in puzzles?"

"You know, I think I've decided that I don't dislike you as much as I thought I did upon meeting you," Micah told her. "I appreciate people who are direct."

"So do I," Sela snapped back through gritted teeth.

"If I had a clearer sense of what exactly is going on, baby witch, I promise I would tell all of you." He shifted back to his human form. "As it is, I'm taking notes and trying to figure it out myself."

"Will you come by again soon, then?" Lyla asked as Micah made his way to the front door. Sela could tell that she also wanted information, despite the level tone her voice maintained.

"Maybe. But Thackeray and I are at Visions every weekend while we're visiting, should you want to find us first." He glanced back at them as he turned the lock on the shop door to let himself out. "I think it might be smart for us to consult Idris, once we have a clearer idea of what's happening. He does know more about our history than any witch I know."

This last remark seemed to be aimed at Alexander in particular, whose eyes narrowed in agitation as the door slammed shut.

"What the fuck was his problem?" Sela asked of the room as soon as Micah had gone.

"Sometimes, those of us who have predator forms take on a bit of the…attitude of the animals they resemble," Lyla said carefully, remaining diplomatic even in the wake of Micah's cryptic rudeness.

"And some people, as you said, are assholes," Sable added, looking up at Sela with a satisfied expression. "Thank you for verbally kicking his ass."

"Not a problem." She turned to Alexander now. "Do you know this guy Idris he kept talking about?"

Alexander nodded. "We've met up here and there over the years. He's more active in the global witch community than we are, but he's pleasant enough. He's even helped me with a couple of difficult orders for customers seeking specialty items in the past. I think Lyla has met with his familiar on occasion?"

"Her name is Reese," Lyla confirmed. "I can't say I know her well, though. She's taken on the nocturnal habits of her animal form, probably because she's so active with the club business. Idris has her closing the place each night, I believe."

"So, Visions is a witch club?" Sela asked, confused. Aside from the strange interaction with Jackson and her sister, the place hadn't seemed particularly magickal.

"Not exactly," Alexander replied. "It services ordinary people, but Idris has done exceptionally well for himself and cut out the competition by way of culinary magicks."

"The drinks," Sela remembered after a moment. "They were amazing."

"Yes, he has a knack for flavor. Beyond that, there's a VIP area exclusively for magickal folk." Alexander half-smiled. "The few times I've been by during club hours, Idris made it a point to have me up there as his guest, even if the visit was only for a quick verification on a magickal artifact. He's quite proud of it."

"I think the two of you need to be heading home about now, don't you?" Lyla interrupted, and Sela could see that she wanted to speak with Alexander alone.

"It wouldn't hurt to do another protection spell on the apartment, honestly, now that the new windows have been installed," Sable agreed. "More practice is always good, and I'm not much use in this form should anyone break in again."

"Here." Alexander went back behind the counter and grabbed a small pouch. He handed it to Sela. "I put this together after Sable told me what happened last night. We know you've shown some talent for plants, so I've gathered a pinch of every major protective herb we stock. They should help secure your home."

Sela began reaching into her pocket for money, but Alexander stopped her, shaking his head. "We're always happy to help friends. See you both soon."

The bizarre combination of distress and comfort filling Sela's heart as she and Sable made their way to her car was a contradiction that was getting increasingly familiar. On the one hand, she had Jackson to worry about. But on the other, Alexander and Lyla were turning out to be wonderful friends, and the loneliness that had filled her life just weeks ago was fading into distant memory. She was becoming used to the constants of anxiety and happiness; maybe they just came with the new-witch territory.

On the ride home, she decided to mention some of what she'd just learned to Sable. She knew it wasn't his favorite topic of conversation, and after today, Sela felt like she finally understood why. But she wanted to know her familiar better.

"So," she began, "Lyla talked to me about witches and familiars."

Sable didn't respond, but she felt him tense.

"I learned a lot," she went on. "Some of it wasn't easy to hear. But I'm glad I know more about us—I mean, about where familiars and witches come from and everything."

"Lyla told you the facts of life," he said coldly. "That's nice. Saves me the trouble."

"Sable, why won't you talk to me about your life before we met? I mean, you got to meet my family. Hell, you slept with my family!" She laughed a little, in part because it all seemed so ludicrous in the wake of what she'd discovered, and in part to let him know she'd truly forgiven him for Natalie. "Why don't you tell me about yours?"

"I can't do that, Sela," he told her, his voice low.

"Why not?" she pressed, knowing she was entering sensitive territory but nevertheless wanting to hear from Sable about his life. It was only fair: if she'd upended everything, she needed to know exactly what she'd ruined. "Did your parents split or something? Is that why you don't want to talk about it?"

"It's because she died," he snapped. "My mom died before I could learn anything from her, before I could even get to know her. That's why I need Lyla to help me guide you. It's why I'm a shitty familiar and I can't answer every one of your questions. It's why I find some of your magick—the things you do without trying—fascinating." Bitterness filled his voice. "I grew up with none of the guidance of a witch. She was dead before my fourth birthday."

Sela could barely get the next word out. "How?"

Sable wouldn't look in her direction, his head turned towards the passenger-side window. "They should have broken up, but they didn't. They fell stupidly in love, and when they had me, they got cocky. They thought they'd only have small-form familiars. His form was a field mouse, of all things."

Sable shook his head. "But she got pregnant again, and they

knew right away something was wrong. She got huge so fast; I remember it, how it terrified me. She couldn't move, she... They were trying to contact a coven for help, I think. But it just happened too fast. My father sent me away when he knew she wouldn't make it. I went to the nearest person in the community we could contact."

"Who was that?"

"An old woman who was never initiated," Sable replied. "She knew about us and would help the community from time to time, but she'd been too frightened of her own powers to accept them or her familiar when her Nascent Eve arrived. She was one of those few who choose an ordinary life. And she had nothing to teach me."

Sela paused to take in everything Sable was telling her. "Why didn't your father go back and get you?"

"I don't know," he answered darkly. "If I'd killed the woman I loved, maybe I wouldn't feel right taking her child back, either."

"Sable, I don't think—"

"What? That he killed her?" He snorted angrily. "He damn well knew he'd been lucky once, with me. Why wasn't I enough? One familiar child that doesn't kill a witch is a miracle in and of itself. He should never have let her risk a second pregnancy, especially not where we were—out in the middle of nowhere, pariahs the community didn't want any ties to, and no local coven to be found."

"So, what was the old lady who raised you like?" Sela asked after a moment, trying to find a hint of light in Sable's story. "Was she nice?"

"Nice enough, for the three years I was with her."

"But if your father didn't come back for you..."

"She died too, Sela." Sable turned to face her, and instead

MELISSA BOBE

of anger, there was only sorrow in his face. "She was too old to care for a kid. I was bounced around to different members of the community, some of whom taught me what it meant to be a familiar—like Diana, who I told you about. Others didn't bother to try." He sighed heavily. "I'm still considered one of the lucky ones. I made it to my witch, and I had some magick and care in my life. But you'll have to forgive me if I don't see it that way."

"I don't have to forgive you. All of that fucking sucks."

"Yeah. It really did."

They drove the rest of the way without speaking, but when it was time to get out of the car, Sela stopped. "Are you glad we talked?" Sable didn't respond, and she added, "Because I am. If we're going to be family, we should know about each other, even if it's shitty things."

They went upstairs, still in silence, but when they entered the apartment, Sable asked, "Do you have enough money for a pizza?"

"Yeah. You want one for dinner?"

"After the conversation you just put me through, I absolutely fucking do," he replied. "And I expect ice cream to follow, so if you're not stocked up, you'd better run back out to the store."

She grinned at him. "I know better than to ever be out of ice cream now that we're together."

As Sela was digging through her closet looking for a cozy pajama top for the cool night, she noticed a gleaming piece of jewelry in the box she kept on the shelf above her clothes. Lifting it, she found a stunning strand of glistening pink pearls.

"Sable," she called out uncertainly. "This isn't mine."

He came to investigate. "Did Jackson leave it here when he broke in?"

She shook her head. "Believe me, I would have noticed. In

fact, I feel like I almost remember this, somehow…"

"Sela, think," instructed Sable. "If this wasn't Jackson's doing, it's probably another one of the spells you cast in high school."

At those words, a light went on in her memory. "Of course! Maria and I did this just before prom! We wanted to borrow real jewelry from our moms and they both refused." She chuckled. "They weren't wrong—we probably would have lost anything they gave us."

"What was the spell?"

"We each took a piece of costume jewelry that was close to what we wanted to wear," she told him, reminiscing over excitedly sitting with Maria in her parents' attic and casting the circle together. "We tried to enchant them so they'd look more like real versions of themselves. I chose a string of plastic pearls, and Maria picked a set of crystal earrings she wanted to look like diamonds."

"And you're sure this isn't just a string of pearls you forgot you had?"

She gave him a look. "Believe me, I've never had a string of pearls to forget. They are really pretty, though. I'm not complaining about this past magickal choice."

"Well, don't get too attached," he told her, making his way to the second bedroom. "We'll need to try to reverse that spell as practice."

"Why?" she called after him sulkily, wanting to keep this newfound luxury.

"To make sure you know how to do a proper reversal so we can get rid of this stalker you've enchanted once and for all."

Thirty

Sela spent every moment that week focused on her magick. While Sable decreed that much of what she'd brought back from her parents' place was good for nostalgia and little else, he did approve of a few dictionaries of magickal tools and their uses. So, Sela brought the books with her to every hustle she had lined up for the week.

While Ashton did his science homework, she studied crystals. While Annabelle ate her wheat-free and dairy-free snacks after school, Sela reviewed the properties of different colors used in magick. She worked to memorize every variation of jasper in between calls at a podiatrist's office. She pored over the uses of herbs as she signed in sick dogs, cats, and birds at the emergency vet clinic.

And when she finally got home at whatever time work ended, Sela worked two nightly spells. For the most part, they were protective: Sable had her cover the apartment, the car, even the both of them. She would have liked to do more than just two a night, but the effort it took to translate the will for each spell into specific, accurate language was much more challenging than she'd thought it would be. Once she finally felt like she had the knack of things, she pushed Sable to let her attempt something they could see; after all, how could she be sure the protection spells were working if all they did was provide an invisible shield?

"I promise you, it's been working," he said. "With the number of spells you've cast, I don't think you're going to get so much as a hangnail. We're beyond protected; in fact, I think we may have accidentally sterilized ourselves."

"Well, I wouldn't trust a condom I couldn't see," she retorted. "So, forgive me if I want to actually watch something magickal happen, just to make sure."

"I have no objections if it'll make you happy," Sable shrugged. "Besides, it's probably a good idea for you to try something other than the same type of spell."

"So, what do you think we should tackle? You like ice cream. Should I make some magickally appear?"

Sable frowned. "Conjuring is tough, and I don't really want to eat anything whipped up by a new witch—no offense."

"No, that makes sense," she sighed, longing for the day she could summon a whole feast. She would never say as much to Sable, but she'd been working more hours than usual to make sure she would have enough cash to feed the both of them.

"You know," Sable mused, glancing around the living room, "you've got a lot of dried plants in here. What would you like to see living again?"

"Really? Conjuring a little Half-Baked is a no, but you want me to reanimate something?"

"They're plants, Sela. I'm not asking you to raise the dead."

She ambled over to a candle she'd made a couple of years before, which had dried lavender within its base. "It would be cool to see these as living blossoms, I guess."

"While inside the candle?"

"Why not?"

"It's an interesting choice," he said approvingly. "If the spell works, maybe this will be something you can use to make your line of products even more appealing. I don't know that

I've ever seen live flowers preserved within candle wax before. And I'm sure someone would want to buy it."

That was another thing she was growing to love about Sable: he'd shown the same interest in helping her thrive in her business as in her magick. "Let's do it."

Twenty minutes later, Sela sat in a circle of crystal quartz, tree agate, and dried thistle, fennel, and forsythia. The lavender candle rested directly before her within the circle.

"Is the spell ready?" She blushed at the question, and Sable rolled his eyes. "What is it now?"

"Just feeling a little…insecure about the rhyme in this one."

He walked over to take a look at the spell. "Get over it. This should work fine."

"Do you think I should light the candle?"

"Absolutely not. I've already told you, you need a *lot* more practice before you start playing with fire again."

"God, Sable, it was one time! I was literally being initiated!"

"Is that what you're going to tell the fire department when you have to explain the source of a little spontaneous combustion?" he shot back. "Explaining the windows to your landlord wasn't enough for you? Now, come on: focus and get started with the spell."

Sela closed her eyes and began calling forth her will. She started to find the edges of something within herself, something she was recognizing a little more with every spell she cast. It was an odd but exciting sensation she didn't have a name for, the feeling of touching something that was new and strange, but also familiar. Sable had told her it was the magickal seal, which would become ever so slightly clearer to the two of them with each spell she cast. Once she felt its presence and made that fleeting contact with it, she prepared to recite the incantation.

Pushing aside whatever self-consciousness she felt about her spell-writing abilities, Sela focused only on what she now intended: to turn the dried lavender flowers within the candle back into living blossoms. She imagined the smell of fresh lavender and the feel of soft buds on her fingertips as she recited the words of the spell:

Within this candle, blossoms rise
from dried-out husks to greenery.
Reanimate before my eyes
and bud with new vitality.
Once dry, now grow and sprout and live.
Enjoy this second life I give.
With this spell, these blooms will thrive:
Lavender come back to life.

"Sela." Sable's voice brought her back from the trance-like state into which she always fell when casting, and she grinned to find the lavender alive and fragrant in the candle before her, growing as though it had been planted there from the start.

But a feeling of tension from Sable made her look up. She saw her familiar staring around the room, looking bewildered and a little afraid. She followed his gaze, and then, breathing in the scents of a garden, Sela realized: she was no longer sitting in a circle of stones and dried plants.

The forsythia, thistle, and fennel had blossomed in rich hues of green, yellow, and fuchsia. Beyond the circle, every dried plant and flower that Sela had incorporated into her work—in the art that hung on the walls, in other candles set around the living room, even in the soaps that rested alongside the kitchen sink—*everything* had come back to life.

"Check the bedrooms," Sable instructed, and she bolted up to do so.

Sela found the few plants in her room all rejuvenated. When she reached the second bedroom, the breakfront's drawers were overflowing with lushly blooming flora.

"It's the whole apartment," she said in panic as she came back into the living room. Sable emerged from the bathroom, nodding to confirm that the soaps in there had turned, as well.

Suddenly, they heard a loud commotion from beneath the living room, where the kitchen of the restaurant was located. Sela's eyes grew wide as she met Sable's gaze in horror. "You don't think…"

She didn't bother to finish the question. She ran down the stairs outside her apartment and circled to the front of the restaurant. There were no customers; it was late for a weeknight, and normally, the staff would've been closing about now. The entry door was open when she pushed it, but not a soul was present in the dining room. Several exclamations sounded from the kitchen, and Sela tiptoed over to peek through the circular windows of the swinging doors.

"Who in the hell could pull a prank like this, Marty?" one of the cooks was saying to the night manager, shaking his head. "I mean, none of us has left the kitchen for a second!"

"And you said it's all the spices?" Marty asked.

"Take a look!" The cook swept his arm out towards an industrial spice rack, and Sela's mouth dropped as she saw that every container, from the oregano to the cinnamon, had burst open with greenery.

"Even the damned lettuce has roots coming from it!" another cook told them, pulling a head of green leaves from the fridge.

Sela crept out of the restaurant and hurried back up to her

apartment.

"What happened?" Sable asked anxiously.

"Well, apparently, my spell's outcomes weren't restricted to this apartment." She winced. "How far do you think it could have spread? I mean, did I bring the spice cabinets of every restaurant on the street back to life?"

"I honestly don't know." Sable's face was troubled, and Sela could almost taste his confusion. "The incantation was fine, and if you were focused on just the flowers in the candle..."

"I *was*," she insisted. "No other plants entered my mind for a second while I was casting, not even the ones that were in the circle."

Sable sighed. "I'll call Lyla in the morning. For now, we should get some rest. There's no way we can figure this out tonight, and tomorrow, I want you to try the reversal on that string of pearls."

"Already?" she pouted. "I was kind of hoping to wear them when I saw Pete this weekend."

"You can try to re-enchant them after you complete the reversal. But I want to see you reverse a spell in a way that's concrete—the sooner, the better."

Sela knew Sable was right. The only way she would be able to reverse the spell on Jackson, which her familiar had reminded her several times was particularly powerful, was if she practiced on something small and tangible. And even though their emotional connection was calming down and they were regaining more privacy from one another with every day that passed, Sela could sense Sable's concern. More troubling than that, though, was the bewilderment she felt from him. If her familiar didn't have a clue as to what was going on with her magick, who would be left to help her?

The following night, Sela came home from her catering gig

right before the skies cracked open in a powerful autumn thunderstorm. Feeling lucky she'd made it inside before the rain, she happily jogged up the stairs, holding a bag of leftovers she knew Sable would appreciate. But when she came in, she found her familiar waiting for her impatiently in the living room.

"Where have you been?" he demanded as she slipped her shoes off.

"Um, work—where I always am. What's up?"

"You need to come take a look at something." Sable stalked into her bedroom, and Sela rolled her eyes as she followed her moody familiar.

Sable was on the windowsill, gazing at her intensely. "Notice anything alarming?"

She looked around the room, but whatever it was that Sable wanted her to see wasn't making itself apparent to her tired eyes. "Sable, this job was a really rough one and I'm beat to shit. Maybe just tell me what I'm supposed to be looking at?"

"What's wrong with the windows?"

Now Sela looked at the windows, trying to push aside her agitation at her familiar's decision to remain cryptic. It was raining pretty heavily, although there was something about how the rain looked...

"It...it's not hitting the glass." She shook her head, not understanding what was happening. "It's pouring, there's rain everywhere, but...why won't it touch the windows?"

"Still think you wouldn't trust that invisible magick condom?" Sable pointed to the storm. "Sela, this place is a fortress! Your protection spells are so powerful, even the damned weather can't get past them!"

"Is that bad? I know it's weird, but it means we're really safe, right?"

"Oh, we're safe. We're safe from everything but the

scrutiny of anyone walking by who might look up and notice an apartment that remains bone-dry while the rest of the world around it gets soaked. This is totally conspicuous magick, Sela—it's not good!"

She sank down onto the bed, rubbing her eyes vigorously as the exhaustion of work and worry compounded in her mind. "Sable, help me understand something: how am I fucking up? I can tell from how freaked you are that this isn't normal, but how do I fix it? Are my incantations bad, or am I focusing my will wrong?"

"You're doing everything right," he insisted. "We're going totally by the book."

"Maybe it's the number of protection spells we cast? We did do a fuckton."

Sable shook his head. "Magick doesn't work that way—or at least, it shouldn't. It's not that you're saying the wrong words, or even that you're getting the wrong results." He paused, trying to find the right explanation. "What's worrying me is that your spells are too *loud*, I guess. They do what you want them to, but they reverberate way beyond what we're attempting. They echo too much."

"Well, have you ever heard of anyone else that's happened to?"

"No." He must have sensed the stab of helplessness that answer shot through her, because he added quickly, "But Alexander does a ton of research. We'll call the shop tomorrow; I'm sure he'll have an idea of what this is."

Thirty-One

Alexander didn't have any ideas at all about what Sela's magick was doing.

"Nothing? No theories whatsoever?" Sela half-yelled into her phone, trying her best to keep hold of the five dogs she was walking with her other hand.

It was a beautiful day, and the park she was headed to with the dogs would be nice and empty at this time—schools were back in session, and they'd get there way before the kids got out. There was even a dog run that she knew every one of her four-legged clients was looking forward to playing in, something she usually enjoyed watching.

If only she wasn't on the edge of yet another magick-related panic attack.

"I know it's not great news," Sable replied. "But maybe it's tied to all of your teenaged dabbling. Maybe the fact that magick was practically all you did throughout adolescence is giving your spells a little more kick now."

"Is that a thing that happens?"

He sighed. "I don't know, Sela. It's actually pretty unusual for someone who engages in witchcraft as a modern-day religion or spiritual practice to turn out to be a true witch. You're in the minority, I'm afraid."

"Great. I'm so glad I'm special." One of the dogs looked up and whined at her, hearing the dejection in her tone.

"Don't give up hope. Worst case scenario, we call this Idris guy from Visions. Alexander said he'd be receptive to us asking for help, and if he doesn't have his number, we could always head directly to the club."

On the subject of numbers and phones, Sela had a sudden realization. "Sable, how are you talking to me right now?"

"What do you mean?"

"I mean, where did you get a phone?"

"Oh. I may have borrowed one from the restaurant."

"What?" Now she actually was shouting. "Sable, after everything I did to that place last night?"

"Well, all the more reason to steal it in the midst of their confusion. You caused so much chaos, who's going to get upset about a missing phone? Besides, how else was I going to call Alexander?"

She rolled her eyes. "As long as you give it back before anyone notices."

"I will, I promise. Now, when are you getting home? We have to try that reversal on your pearls today."

"Do you think that's a good idea? I mean, should I even be doing spells if Alexander's stumped and we have no clue what's happening?"

"I think it's a bad idea for you to stop doing magick right now," Sable told her. "If we want this to work itself out, you have to keep practicing."

"All right," she sighed, not feeling at all confident in her magick. "I'll be home in the early evening. After I drop these dogs off, I'm doing some after-school pickups for this one family, but the mom said she wouldn't be home too late. I've got to hang up; these guys want to go off-leash."

Sela brought the dogs into the run, where they leapt and rolled to their hearts' content. Normally, she'd be playing with

MELISSA BOBE

them—throwing a ball or engaging in tug of war with a rope toy. But all she could do was worry. Why was everything she did with her magick turning out...well, the same way everything else she did with her life seemed to turn out?

"You know," she told one of the dogs, a Boston terrier who had come up to her demanding she play with him, "this is starting to feel a lot like senior year of college."

Her phone suddenly buzzed again, and Sela prepared to tell Sable to stop using up this random stranger's minutes when she saw that it wasn't her familiar calling, but her boyfriend. An automatic smile spread across her face.

"Hey, how did you know I was having a bad day?"

"Oh no," Pete's voice came over the other end of the line, full of sympathy. "I was hoping to talk you into meeting me for an impromptu dinner, but maybe it's a bad time?"

"I can't tell you how much I wish I could. Work is just ...killing me." It was as close to the truth as she could get; besides, being a witch was beginning to feel like a job that she wasn't doing particularly well.

"Let's meet up this weekend, if you're free? I promise I'll cheer you up."

She smiled. "I have no doubts there."

"What night works best for you?"

"Hmm, maybe Friday? By then, I should be just about climbing the walls."

"So...tomorrow night?"

Sela laughed. "Wow, it is a good thing you called me because I literally did not remember what day it was."

"Sounds like you could use the night out," Pete replied. "I'll pick you up tomorrow at seven?"

"Yes. And Pete: thank you."

"For what?"

"For making this day suck less."

By the time she got home, Sela's spirits had lifted. Making a date with Pete had definitely helped, and the kids she'd been watching were unusually chill until their mom came home. She'd even had a chance to work on the reversal spell for the pearls.

When she walked into her apartment, Sable was waiting with a bag of Thai food by the door.

"How did you manage that?" she asked him, ecstatic that she wouldn't have to cook.

"Well, before I gave the phone back, I called in an order and told the guy to leave the food in front of the apartment door. I said I'd leave the money under the welcome mat and tip well if he didn't ask questions. He went for it."

Sela rolled her eyes. "Great, now he probably thinks I'm doing something bizarre and illegal in here." But she didn't complain any further after spying the order of pad kee mao Sable had gotten her.

"You need your strength, witch—we've got a reversal to try tonight. Now, let's eat before my pad thai gets cold."

Sela threw together a pot of tea and they proceeded to dig in. Her familiar might be acting like a criminal mastermind, between stealing phones and shoving money under mats, but at least he knew exactly what she needed at the end of the day.

"So," Sable told her between bites, "I made one other call that you should know about. Well, I made a few calls to get the number I needed to make that call, but whatever."

"Oh my god, this poor bastard whose phone you took," Sela said, shaking her head. "I hope you erased his call history."

"What kind of familiar do you think I am? Of course I erased it. Anyway, I managed to track Diana down."

"Wait, Diana who was like the big sister you never had?

That Diana?"

"The one and only," Sable confirmed. "We caught up for a bit, and she's decided to come for a visit."

"What?"

"Well, her witch is apparently away on a business trip, so she's got some free time. Besides, they've moved recently, so she only lives a half day's drive from here."

"Whoa," Sela said, taking all of this in. "Sable, are you okay? I mean, this is a lot, isn't it?"

"Oh, you mean Diana coming?" He laughed. "Sela, as fucked up as I am over my whole sorry past, Diana's amazing. I mean, she's like a shining spot in the giant bucket of crap that's been my life."

"But won't seeing her be a little emotional for you?"

"It'll be a good kind of emotional," he reassured her. "Anyway, she wants to try and help us, if she can. She's not particularly knowledgeable the way Alexander is or anything, but I figure the more familiars and witches we can get to look at our situation, the better."

"I definitely won't turn down any help, at this point," Sela told him. "I'm sorry your witch turned out to be such a fuck-up, Sable."

"I don't think these are necessarily fuck-ups, Sela."

"What do you mean?"

He looked at her thoughtfully. "When I consider everything—the excess that your spells are causing, the wild growth of all the plants—I think there might be something significant at work here."

"Like what?"

"I don't know. That's why I want us to get help."

She nodded in agreement. "Sounds good. In the meantime, I'll keep doing my best to not fuck up, at least magickally."

"Speaking of magick, should we get started on the necklace?"

"Yeah, I actually have an incantation written. I thought it up while I was baby-sitting."

Sable shook his head. "Reversals don't work that way. We need to consult your original spell in order to reverse this one."

"That's a horrible rule!" Sela exclaimed. "What if I didn't write one of my spells down?"

Sable narrowed his eyes. "Did you not write one of your spells down?"

She thought about this. "Well, no—I was actually pretty intense about that. I even wrote them out on scrap paper first and then copied them into the Book of Shadows so they'd look pretty and I wouldn't have to scratch any words out."

"Good," he replied, heading to her room. "Let's find the spell. We also need the gossamer chain."

"I'll get it—it's still in the breakfront drawer on top of the amethyst point."

Sela went to retrieve the chain from the second bedroom. She was amazed once more at how silken the webbing was to the touch. If Sable hadn't assured her that it was metal, she would've been convinced it was the softest fabric she'd ever encountered.

"What do I do with it?" she asked, holding the chain out to Sable, who had come to join her in the second bedroom.

"Let it rest over the blue goldstone sphere until we start the spell," he advised. "You'll drape it over your hand once you're casting. First, though, we need to write the incantation by directly inverting as many of the original words and phrases from the spell that changed the necklace in the first place."

"Does it have to rhyme?" Sela asked skeptically. "Because that's a tall order."

"It never has to rhyme," Sable reminded her.

She found the spell and began working on reversing the words she'd written all those years ago.

"Shaping your will in a reversal is a little different," Sable instructed as she wrote, "because you have to focus on undoing *exactly* what your will was originally. So, think about what you wanted, and then aim to undo that as you think about what you want now."

"Sure, that's not like patting your head and rubbing your stomach at the same time," she muttered, more than a little nervous about getting this right.

"Get used to multitasking," he told her. "That's what witches do."

When the spell was finally ready, Sela sat in a circle of lit candles. This made Sable beyond anxious, of course, but she needed to do everything as she had done it originally.

"Once you've managed to focus on your will, lift the gossamer chain and drape it over your hand. Then position that hand above the necklace as you speak the words of the spell."

Sela did as Sable instructed, tapping into her magickal seal and breathing into the power she felt. Holding her hand with the webbing over the string of pearls, she spoke aloud the reversal spell:

No longer must this necklace shine like the sea:
I release its beauty and ask that it return to its original form.
Plastic beads manifest once more,
and this string of pearls exist no longer.

Nothing happened.
Sela waited expectantly.
Still nothing.

"Sable?"

"I can see." Sable's face was heavy with concern.

"Do I say it again?" she asked earnestly, growing more uneasy with every second the shining strand of pearls remained. He shook his head. "You did everything right. I felt your magick, felt the seal, and we have the chain, which should have cemented your efforts. The spell you wrote is good. It should have worked."

Their eyes met, and Sela asked the question they were both thinking: "If this didn't work, what's going to happen with the enchantment on Jackson Woods?"

Thirty-Two

"Sela, you know you're obsessing, right?"

Sela and Sable might finally have their psychic link under control, but keeping Natalie off of her emotional radar was an entirely different story.

"I know," Sela replied, switching on her turn signal as she waited for a red light to change. "I was just hoping that magick would be the one area where I'm not...you know..."

"A failure?" Natalie filled in helpfully.

"Yep."

"You're not a failure."

"But—"

"Sela! You're not a failure! Look, you just started all this weird witch crap. You're not going to just get it overnight."

"This isn't normal, though. I'm really fucking up."

She could practically hear Natalie's eyes rolling through the speakerphone. "Whatever! So you're fucking up—you'll learn how *not* to fuck up, eventually. Meanwhile, this box of products you sent me is amazing! The lip gloss is my favorite; it's totally inspired."

Sela smiled. Her business was coming along slowly; so far, her only customers were her sister, her mom, and Pete's sister and her friends. But she was hopeful that word would soon start to spread.

"Plus, who cares if your magick is a little iffy? Your

boyfriend's hot as fuck."

This was also true. "You know, you're hard to argue with sometimes, Nat."

"Of course I am! I'm always right. And how is my future brother-in-law, by the way?"

Now, Sela rolled her eyes. "Pete's great. We have a date tonight."

"Good!" There was a pause, and then Natalie said in a voice that was more reserved, "He seems like he's a good guy, Sela."

"He is a good guy." She also hesitated, not wanting to scare her sister off the phone. "Hey, Natalie, are you ever going to tell me about what happened? You know, about why this freaky magickal stalker shit is especially freaky for you?"

"Not today."

And Sela had no choice but to leave things there, the concern she felt for her sister only assuaged by the knowledge that Natalie was safely at home, far away from where this thing she couldn't talk about had happened, and far from Sela's own problems.

Work had ended earlier than planned, so she had time to run a few errands. She got her familiar a cheap phone so he would stop stealing other people's, and was pleasantly surprised to learn that adding another number to her plan somehow lowered the cost per line. Then, she picked up a decorative basket and some tissue paper. She'd decided she would bring Lyla and Alexander gifts as a thank you for all of their help at some point that weekend. It seemed like the least she could do.

As she unlocked the apartment door, she heard laughter coming from inside.

"Sela, you're home!" Sable greeted her, happier than she'd ever seen him. "What's all that?"

She pulled out his new phone. "This is so you don't keep stealing from the guys who work in the restaurant. The plan's already active, so you can start making calls whenever. Within reason."

"Fantastic! I swear, I'll only call expensive international locations on weekends."

"Oh, you tell jokes now. Great."

"You must be Sela."

A young woman emerged from the back of the living room. The first thing Sela noticed about her was her hair: sleek and black, it was cut in deliberately blunt layers all the way down to her hips. Outside of an old Florence + the Machine video, Sela had never seen such a dramatic style. Beneath a heavy straight bang, the woman wore a subdued smoky eye, and her coral matte lipstick popped as she offered Sela a warm smile.

"Diana?" Sela asked, though with a haircut like that, she knew this had to be Sable's mentor in magick and styling.

"It's so nice to meet you! I'm happy to know Sable has found himself with such a kind witch."

"Thanks," Sela smiled. "I just wish he could say she was a talented witch, too."

"I wouldn't be so quick to assume otherwise," Diana told her, dark-brown eyes showing gentle concern. "It seems like your talents may just need a little…redirection. We'll hopefully know more this evening after Sable and I talk."

"I wish I could introduce you to Pete," Sable remarked sullenly. "It sucks being stuck in this form again."

Diana let out a frustrated sigh. "I wish you wouldn't talk about yourself that way, Sable."

"I happen to find you equally snarky in both forms," Sela added helpfully.

"See?" Diana grinned at her, and Sela was once again

amazed at how likable everyone she met in the magickal community was. Maybe she'd only had trouble making friends since high school because she hadn't met any witches or familiars until now.

"Sable tells me you're about to head out on a date," Diana went on, a mischievous sparkle in her eyes. "Would you like some help getting ready for the night?"

"So, this is like a thing with you guys."

"I personally believe that familiars should help their witches succeed in all aspects of life," Diana told her. "What's the point of helping with magick if we sit by and watch you flounder in business or fashion? A successful individual makes for a successful witch."

"Wise words from the queen herself," Sable remarked affectionately. "You should let her dress you, Sela. She's better than I am."

"I did teach him everything he knows," Diana confirmed. She glanced knowingly at Sela and added, "He did a great job with that haircut."

"Well, between your haircut and that dress you're wearing, I can tell I'm in the presence of greatness," Sela replied. "Just don't judge the state of my closet, okay?"

"Cross my heart," Diana laughed, following Sela to the bedroom.

Sela settled herself on the bed next to Sable, who was chatting away happily with his old friend. She was glad to see him in such good spirits, and made a mental note to invite Diana to visit more often.

"Magick gives you a sense of things," Diana told Sela as she sorted through the mess of a closet. "That includes what a person is like. And once you know what she's like, you know how that should be reflected in what she wears. And you go from there."

"Just like that?" Sela felt like she didn't even have a sense of herself, never mind everyone else around her.

"It takes time." Diana smiled kindly at her. "You two just started, don't forget! I spent the better part of my first year as Darius's familiar getting his wardrobe under control."

"Darius is your witch?"

Diana nodded. "And don't worry, you'll have a chance to pay it forward once you and Sable become a little more seasoned."

"I've heard that before," Sela said, thinking fondly of Lyla.

"We all do it," Diana went on. "If you feel like every magickal person in spitting distance is lending you a hand every now and again, then as a community, we're functioning as we should. There's more unity in magick than many people realize." She shot a quick glance at Sable as she said this, but he either didn't notice or pretended not to. "Anyway, we tend to be more well-dressed than ordinary people. This should work!"

She'd surfaced from the nightmarish depths of the closet victorious, holding out a royal blue tunic that Sela had totally forgotten she even owned. It had long sleeves and a wide boatneck, and it flared outward around the mid-thigh.

"Do you have any tights?" Diana asked.

Sela winced. "I have one pair of emergency black pantyhose with no holes in them. Yet."

"Hmm. How long before Pete is going to arrive?"

Glancing at her phone, Sela replied, "A little over an hour."

"Perfect! Plenty of time for a spell."

"I don't know, Di. That's what we've been having trouble with, remember?" Sable looked at his friend skeptically.

"And what better way for me to assess the problem than to watch her doing a spell?" Diana reasoned. "Besides, if we do flowers and vines up the sides of the pantyhose, the outfit will be perfect."

"What do you think?" Sable asked Sela.

She shrugged. "You guys are the experts. Let's just hope my entire wardrobe isn't covered in vines afterwards."

"Once you're dressed, we can work the spell," Diana said.

After some revisions to her incantation guided by both familiars, Sela sat in a circle with Sable by her side. Diana patiently looked on as Sela cast the spell, searching for any anomalies in the magick.

Strangely, though, there were none. When Sela opened her eyes at the end of the spell, she found lovely flowering vines accenting the tights. They appeared painted up either side of her legs, and as Diana had predicted, they made the ensemble pop.

"Just give me one quick second," Diana said, bending over Sela with a handful of eyeliners clutched in one palm.

"Where did you find those?" Sela asked.

"Oh, sweetie: I don't walk around looking this good without a full toolkit in my car at all times. There, that should do it!"

When she examined herself in the bathroom mirror, Sela saw that Diana had drawn impossibly delicate light-blue blossoms in the outer corners of her eyes. At a distance, they just looked like dramatic evening colors, but viewed closely, the graceful petals and tiny leaves complemented her dress and tights perfectly.

"Dude, you're an artist," she breathed, to which Sable and Diana burst into laughter.

"Glad you think so," Diana said.

"What's funny?"

"Diana actually is a professional makeup artist," Sable explained. "And a painter, too."

"Well, the paintings aren't quite paying the bills, yet." Diana shrugged. "But the makeup keeps me fed and happy for now."

"I know what that's like," Sela said, thinking about her own endeavors to get her line of products off the ground.

The door buzzed, signaling Pete's arrival. Sable went grumpily into the second bedroom, annoyed he couldn't see his friend.

My boyfriend and my familiar, the bromance of the century, Sela thought to herself.

Diana linked arms with her as she walked Sela to the door. "Full disclosure," she said, "I was thrilled when Sable told me his witch was an artist, too."

"Thank you so much for the outfit and the makeup," Sela told her. "And for coming to help us. I know Sable really missed you."

Diana nodded, then shooed her to the door. "Don't keep your date waiting! I hear he's hot."

As she made her way down the stairs, she found Pete grinning a little dazedly up at her.

"What's that look about?"

He shook his head. "I know it's not possible, but you just look more fantastic every time I see you. Words are kind of failing me at the moment."

She grinned back. "I don't know, that's not such a problem. We'll probably want to keep the talking to a minimum tonight, anyway. We'll have other things to occupy us."

Her outfit and haircut were officially out of control, because that was the most Natalie line that had ever left Sela's mouth. But Pete didn't give her a chance to be embarrassed at her own brazenness; he caught her lips with a long, intense kiss, and Sela had to steady herself against his strong frame.

"I hope you don't find this presumptuous, but I thought it might be nice to have a night in," he said, pressing his forehead against hers. "So I cooked."

"You cooked?"

"Is that a problem?"

She sighed contentedly. "No, I was just wondering whether you were completely perfect, and the scales seem to be tipping towards yes."

The drive to Pete's was quick; Sela hadn't realized he lived so close. This was an exciting development. If tonight went well, then the closer his place, the better.

The apartment itself was also a surprise. It was bright and modern, with large windows Pete had covered with simple grey shades. The kitchen was a small corner adjacent to a larger joint living and dining room. The furniture was black, white, and grey, including a suede ash sofa and gunmetal coffee table with glass accents.

But what surprised Sela was the impressive amount of autumnal décor Pete had set out. The sofa was brightened by a vermillion throw, and he'd piled wicker balls in a brass decorative bowl in the center of the coffee table. Apricot candles stood in a delicate wire holder on the dining table he'd set, complete with a gold table runner. And the dishtowels in the kitchen were a warm shade of burnt carrot.

"I didn't think you'd do seasonal decorating," she teased as she made her way around the living area, admiring the granite mock-fireplace along one wall that Pete had filled with creamy peach pillar candles.

"Are you kidding? You should see this place during the holidays. I do particularly impressive work for Halloween." He gestured to the sofa. "Please, get comfortable. I'll start heating up the food. Do you want a drink?"

"Sure, whatever you're having," she replied, smiling. "Why is Halloween so special?"

"Caroline's kid, my nephew Joey," he answered, pointing to a collection of framed photos on the mantel above the mock-fireplace. "He's the half-toothless Boy Wonder."

Sela went to investigate. She could see Pete's sister was a good deal shorter than he was, with a beautiful smile like her brother's. In some photos, Caroline held a little boy of about six who, as Pete had said, was missing several of his front teeth, resulting in some especially adorable and impish looks. Pete was in some of the photos with his nephew, as well. In one of them, Joey was grinning from ear to ear, posed heroically in a Robin costume with Pete standing stoically behind him in full Batman garb.

"Completely perfect," Sela murmured to herself.

She felt a stab of irritating but unavoidable guilt as she thought about how open with his life Pete was. She hated lying to him, but she couldn't control her magick well enough for a demonstration, and even if she could: what if he turned on her? Things were going really well between them and she trusted him, but could she tell him she was a witch? Not for the first time, Sela longed for a manual that would solve all of her witchcraft-related problems. Never mind a Book of Shadows; where was *that* magickal book? And more importantly, did it have a chapter on how to tell your non-witch boyfriend who you really were?

"Did you say something?"

She turned. "These are so cute! How old is Joey?"

"Seven now, so a little older than he was in most of those photos." Pete glanced affectionately in the direction of the mantel before turning his attention back to the wine he was pouring. "We're negotiating costumes for this year already.

Once September hits, there's an extensive bargaining process in which we attempt to find something cool enough for a kid that doesn't involve me looking too unsexy."

He walked over and handed Sela a glass of rosé.

"You remembered I prefer pink," she remarked, sipping the wine in delight. It was sparkling and sweet.

He nodded. "It's easy to pay attention to you," he replied, looking down at her mouth thoughtfully. "You're breathtaking."

Sela started to laugh the compliment off, but caught his gaze once more and instead, took his glass and hers and set them pointedly down on the coffee table. "Do you think dinner can wait?"

"I wasn't hungry," he said into her neck as he came up next to her and wrapped her in his arms. "Did you say you were hungry?"

"I'm positive I did not," she managed before they found themselves tangled up in one another on the suede sofa. In the brief moments she came up for air, Sela started unbuttoning Pete's shirt, wondering if they should make their way to his bedroom but finding herself far too preoccupied there on the sofa to suggest as much.

Suddenly, in the midst of passionate kissing and further removal of clothing, Pete's voice cut through her bliss in a confused tone. "Um...Sela?"

Not something she wanted to hear after someone had just removed her tights. "Yes?"

"I'm just wondering, did you always have these tattoos? I feel like I've seen you in a skirt before, and—"

"*What?*" She sat up abruptly and looked at her bare legs.

Apparently, the spell had echoed after all, just not onto Sela's other clothes as she'd thought it would. Down the sides of both of her legs were lush illustrations of vines and flowers, very similar to the ones that she had made appear on her tights, except these were even more vibrant. She would have been caught up in the beauty if she weren't so appalled.

"Oh, right." She forced a fake-sounding giggle from her throat and hoped Pete wouldn't notice. As quickly as possible, she swallowed her guilt and thought up a lie that might be close to believable. "So, remember how Sable used me as his yoga guinea pig?"

"Yeah," a still-confused Pete responded. Thankfully, he did seem a bit distracted now that the lower half of her body was mostly bare.

"Um, I kind of lent myself to another friend, Diana, for some work-related experimentation, too."

"You let her give you tattoos as an experiment?"

"She's a makeup artist, so they're painted on. It's just temporary." *It certainly will be temporary!* she added silently to herself. *I don't care how difficult my powers are being, we're fucking reversing this one!*

"Oh. Well, they're nice," Pete murmured, clearly more interested in resuming their previous activities than in how many weird friends Sela had that she let experiment on her.

Okay, Sela, she thought to herself, *you have two choices: continue freaking out over what are actually kind of beautiful paintings on your legs, or keep getting this very hot man out of his clothes.*

She leaned forward and pressed her mouth against Pete's once more. "Where were we?" she asked with a coy smile, forgetting about the flowers on her legs entirely.

Some time later, Sela was nuzzled up against Pete's chest, the soft throw blanket wrapped around them both. She couldn't stop smiling, her happiness extending right down to her toes.

Very long moratorium on sex officially over, she thought.

And what a way to end it!

Pete kissed her on the nose and asked, "Are we hungry now?"

"Starving, actually." She pushed herself up on one elbow. "Can I help?"

"No." He kissed her again, then grabbed his shirt and boxers and started getting back into them. "You can keep relaxing. It'll be ready in no time."

Sela quickly tucked her pantyhose into her purse rather than putting them back on; the fact that the vines painted on them were a perfect match to the "tattoos" on her legs might raise more questions that she didn't want to have to lie to answer. Then, she slipped back into her tunic and panties and made her way to the table, where Pete was lighting the candles and setting out dinner. He'd prepared baked stuffed acorn squash and a pear arugula salad.

"How did you know that I craved healthy and delicious after sex?" she asked him, mock-suspicion on her face.

"Hmm. It could be because I'm an all-knowing dental genius who senses your every whim and desire." He reached out to interlace his fingers with hers. "Or maybe we're just that good together, because it happens to be what I like eating after sex, too."

They made their way to the bedroom after dinner, though it would be a while before they'd decide to get some sleep. The whole time, Sela kept thinking: witchcraft notwithstanding, this had to be the most enchanting night she'd ever spent.

Thirty-Three

Sela's sleep took her from the comfort of Pete's warm embrace to the hazy alley of her dreams.

By now, the scene was familiar. Though she hadn't remembered anything upon waking after the last time she'd had the dream, returning to the alley sparked the memory of her previous visits. To her left was the gathering of witches and their familiars; to her right, the silhouettes of the woman she knew from somewhere and the lizard on her shoulder, with Jackson Woods a few feet behind them. That faceless voice still called her name in the background where her eyes could not grasp anything clearly. And Sable stood stalwart by her side.

Now, she realized, she recognized Micah among the collection of familiars. His witch was the pale, long-haired blonde man who had helped her and Natalie at Visions on her birthday.

Thackeray, Sela thought to herself, putting the name Micah had given her to the face she'd now seen multiple times.

Even in the dream, this gradual revelation of familiar faces troubled her, though it was comforting to realize they weren't strangers. Why this slow unmasking of people she knew, or would apparently come to know soon? And why did that voice persist in calling to her?

The woman with the lizard on her shoulder turned, fearful, as Jackson made a few bold steps forward. His expression was dull and frightening, his gaze wooden with enchantment.

But what drew Sela's attention was not Jackson stumbling towards her, but Sable's reaction. His face was full of astonishment: as Sela followed the path of his gaze, she saw that he was not looking at Jackson, but at the woman in shadow, the one with the lizard on her shoulder. The woman was moving away from Jackson, but instead of running past him to safety, she was making her way to Sela, reaching out a desperate hand.

Sela knew Sable was struggling to tell her something important, but before he could, glass shattered, and now Pete's voice was the only sound she could hear.

"Sela, stay here! Shut the door behind me!"

She sat up, wrapping a sheet around her in confusion. "What's happening?"

"Just stay here," he repeated, and she could see him digging in the back of a nearby closet. He emerged with a crowbar in his hand and went towards the bathroom adjacent to his bedroom.

The sound of more glass breaking woke Sela completely. "Pete!" She opened a drawer, threw on one of his t-shirts and ran up behind him, even as he tried to stop her and make his way alone into the bathroom.

"Sela, stop it!" he hissed, trying to restrain her without hurting her.

That Pete would try to keep her safe even in crisis made her realize how deeply she was feeling for him. Nevertheless, she shoved herself at the door. "I have to see who's breaking in!"

"You need to call 9-1-1!"

"I might know who it is!"

"*What?*"

"Pete, just let me look!"

The door swung open. Sela had but a moment to wonder whether her powers had allowed her to win the battle of strength against her boyfriend, or if she was that determined to see inside. Then, Pete threw on the bathroom light and raised the crowbar.

The window loomed large above a long, white bathtub. The shower curtain had been torn down. Most of the glass in the large bottom pane had been shattered into the tub. And through the empty frame of that window, Jackson Woods in his brown leather jacket began retreating down the fire escape.

"Hey!" Pete yelled after him, though he didn't seem to know what to do beyond that.

Sela softly put one hand on his arm. "We have to talk," she said shakily, and went to sit on the edge of the bed.

At the sight of her reaction, Pete set his own emotions aside for the moment. He sat on the bed next to her, and gently took her hands. "Sela?"

She was trembling, despite her efforts to stay calm. How had Jackson found her at Pete's? She'd thought that, even in the context of the spell on him, he was simply stalking her—that he'd looked her up online, found her apartment, started tailing her car. When Lyla had told her someone was tracking her magickally and then she'd learned it was Jackson, she'd just assumed that meant he was tailing her *because* of her magick— not by way of it.

But Pete had picked her up that evening, and while it occurred to her that Jackson could have followed them from her apartment, he was never exactly subtle when he was around her. It didn't make sense that he would take such a long time to act if he had been in the area since they'd arrived.

What was scaring Sela now was the growing realization that it must be the enchantment itself leading Jackson to her. He might not even know her schedule, her car, or where she lived. It seemed like he sensed *her*, magickally—no standard run-of-the-mill stalker information required. And that was truly terrifying, because it meant that there were no rules or safe places: he could find her at any time, no matter what she did or where she went.

"What's going on, Sela?" Pete's voice brought her from her frightened train of thought.

Where do I even start? she wondered, at a loss as to how to explain Jackson without outing herself as a witch.

"So," she began hesitantly, "that guy has been following me."

"For how long?"

"I don't know. A few weeks?"

Realization dawned on Pete's face. "Wait, the guy at the restaurant?" Sela nodded, and Pete looked at her with doubt in his eyes. "I thought you'd said you didn't know him."

"I didn't, at the time," she said truthfully. "I didn't remember him. He...we went to school together a really long time ago, and—"

"And that's why you don't want me calling the cops? Because you know this guy?" Pete was obviously fighting hard to keep his patience now.

She let out a sharp sigh. "No, Pete. I think he's sick or something. I haven't seen him in over ten years, and we barely knew each other at school. I think he needs help." Again the truth, even if it wasn't all of it. "Haven't you noticed that he seems really, I don't know...like he makes no sense?"

Pete raked a hand through his hair. "But this is dangerous, Sela. I mean, if he's sick, he needs to get that help. And he certainly can't be breaking into my apartment in the middle of the night, trying to get to you!"

"I know," she said quietly. "And I'm so sorry. I'll take care of the window, I promise." She squeezed his hands imploringly. "But please, Pete: I want to see him get help, real help. If he got arrested, I just don't think it would go well. I know it's silly because he's been following me and scaring me, but I feel bad for the guy."

Now Pete sighed. "I don't care about the window, Sela. My brother-in-law's a contractor, he'll take care of it." He brought his hands up to cup her face now, and she saw his brown eyes were full of concern for her. "Just promise me you'll contact the right authorities to help you with this: domestic violence center, local hospital, whatever. I get that you want to be compassionate here, but you have to report this to someone. Don't ignore this anymore, okay?"

She'd be going to the authorities, all right; she was planning to head straight to Essential Elements as soon as she got the chance. "I promise."

Pete got up and shut the bathroom light, firmly closing the door and placing a chair in front of it. He put the crowbar next to his side of the bed, then gave her a long look of concern and frustration. Sela knew he wanted to say more about how she was handling things, but that he was also trying not to push her.

"We can't do much more now," he finally said. "It's three in the morning. Let's go back to sleep."

Even with Pete's arms wrapped around her, Sela couldn't get to sleep for another hour, feeling anxious, angry, and most of all, powerless. When she finally did drift off, she slept dreamlessly and didn't notice when Pete got out of bed before her.

The sweet smell of French toast and coffee woke her in the bright light of early morning, and she sat up with a start. It took her only a few seconds to remember where she was, and despite the fact that Jackson had tried to break in only hours before, sleep had faded the intensity of her emotions. She could hear Pete humming tunelessly to himself as he moved around the kitchen, and she let a smile spread across her face as she got out of bed, still wearing the t-shirt she'd grabbed from his drawer.

"Oh, damn," he remarked on her entrance, though he looked happy enough to see her. "I was hoping to surprise you with breakfast in bed."

She curled up into the sofa and eagerly took the cup of coffee he approached her with. "That's okay. I like watching you cook."

It turned out he'd not only made French toast, but also scrambled eggs with a side of fresh melon and berries.

"You know, I sense our relationship is going to leave me spoiled," she commented between bites as they ate at the table.

"I guess that's possible," he replied playfully. "I'll do my best."

They spent another few hours in the bedroom after breakfast, until Sela looked at a clock nearby and groaned.

"What?" Pete murmured into her hair, kissing her on the head.

"I have to go home and get ready for work."

"Really? Today?"

She put her chin on his chest and gazed up at him glumly. "Yeah—that's the part-time hustle for you. No such thing as a weekend. I've got to go baby-sit these kids."

"Well, kids are important. You want company?"

She laughed, sitting up. "Somehow, I don't think the parents would be thrilled with me acting like a high school baby-sitter who sneaks her boyfriend in." Then she added knowingly, "I bet parents fucking love you, don't they?"

Pete grinned. "Generally, that's the case. But it sounds like you'd better fly solo this evening. When's our next date?"

She almost suggested the next day, but then remembered she had to get to Lyla and Alexander immediately. The situation with Jackson was getting too dangerous and she needed help, because right now, there was no way to stop him. She quickly flipped through her upcoming work schedule in her mind. "How would you feel about Wednesday?"

He took her hand and kissed it. "Like I wish it would come sooner than it will. But that works."

By the time Pete dropped her back at her apartment, Sela only had about an hour to get ready for work. "Sable?" she called as she opened the door.

"Welcome back," he said, and she could hear the grin in his voice. "That was a long date."

Sela rolled her eyes. "Yes, it was, and for the most part, it was awesome."

"For the most part?" Diana greeted her.

"Well, it would have been perfect if Jackson hadn't broken into Pete's apartment at three in the morning."

"Why didn't you signal me?" Sable demanded, worry filling his eyes.

"With what, Catman? A light in the sky?"

Her familiar glared at her. "Why do you think witches and familiars have a psychic link in the first place, Sela?"

She paused for a second, considering this. Their emotional connection was so under control at this point that apparently, she'd forgotten about it. "Oh. Right. Well, in my defense, the shattering glass and looming stalker on my boyfriend's fire escape had me a little too distracted to think about sending you an S.O.S."

Sable turned to Diana anxiously. "You see, this is what I'm talking about. We have to find a way to break the enchantment immediately. You've seen the spell—he's only going to get worse."

"Do you have a minute to talk?" Diana asked Sela.

"I have to leave for work in like an hour, but I can sit for a little while."

"We've been having tea. I'll pour you a cup." Then Diana blinked at her. "Um, how did the designs from your tights end up on your legs?"

"Yeah, so you guys know how we thought that yesterday's spell went normally?"

Sable's eyes widened. "You're kidding."

"Nope! I apparently have temporary tattoos."

"Wow," Diana said. "I mean, they look fantastic, but: wow."

"I actually might leave them for a few days," Sela admitted. "I mean, it's not like my spell reversals are working, anyway. Why not have some cool tattoos for my troubles?" Now she turned to Sable. "Have you filled Diana in completely on everything?"

"Yes."

"And?"

Diana brought the tea over and sat next to them on the sofa. "It seems like you could probably use this."

Sela took a grateful sip, but didn't want to get distracted. "Do you guys know what's happening with my spells? Why they're doing the...echoing thing, and why the reversals won't work?"

Diana sat back, her arms crossed in apparent frustration. "I have no ideas at all about the echoes. You're going to need to do some research within the community, I think."

Sela sighed, bringing her hand to her forehead. "I was worried you'd say something like that. What about the reversals?"

"The only thing that makes sense," Diana continued hesitantly, "would be if there were another witch involved in these spells."

"How does that make sense?" Sela countered. "The only other witch I know is Alexander, and he hasn't done any spells with me."

Diana looked at her steadily. "Are you sure?"

"Positive," Sela insisted, turning to Sable, who nodded in confirmation.

"I've been with her through all of her spells," he said. "It's only been the two of us. We haven't worked with any others."

A thought nagged at the back of Sela's mind. "There was something…"

"Sela?" Sable pressed her.

"Lyla said something like this, too. Something about…if she didn't know better, she'd guess there was another witch." Sela met Diana's gaze. "How would another witch be involved in my magick without my knowledge?"

Diana frowned. "That I can't tell you. I don't know of any way it might happen, which doesn't mean that it couldn't, of course. But I can't guess how."

Sela turned to Sable. "I think we really do need help." The words reminded her of the conversation she'd had with Pete in the middle of the night, and she echoed the sentiment he'd expressed to her. "Jackson is not going to just go away if we ignore him and hope for the best."

"How'd you get rid of him, anyway?" Sable wanted to know.

She shrugged. "Pete had a crowbar in one hand and was going to…whatever. I guess it scared him off, but does that make sense if he's tracking me through my magick?"

"Pete's great," Sable remarked a little dreamily. "I can't wait till I have control of my form so we can hang out."

"That depends," Diana said, ignoring Sable's waxing

bromantic. "When you knew Jackson years ago, was he likely to fight or flee if confronted?"

Sela shrugged. "I mean, I know I had that intense crush on him, but I didn't really know him all that well. He didn't seem like much of a fighter, though—more the type to cut class so he could sit around reading Jack Kerouac. He was really shy, from what I remember."

"That's probably how Pete managed to frighten him away," Diana mused. "The spell shouldn't change his character beyond his actions towards you—not at first, anyway. If he's not confrontational, then he's not going to become confrontational. At least, not with other people."

Sela let out a long breath. "Okay, well, he seems to give me at least a few days between break-ins, so: I'm going to take a shower because I have to watch these kids tonight. And tomorrow, maybe we can all go back to Essential Elements and see what Alexander can do for us? I know he said he's reached the limits of his own research, but maybe he can get us in touch with someone else, like Idris from the club."

"I can't come with you." Diana smiled apologetically. "I'll be leaving for home again in a little bit."

"Oh." Sela was disappointed. She really liked Diana, and it was clear she was a huge part of Sable's life. "I wish we'd had a longer visit."

"It won't be our last," Diana assured her, giving her a hug. "Don't worry, Sela. One way or another, your magick is going to work itself out."

Sela smiled tightly in response; it was, after all, exactly *how* things were going to work themselves out that had her so worried. But she said nothing, wanting to send her new friend back home feeling like she and Sable would be okay, somehow.

Thirty-Four

Sela woke early the next morning to assemble the gift basket she was bringing Lyla and Alexander. She popped a tray of orange-cranberry muffins in the oven before going to gather their gifts. It took some extensive digging around in the breakfront in the second bedroom—Sable objected greatly to being woken up by the noise—but she finally found what she was looking for.

For Lyla, she grabbed a bottle of bath salts she'd made. They smelled of lilac and bergamot, and from that shower on her Nascent Eve, Sela knew that they'd go perfectly with the scent palette of Lyla's bathroom. She also selected four lilac dipped taper candles and a bottle of honey-mint hand cream she'd made.

As for Alexander, she chose a thick journal of natural paper that she'd bound in leather, back when she was doing more complex handmade projects. She had pressed flowers and leaves against several of the pages and used warm water and natural dyes to leave their silhouettes behind, creating subtle designs throughout the book.

"This is a lot of trouble to go to early on a Sunday morning," Sable grumbled, but he added quickly, "Make sure you let them know it's from both of us."

"Aren't you coming with me to the shop?"

He blinked at her groggily. "Now? Do you even think

they're there?"

"Sable. Wake up. They live there."

Sable stretched, then trailed off to the kitchen, calling over his shoulder, "You're lucky I'm worried enough about your stalker to drag my ass out of bed this early."

"You're not the only one who's worried," she muttered under her breath as she brought the gifts with her into the living room.

While Essential Elements technically wouldn't open for another couple of hours, its owners were already tidying the shop. Lyla came to the door with a smile.

"What's all this?" she asked Sela. "Good morning, Sable. Mind you, Pluto's on the floor."

"Wonderful," he snarked, leaping up onto the front counter to avoid Pluto's domain. Thankfully, the latter was snoozing deeply under a bookshelf in one corner and didn't notice their entrance.

"I just wanted to thank you both for everything," Sela said as she set the basket of muffins on the counter next to Sable, handing the wrapped journal to Alexander and the bundle of bath products to Lyla. "I—" She caught a sharp glance from Sable and corrected herself, "I mean, *we* would never have made it through the past couple of weeks without you, and I can't tell you how much we appreciate it."

"Though completely unnecessary, this is quite the gesture." Alexander was handling the journal with utmost care, and Sela was pleased to find a broad, rare smile had swept across his face. "I'll treasure it."

"These are lovely, Sela," Lyla told her as she opened the bottles and breathed in their aromas. "You made them?"

Sela nodded, thrilled that they both liked their gifts. "The journal, too. I've been trying to get back into making products, maybe setting up an online store or something."

"Ah—that's what you wanted business advice about, I take it?" Lyla seemed to consider the products in her hands, sharing a surprised but suggestive look with Alexander.

"You know, Sela," he turned to her, "if you wouldn't mind holding off on the online store, Lyla and I have actually been hoping to launch a botanicals and aromatherapy line within the shop. We were in the process of trying to find a manufacturer who would be willing to sell exclusively through Essential Elements."

Sela's mouth dropped open. "Seriously?"

"If you could make candles tailored to specific spells and magickal uses that also smell this nice," Lyla told her, "I think you'd turn quite a quick profit. Can we talk terms over coffee?"

"Of course!"

Sela was beside herself. Selling through Essential Elements would be a dream! Over the years, she'd had mostly good employers—some awful ones—but none had ever been friends. Beyond that, the shop was feeling more and more like a magickal home away from home; now, it might become home to her products, as well.

While Alexander went to prepare a tray of coffee and fresh fruit, Lyla showed Sela where they kept a spare folding table behind the front counter for occasions like this one. Breakfast was full of exciting plans, order forms, laughter at Sable's aversion to Pluto, and delicious food and coffee. There were more sober moments, as well, with Sela filling Alexander and Lyla in on Jackson's most recent attack.

"I'm going to call Idris in a bit," Alexander told her, and he took her hand suddenly, surprising Sela. He squeezed it firmly, saying, "Don't worry. We are going to figure this out, and I promise, we'll help keep you safe. Both of you." He turned to Sable as he finished the thought, and let go of Sela's hand to resume drinking his coffee.

Sela felt her heart swell. While Lyla had been the more demonstrative of the two—and probably always would be—the fact that Alexander, the only other witch in her life, had shown his care for them meant the world. She thought with gratitude once more on how lucky she and Sable were to have stumbled upon another witch and familiar who were not only great guides, but also generous friends.

The tail end of their meal was interrupted by someone opening the front door of the shop.

"That's odd," Lyla remarked. "I was sure it was still locked."

"I hope you don't mind," a bell-like voice came from the door as one young woman and then another entered. "We thought we'd let ourselves in. We've been hoping to meet the local community, and clearly, we've found you!"

The woman who'd spoken had a summer tan that made Sela immediately think of her sister, who'd burned herself many times in an effort to gain the same glowing complexion. She seemed to be about Sela's age, with blonde curls that hung just to her shoulders and a smile that could only be described as adorable. She wasn't very tall, nor was her companion, who also entered the shop with an endearing smile on her face.

The second woman's skin was brown, and unlike her friend's curls, her own thick hair fell in layered black waves to her waist. She had huge, long-lashed brown eyes under thick brows, and Sela noticed that one of her canine teeth had grown in at an angle, adding a charming, youthful aspect to an otherwise perfect smile.

Alexander stood to greet them, and Sela observed that both he and Lyla seemed cautiously welcoming. She realized that she herself felt only good vibes coming from the two strangers, and her first instinct was to trust both women. But as she looked more intently at them, something tugged at her memory.

Not again, she thought. *Can I meet a person for once and just have it be nothing more than that?*

"I'm Lyla, and this is Alexander, my witch."

"It's really nice to meet you," the woman with the black hair greeted Lyla. She had a gentle and shy manner of speaking, very different from the blonde woman's cheerfully ringing tones. "I'm Ritzy, and my witch is Sybil."

"What brings you to Essential Elements?" Alexander asked, not unkindly.

"Well, that's the thing," Sybil replied, and she turned to Sela and Sable, still smiling but looking perplexed. "We're not sure, but the moment I saw you two, I thought that it must be something to do with you."

"With us?" Sela managed, a piece of muffin in the side of her cheek.

Ritzy nodded. "I had the same feeling upon seeing you both. Sybil and I have a knack for knowing what's to come."

"Premonition? Both of you?" Sable asked in surprise.

They nodded together.

"We found each other way before my Nascent Eve last year," Sybil told them. "I was looking for Ritzy as much as she was looking for me."

"It's true," Ritzy confirmed, smiling fondly at her witch. "It made finding an apartment together much easier."

"It's quite rare for a witch to aid her familiar in finding her," Alexander interjected, clearly interested.

Sybil grinned. "Apparently, I was aptly named."

"A rat," Sela said aloud, and they all turned to her.

"Wow," Sybil responded. "Are you prone to premonitions,

too?"

"What do you mean, 'a rat'?" Sable demanded. "Sela, I swear, if you're keeping things from us again, I'm just going to let Jackson find you."

"She means me," Ritzy offered helpfully, before transforming from her human form into a small black-and-white rat. "This is my other form."

"How could you have possibly known that?" Alexander turned to Sela, the same suspicion that Sable had expressed entering his voice.

Sela sighed, knowing an explosion from Sable was imminent. "So, I didn't think anything of it, and I didn't really remember until now, but...I keep having the same dream, and you guys are all sort of in it."

"That's it!" Sable shouted angrily. "I can't take any more. You've been having foretelling dreams, and it never occurred to you to tell me?"

"They keep getting interrupted!" she said defensively. "The last time, Jackson breaking in woke me up!"

"Who's Jackson?" Sybil asked, fascinated.

"Sela, I'm afraid Sable's right to be vexed about this." Lyla turned to her, her face grave. "Foretelling dreams are nothing to take lightly, and certainly shouldn't be ignored."

"That is true." Ritzy returned to human form. "Would anyone mind if I had a muffin? Changing forms always make me hungry."

Sela took a muffin and put it on a spare plate, handing it to her.

"If you think dishing out baked goods is going to save you," Sable commented tersely, "think again. Now, you'd better tell us about these dreams."

"Well, I'm still piecing them together, I guess," she

admitted, trying to make sense of everything she'd seen while asleep.

Lyla had found two more chairs, and she brought Ritzy and Sybil to join them at the table.

Sela tried to recall details from her dreams. "Jackson Woods was there, and I think my dream might have been trying to warn me about him. The first time I had it was just after I'd met Sable." Sable seemed about to interrupt her with more fury, so she hurriedly continued, "But there were also five witches and five familiars there each time, and they—well, all of you—started to get clearer as I met you in real life."

"You've encountered everyone?" Alexander probed.

She shook her head. "Not yet. So far, you and Lyla were the first people from the dream I met. Then, I think I ran into Micah's witch, Thackeray, at Visions when Natalie and I went for my birthday."

"Really? And you never thought to tell me that?" Sable managed to interrupt.

Sela shrugged. "I didn't put together who he was until the night before last. Then we met Micah, and now, Ritzy and Sybil. The others are still a mystery." She paused for a moment. "And I think there's another witch and familiar pair in my dreams, but they're not standing with the rest of you. They weren't there at first, either. They're sort of more recent additions."

"Where are they standing?" Ritzy asked. She put a kind hand on Sela's arm and added, "Even the smallest details can matter in a foretelling dream."

"The last time, they were between me and Jackson, and I felt like the witch was trying to tell me something. Sable was, too." Sela looked at him, troubled. "Is there something you're trying to tell me?"

"I think I've already threatened you amply for withholding

this information. Beyond that, I have nothing to add."

Sybil chimed in comfortingly, "Don't worry, foretelling dreams aren't always so literal, either. But Ritzy's right—you do need to get all the details, if you can. Was there anything else?"

Sela realized she couldn't quite answer the question. There was something she was leaving out, she knew. She just couldn't place what it was. She went through a whole checklist of the dream's contents aloud with present company: gossamer chain, blue goldstone sphere, Sable, witches, familiars, Jackson Woods, even her outfit and haircut. But she couldn't recall anything beyond that.

"I'm sorry," she told them. "I'm guessing that must be everything, but I can't say for sure."

Sable sighed. "Well, at least you've finally told us this. Of course, I haven't the faintest idea of what it means. Does anyone else?"

Ritzy smiled apologetically. "We're almost as new to magick as you are. Sybil and I were initiated just over a year ago."

That sparked some small hope in Sela. Ritzy clearly had control over her form, and Sybil had only been an active witch for about a year. Surely, that must be good news for Sable?

"I have only vague hypotheses in mind, at this point," Alexander said. "But again, Idris will be the one to ask. Hopefully, he'll be able to tell us what's happening. Are you free to see him this evening?"

"I have a few afternoon dog-walking jobs, but I should be done with everything by no later than seven."

"Good," Alexander nodded. "We can meet you at Visions at ten, after we've closed."

"Now, I'm afraid it's time for us to begin our day—we're

already a few minutes late opening." Lyla stood and began gathering dishes. "Sela and Sable, thank you so much for the gifts. You've started our week very happily."

"And thanks for inviting us to join you this morning, everyone," Sybil added. "We're so happy to meet all of you, even if we're not sure yet why we're here. It sounds like you're all about to find out tonight, though."

"Why don't you two stick around?" Alexander suggested to her and Ritzy. "We'll help you get more acquainted with the neighborhood. You may even want to join us tonight."

"That would be great!"

"Sela, wait just one moment." Lyla disappeared into the part of the shop where her clothing line was displayed and returned a few moments later with some folded clothes and a familiar, rose gold anklet in her hands.

"Lyla, I couldn't. You already gave me the beautiful Nascent Eve dress, and I—"

"According to your dream, these are yours," Lyla said, placing them in her hands. "And besides, you'll need something to wear this evening, won't you?"

Sela wrapped her in a grateful hug, then gingerly placed the soft fabrics and shining jewelry in her bag, cherishing the gifts.

As she and Sable got ready to leave, Ritzy suddenly turned to Sela and grasped her hands. "You should go home, at some point. Do you have time before work?"

"Not really," Sela replied dubiously. "I mean, I'm dropping Sable off, but I have to hurry to my first walk after that."

Ritzy pressed her lips together. Even through her shy demeanor, Sela could see urgency in her brown eyes. "Well, as soon as you get the chance. I have a feeling there's something in your home that you need to discover. Something you've overlooked."

Sela studied her new friend's face carefully. "Is Ritzy a nickname?"

Ritzy smiled, though the intensity didn't leave her face completely. "Yeah, my full name's a little long."

"What is it?"

"Euridys," she replied, a little bashful. "It's one of the first things Sybil and I discovered we have in common—our given names are mythological."

At the sound of her name, Sybil joined them. She put an encouraging hand on Sela's arm, still stretched out in front of her as Ritzy hadn't let go of her hands. "You should listen to her, you know," she advised. "Her gut feelings are even better than mine. And honestly, I've got the same one: there's something about your magick at home that you need to figure out. It's going to help with whatever is troubling you."

Sela hesitated for only a moment before assuring them, "I will. As soon as I get in from work, I'll look."

Thirty-Five

"So, what exactly are we looking for?"

Sela and Sable were standing in the middle of the second bedroom, all of the magickal tools and books Sela had acquired in the past weeks laid out on the table. She had emptied the contents of every box and bag she and Sable had found in her parents' attic, along with her Book of Shadows, the gossamer chain, and her blue goldstone sphere, which glowed persistently.

"I really wish that thing would calm the fuck down," Sable grumbled, indicating the goldstone.

"I don't think it will," Sela responded. "At least, not until my stalker is no longer stalking me."

"And you're sure that Ritzy and Sybil had no clues to offer beyond 'check everything again'? It would help if we knew even the general direction in which we should be searching."

Sela shook her head. "At least we have a couple of hours, minus the time I'll need to get club-appropriate. I guess we should get started."

After an hour of looking through every drawer in the breakfront, examining every object she'd crafted, and poring over several of the books on the table, it occurred to Sela to check her Book of Shadows again.

"Sable," she murmured as she opened the front cover, "do you want to do this with me? It can't hurt for you to get more acquainted with all the spells I put in here."

He yawned. "Why not? I'm certainly not getting anywhere with this old tarot journal of yours, other than learning that you were dramatic about *everything* when you were a teenager."

Together, they paged through the book, Sable remarking snarkily on some of Sela's spells, and Sela smiling fondly at memories that arose now and then.

"Wait a second, Sela," Sable said suddenly as she was about to turn a page.

"What?" she asked, surprised he'd stopped her. "The incantation for success on my exams? You think that's what we missed?"

"No." He rolled his eyes. "This other spell, over here."

She glanced at it. "Oh, yeah," she chuckled. "I think this was after a re-watch of *Practical Magic*. Kind of makes you think we missed the point behind the appearance of the roses in the movie, though."

The spell was a simple incantation for a green thumb. She remembered thinking in high school that the best witches must have the coolest gardens, but Sela herself had managed to kill every plant she'd ever tried to grow at the time—even her cactus. The spell had been an effort to create a witch's garden:

> *From driest earth, green life come forth*
> *and thriving vines with leaves extend.*
> *We summon nature's power here.*
> *Give us reign o'er seed and stem.*
>
> *May our joined magick offer life.*
> *Plant, soil, stone our shared domain.*
> *And should we find a desolate place,*
> *we vow to make it green again.*

Our greatest power sealed in flame,
this sacred gift we both now claim.
Witches of rock, vine, and tree,
as is our will, so mote it be.

"Sela, why is this spell plural?"

"What?" She looked again and shrugged. "Oh, Maria and I must have written it together."

"Who?"

"Maria Gonzalez, my best friend in high school. Remember? I told you about her—we did the spell on our prom jewelry together." Sable's mouth actually fell open as she said this, and Sela prompted him, "What? Why does this spell matter?"

"What are the fucking odds..." He shook his head in disbelief. "Sela, think about it: the spells you've cast have echoed in a way that indicate more than one witch. And your magick manifests in ways that could have been directly the result of a spell like this one! It's intensely generative, and has to do with plants and nature."

"What are you saying?" she asked him, not seeing whatever it was that seemed so significant to Sable.

"I'm saying that I think your high school coven had more than one true witch in it," Sable told her.

"Wait, you mean Maria?" Sela stopped and thought. Maria had been there through most of the spells she'd cast in high school. They'd helped one another write incantations, had pooled their savings for coven supplies, and they'd done countless circles and spells together. "But I thought it was really rare for a witch to have practiced magick before her initiation. Wouldn't this mean..."

"...that two true witches found one another before their

initiations, became best friends, and went on to practice together," he finished for her. "Sela, the odds have to be absolutely astronomical, but it's the only plausible explanation."

She paused, thinking hard on the spell in front of her. "The flame," she remembered finally. "Sable, when Maria and I were casting this spell, we'd put a metal dish of flame between us."

"What did you use as fuel?"

"Olive oil, I think; it was the only flammable liquid I could get my hands on that didn't smell awful," she recalled. "And we put a bunch of herbs in it before we lit the flame."

Sable looked impressed. "That's a powerful green thumb spell for two novices to think up."

"But when we were chanting the incantation," Sela went on, "I remember there was this…spark that happened."

"How do you mean?"

"We had our hands pressed together over the flame," she recounted. "And as we chanted the words of the spell, there was a bright flash of light and we felt a spark in the palms of our hands. It was so fucking cool—the first time either of us was convinced that what we'd done must have worked."

"And so it did," Sable confirmed.

"But what do I do now? I have no idea how to get in touch with her."

"Why not?" he demanded. "Doesn't her family still live in the same town as yours?"

Sela shook her head. "Maria's stepdad was a fucking asshole. He could never hold a job for long because he drank so much, and she told me around the time we were applying to college that he was planning to move them out of state, to take them to his mother's house." She remembered the man with revulsion. "Apparently, she was elderly enough for him to take advantage of."

"And you don't have a number for Maria?"

"She never had a phone for very long." Sela remembered loaning her friend her own cell on a regular basis. "They couldn't afford it. He kept drinking away the money for even the most basic things. He was a real bastard; he used to give Maria such shit about how she looked."

"How she looked?"

"Her parents were immigrants. Her mother was light-skinned, but Maria's dad was darker and she took after him. Her stepdad didn't have any great love of my origins, either; whenever I visited, he used to call me 'that ugly Jew girl' right in the next room, with me and Maria within earshot. She'd get so embarrassed, but it's not like I blamed her. It wasn't her fault her mother married a piece of shit."

"Some people deserve the worst curses we can dole out." Sable put an urgent paw on Sela's knee. "But we are going to need to find Maria as soon as possible."

"Oh my god," Sela realized aloud. "I can't reverse the spells without her, can I?"

"If you cast them together, you have to break them together," Sable confirmed. "She'll likely have a gossamer chain herself. You'll need both, and each other, if you're going to stop Jackson."

"But the spell on Jackson was mine. Maria didn't cast it with me."

Sable thought about it, then shook his head. "If you practiced with each other frequently enough, your magick is interconnected. Even if she didn't cast that particular spell with you, were you close enough that she could have contributed to the spell's intent? Do you think she wanted you to succeed?"

"Of course. We were best friends."

"With the power behind two adolescent witch best friends'

desires, I'd say that would be more than enough to do it."

Sela sighed. "How am I going to find her?"

"We can try to cast locator spells. But first, you should get dressed. We need to leave for Visions soon."

"Shouldn't we call Lyla and Alexander and tell them that we've figured everything out? I mean, now that we know Maria's the other witch involved in my spells, we don't really need Idris's help anymore, do we?"

"Sela," Sable said gently, "this may explain the echoes in your magick and why we haven't been able to reverse any spells, but it doesn't begin to tell us why all of these witches and familiars who you seem to be dreaming about keep turning up. I don't want us to assume that we know how to fix things and end up in an even bigger mess."

She threw her arms up in frustration. "So, I guess we are basically being forced to go clubbing."

Sable laughed. "Don't be so down, witch! We've made a really important breakthrough tonight. Come on, I'll help you pick out your makeup."

Thirty-Six

Visions was so packed that, even with her newfound ability to sense magickal people, it took Sela a good ten minutes to find Alexander. He was off to the side of the main floor, standing near the elevators and waiting for them to arrive.

"Here." He handed Sela a drink.

She tasted elderflower, white peach, and sage, but no liquor. "Is this a virgin drink?" she asked, not necessarily disappointed; alcoholic or not, it was delicious.

"We need to be clear-headed," Alexander told her, holding up his own drink for reference, which looked the same as what he'd given her. "Everyone's waiting up in the VIP room. I assume Sable is nearby?"

Sela held up her purse, the largest she owned, and Sable briefly poked his head up. "Hi, Alexander. Don't worry, I'm here being humiliated as usual."

"I can't believe they didn't search my bag," Sela remarked good-naturedly, ignoring her familiar's angst.

"They were told not to," Alexander informed her. "Idris is expecting you both."

As they made their way through throngs of people, Sela started to feel she was styled conservatively for the occasion, despite the beautifully dramatic clothes she'd received from Lyla. She wore a smoky sapphire eye to match the glossy, deep blue heels Sable had chosen to go with her midnight blue skirt.

But everyone around her seemed to be wearing tons of glitter, feathers, and giant costume gemstones. Professional dancers filled the main stage, wearing wings as tall as they were, streamers extending from their wrists and ankles and trailing ethereally about them in endless spirals as they moved in dizzying formations. Several people dancing in the crowd also sported iridescent wings, and Sela consoled herself by remembering that her own top had wing-like sleeves and her leg was graced by the twisted rose gold anklet, fit for a warrior goddess.

"Was I supposed to dress a little more...whatever this is?" she called to Alexander over the electronic optimism of an Allie X song blaring from the club speakers.

"It's apparently fairy night," he called back to her as they made their way up a staircase. "I think you're passable, even if you left the glitter at home. If it makes you feel any better, both Lyla and I missed the memo, as well."

That much was true. Alexander had handsomely combed back his thick, black waves and was wearing a smart navy suit jacket over a button-down black shirt, but he had no glitter or gems anywhere. The only sparkle on him came from the lights of the club dancing reflectively off of his platinum glasses.

They turned down a neon-lit purple hallway that split like a forked road in the middle; Alexander led her to the left, and Sela felt a spark move down her body, at which point Sable sprang from the large bag and began walking beside them.

"What was that?" she asked, a little freaked out by the sensation as well as the fact that her familiar was out in the open.

"We were magickally scanned into a private area, so to speak," Sable replied, moving forward along the hall, which curved dramatically and sloped up at an incline. He was at least dressed for the night's theme, Sela noted, the blue goldstone pendant Lyla had given him on their Nascent Eve glittering brightly against his fur. "No one who isn't in the magickal community will be able to find us from this point on."

"Here we are," Alexander told them as the hall suddenly opened into a large room with a wide window overlooking the club. The room was painted completely black, Sela realized after a moment, though the bright lights of the club made it seem alive with color. There were multiple chaises and armchairs around, and a bold red carpet filled the floor under the furniture, all pieces of which were velvety and black as the walls and ceiling. Little metal tables were dispersed among the seats, filled with fragrant drinks, fresh fruits, and lush flowers.

Lyla sat in a small armchair next to a chaise where Ritzy and Sybil were relaxing, the two of them apparently more prepared for fairy night than anyone else in the room: both had on glittering sequined dresses that caught the flashing club lights dramatically. Lyla was wearing a deep red floor-length gown and had drawn her locs into an elegant up-do, accented with fresh orchids. She greeted them with a smile.

Sela recognized Micah in his panther form, stretched along the length of another chaise, while Thackeray, his witch, stood nearby in a black suit. A pale blue shirt beneath his jacket made his eyes almost glow under the club lights. He nodded in acknowledgement as he met Sela's gaze, and she smiled tentatively in reply.

In a larger armchair sat a man who looked to be in his fifties, with green eyes and salt-and-pepper curls combed carefully back from his weathered, ruddy face. He wore a metallic green shirt, and his shoes were bright with silver glitter.

A long-eared brown hare sat on the armrest to his left, gazing steadily at Sela and Sable. After a few moments, she transformed into a curvy woman in a tight copper dress, her jet-black straight hair cut dramatically along her jaw in an A-line bob. She was giving them the same appraising look she'd displayed in her animal form.

"Idris, look," she murmured to the witch beside her in a soft voice. "Our new guests are here already."

"I can see that, Reese. Welcome, Sela and Sable," Idris greeted them. "We've obviously been hearing a lot about the two of you, and the attention you've been drawing from our other guests."

Sela noted that while the inflection on some of Idris's words revealed him as having originally come from Canada, Reese spoke with a distinctive Filipina accent. She was struck once more by how far some familiars and witches must live from one another before being magickally brought together.

"It's good to meet you," Sable spoke for both of them, sensing how overwhelmed Sela was by a room full of magickal people, the majority of whom she'd been dreaming about for weeks.

"Sable and Sela have been finding themselves with questions that I'm afraid my familiar and I haven't been able to answer," Alexander said. "They've been coming up against formidable challenges in regards to their magick."

"Actually, we've just made a little progress there, thanks to a suggestion from our new friends." Sable looked appreciatively towards Sybil and Ritzy, both of whom returned the glance with kind smiles.

"We're so glad it helped," Sybil gushed, and Ritzy nodded her agreement.

"Why don't you make yourselves more comfortable?" Idris offered. "There are empty seats and refreshments all around. You can tell us more about what you've learned."

"Hopefully, the baby witch has finally figured out why the

rest of us are here," Micah remarked languidly. Thackeray rolled his eyes at his familiar's tone, but sat next to him on the arm of the chaise.

"We still have no clues about that," Sela replied as she sat with Lyla, Ritzy, and Sybil. "But we did find out why we couldn't reverse any of my old spells. And why the magick I do now has echoes, or whatever." She turned to Lyla. "You were right. It was another witch, even though Sable says the odds are crazy against it."

"Against what?" Micah interjected again. "You'll have to fill us in with a bit more detail, newbie—you're going a little fast for even the quickest of us."

Sela backtracked, remembering that only Alexander and Lyla knew she'd been a practicing witch before her initiation. She made sure to include her foretelling dreams and the magickal echoes she'd experienced since just before her Nascent Eve. The faces of her newer acquaintances registered several emotions as she spoke, mostly combinations of intrigue and surprise.

"And so Sable figured out that Maria must be a witch, too," she finished. "It's the only explanation for why even the gossamer chain didn't work when I tried the spell reversals. And once Sable suggested it, I realized that Maria was the woman in my dreams whose face I couldn't make out yet, the one standing apart from the rest of you."

Thackeray was the first to speak. "But Sela, dear, I have to agree with Sable's assertion regarding the odds of this being the case." He shook his head in apparent disbelief. "To have two witches practicing in the same place before they were initiated—and practicing together, no less! It almost seems impossible, from what I know." He looked to Idris, the brows above his pale blue eyes drawn together in bafflement.

Idris leaned forward. "All of you have found one another very recently, you say. And Sela has history with this other witch, Maria." He glanced over at Reese, who was looking at Sela with an astonishment that seemed to border on wonder. "You know what this means," he remarked to his familiar, who nodded silently, continuing to stare at Sela in open amazement.

"Care to tell the rest of us?" Micah turned his massive feline head agitatedly in Idris's direction.

"Sela," Idris announced, "is what is referred to as a covenmaker."

This caused a small ripple of commotion among the older witches and familiars in the room, but Ritzy and Sybil looked at Sable and Sela with as much confusion as the two of them were feeling.

"I'm sorry, what?" Sela spoke up. "I don't think Sable or I have any idea what that means."

"That makes four of us," Sybil added.

"Are you sure?" There was a quiet but definite shock in Thackeray's voice. "Idris, I mean...we've been initiated for quite some time. You think now?"

"The ages of the other coven members don't matter, my friend," Idris replied with a wry smile. "The coven comes together once the covenmaker is initiated." He turned to regard Sela again. "Unless, of course, she happens to meet another coven member long before that. Then, its magick begins to take shape even sooner."

"Why are we talking about covens?" Sela asked. "I thought those were super-rare."

"They are, Sela," Idris agreed. "And so are you."

"A covenmaker," Lyla spoke up, making efforts to include the four people in the conversation who didn't understand what was happening, "is the witch who catalyzes the formation of a new coven. Covens need to form organically, and they depend on all members coming together at the same time. The way that happens, I believe, is when the youngest witch of the coven is initiated." She turned to Alexander, who nodded in confirmation.

"It has to be the youngest," he added, echoing what Idris said previously, "because the coven is catalyzed upon completion."

"So, I'm special...because I'm new?" Sela asked in disbelief.

Sable blinked incredulously beside her. "What my witch said."

"Yes," Thackeray entered the conversation once more. "Covenmakers are rare because covens are rare. It doesn't mean that you're a leader or anything along those lines—there's really no such thing in a magickal egalitarian collective, which is what a coven is. But it does mean you get things started for, well, all the rest of us."

"So that's why you've been dreaming about us!" Sybil said, apparently relieved on Sela's behalf.

"Us and others, right?" Ritzy added. "Didn't you say there were two dog-form familiars and their witches standing with us in your dream?"

Sela nodded. "Everyone isn't here yet."

"They'll come," Idris assured her. "But we do need to get back to the subject of the other true witch from your childhood coven. If I'm correct—and I'm almost certain that I am—she indicates that you are something of a special case, even among the elite group that covenmakers make up."

"Why?" Sable asked. "If there's nothing about her magick that's special, then shouldn't she be like any other witch once the coven forms?"

Idris shook his head. "Because the magick of two witches began this coven—because Maria was practicing alongside you from the time you began working spells—you, Sela, have ensured your coven will be especially united from the start. The magick of this coven has been, since before its inception, plural."

"What does that mean?" Sable pressed.

Alexander answered, "The more unified a coven is—the more uniform the magickal will of its witches and familiars—the more powerful that coven becomes."

Idris nodded. "Precisely."

"So, again, I'm not special," Sela said slowly, "but because Maria and I did stuff back in the day and I'm the youngest one in the group, we all sort of…benefit?"

Reese grinned at her. "I like this witch," she remarked to Idris. "Optimism is at a premium among millennials. And her haircut's cute."

"When will the others arrive?" Sela asked. "The two other witches with the dog-form familiars, I mean?"

"Very soon, I'm sure," Idris guessed. "And your friend Maria should be finding her way to you, as well."

Sela breathed a sigh of relief. "That's good, at least. I won't have to go searching for her, since she's coming to find me."

Thackeray cleared his throat. "Actually, I'm somewhat concerned about that aspect of Sela's dream. If Maria and her familiar weren't standing with the rest of us, perhaps they aren't part of the coven?"

Idris shook his head. "The spells she and Sela cast together would never have been so successful if she weren't a coven member. It would be forced magick, ineffective at best."

"But Thackeray's right," Sela insisted. "There must be some reason Maria wasn't gathered with the rest of you."

"Maybe it's because you already knew her before you were initiated, and you had to meet the rest of us later," Ritzy chimed in comfortingly. "Foretelling dreams aren't always totally clear."

"Maybe."

Sela regarded everyone around her. So, this was a coven—*her* coven, a coven she and Sable had started, apparently. They all seemed nice enough: Lyla and Alexander were already friends, and she really liked Ritzy and Sybil. Thackeray was odd but had helped her with Natalie that night Jackson attacked her, and Micah was an ass but might not be the worst company, given some time.

The biggest adjustment she was trying to wrap her head around was being surrounded by people who would be part of her life for the long term. Along with the hope of a stable career, she'd sort of given up on trying to make friends since college, and now there was a whole collective of new faces that she was tied to by powerful unseen forces.

"Now what?" Sybil bluntly asked, and Sela could've kissed her for it because it was exactly the question rolling through her mind.

Micah suddenly shifted into human form. "Well, since we've figured out why we're all here, I suggest we get wasted together out on the dance floor. As far as I'm concerned, there's no better way to make acquaintance. Right, Thax?" He winked at his witch.

"While extreme intoxication doesn't seem completely necessary," Thackeray answered dryly but with an affectionate look on his face, "I think some time together might be just the thing."

"Please," Idris told them, as he and Reese rose to their feet. "Reese and I will remain up here—we prefer to oversee club

activities from this space. But we ask that you enjoy our
hospitality for as long as you'd all like. You'll always be
welcome here. It is an honor to play host to the sole coven in our
region of the global magickal community."

That also resonated with Sela: they would be the local
coven, the one group of witches and familiars that others of their
kind would come to for help. This in itself was overwhelming.
But on top of all of the information that had been thrust upon
her in the last day, Sela was more than a little anxious about
heading back onto the dance floor at Visions. After all, the last
time she'd been here, so had Jackson.

Almost as if she'd read Sela's thoughts, Reese said, "By
the way, Sela, you should know that in addition to always being
welcome, you're also safe here. Your enchanted stalker can't
get in."

"He can't?" Sela echoed doubtfully.

"Anyone who behaves the way he did on a first visit is
never allowed in Visions again," Idris confirmed. "Naturally,
we didn't know he was enchanted at the time, but either way,
we've got our own protections."

"He can walk up and down the block all he wants, but he'll
never find the front door." Reese winked at her.

Another thought occurred to Sela. "What about Sable? I'm
not dancing without him."

He turned to her as she said his name, his eyes warm, and
she could feel him sending her strong vibes of affection through
their emotional link. "I actually would like to stay up here and
get to know Reese and Idris a little better. Besides, I literally
have two left feet in this form."

"I'll stay with you," she insisted, not about to leave her best
friend behind.

"You absolutely will not. You'll go dance with everyone

else and get to know our new friends."

"Don't you need to know them, too?"

"I'm definitely the more charming of the two of us, so I'll become friends with everyone faster than you could ever hope to. Now, go make good use of that outfit Lyla gave you."

Lyla and Alexander opted to stay put for a while, as well, promising to join the dancing later. It was clear that they also wanted to discuss coven matters further with Idris and Reese.

As Sela and the others made their way down to the dance floor, Micah surprised her by coming up next to her and saying, "I'm glad to know you're our covenmaker, baby witch."

"Why is that?"

He smiled somewhat wickedly. "You couldn't tell I was rooting for you all along?"

"Don't mind Micah," Thackeray remarked. "He forgets he isn't ruled by his panther form."

"It's half of who I am, Thax—what can I say? Besides, Sela and I have gotten along famously since we met, even if baby witches have no sense of humor."

She was about to snark something back, but felt her phone receive a text. Sela glanced at it: *I miss you already.* She blushed happily at Pete's message.

"Hmm—who's this?" Micah asked shrewdly.

"My boyfriend," she replied, aloof.

"Well, invite him," he called over his shoulder as he passed her and stalked onto the dance floor. "It's a night to celebrate, and we'll have to meet him sooner or later."

"A boyfriend?" Sybil beamed at her. "Definitely invite him!"

"Anyone you're dating is sure to be great," Ritzy added. "We're so happy to be in a coven with you and Sable, Sela. We already know it's going to be awesome."

She squeezed Ritzy's arm warmly in response, but was about to argue that inviting Pete was a bad idea. Then, she stopped herself: why not? If the day came when she'd have to tell Pete about who she really was, what better way than after he'd come to like her friends? He already loved Sable, and Ritzy and Sybil were proving to be incredibly sweet—she was sure Pete would adore them, too. Thackeray was a good person, she knew, and Micah was growing on her. Wouldn't they be more reason for Pete to get comfortable with the idea that he was dating a witch?

She opened the conversation and typed: *My friends dragged me out dancing after work. Want to join?*

He replied immediately: *Sounds fun! Where?*

Visions, the club downtown. Know it?

Yeah! Meet you on the dance floor?

Glancing around at how packed the floor was, and knowing that security would let her back in, she texted back: *Total madhouse! Meet you outside.*

Great. Be there in twenty. Can't wait.

She broke into a broad grin, and Micah, who'd circled back around to her, rolled his eyes. "Now we *have* to meet the guy who put that ridiculous look on your face. Go find him and bring him to your people."

"He'll be here in twenty minutes," she shouted over the music. "I'm going to go outside and meet him."

"Well, hurry back, covenmaker," Micah commanded. "The dance floor waits for no witch!"

She headed for the back exit of Visions, figuring it would be faster to walk around to the front from the street than make her way through the multitude of people dancing. As she left, she saw Ritzy and Sybil in the middle of the floor, looking at her with concern in their eyes and trying to push past the crowd, their mouths saying something to her.

She held up a pointer finger, mouthing, "Just one minute!" at them. *Micah will let them know I've just gone to meet Pete*, she thought, stepping out into the quiet of the night.

It had gotten cool, the way autumn always did before anyone could expect it. Sela shivered a bit, and then glanced around, taking in familiar surroundings. She noted that a couple of storefronts away was the shop where she picked up so many supplies for her homemade products, the one next to the alley she'd kept dreaming about.

"Imagine that," Sela said as she smiled to herself, walking over to the alley and gazing down the length of it. Despite the coolness of the night, it was hazy, just as it had been in her dream. The air must be more humid than she realized.

As she turned to make her way back to the entrance of the club, something suddenly hit her blindingly in the front of her face. She felt a heavy hand over her mouth and only had moments to struggle before she was struck again, and a haze like that she'd glimpsed in the alley moved quickly over her vision, seeming to fill her head.

Just before she fell into deep nothingness, Sela saw a flash of brown leather and thought of Sable, her mind screaming one thought in his direction: *Help me*.

Thirty-Seven

Sela was still in the alley, but it looked strange and her assailant had mysteriously vanished. She stood, wondering at her ability to do so after such a blow to the head. Seeing the endless haze settling all around her and obscuring the street on either side of the alley, and realizing she felt no pain at all, she understood: she was back in the dream again.

This time, though, she found herself without the usual company. Sable and the coven were gone, as were Jackson and Maria. Sela was as alone as she'd been when she was attacked.

"Sela."

Hearing the voice that had called to her every time she'd entered the dream, Sela began making her way down the length of the empty alley, searching for its source.

"Sela."

It sounded again. She glanced to her left and found the familiar expanse of mirror, and her reflection gazed back, a concerned look on her face.

"Sela."

As the voice persisted, the Sela in the mirror shook her head, miming that she should cover her ears.

It's not the one you're worried about, her reflected image warned her, the words sounding in her mind. The reflection reached through the glass to toss Sela something, which she caught with cupped hands.

It was the blue goldstone sphere, shining brighter than ever.
It's not for who you think it is.

"I don't understand," she told her reflection, holding the sphere uncertainly.

You think this is the worst of it, her reflection whispered, lips shaping barely comprehensible words as she glanced nervously around the alley. *But it's not.*

Things are going to get much, much worse.

"Sela."

The voice came close, enough to frighten her reflection back. The mirror frosted over, and Sela could find her reflected self no more.

"Sela, I'll see you soon."

Thirty-Eight

The sound of pacing footsteps brought Sela back from unconsciousness. She remembered that something—no, *someone* had hit her. Despite the impulse to open her eyes, she kept them closed and did her best not to stir. She breathed steadily, as she imagined she would if she were sleeping. Her head and face throbbed with an impossible ache, and the effort not to wince took nearly the full extent of her focus.

The footsteps seemed to circle her, but they weren't close enough to suggest the person they belonged to was standing right nearby. That person was, of course, Jackson; she knew it must be him. She'd seen his jacket before he'd knocked her out completely.

Her pulse quickened with fear, making her head swim even more, and she told herself sternly: *Get a fucking grip, witch. Are you a covenmaker or not? Keep it together; Sable will find you.*

Still trying to appear unconscious, Sela used her other senses to attempt to figure out where she was and what was happening. Her captor seemed to be pacing around her in a wide circle, so the room they were in must be large. As she listened more carefully, she realized that he was also muttering under his breath; the sound was barely perceptible, but once she'd latched onto it, she knew without a doubt that it was there.

His footsteps seemed to echo. Perhaps there was a particularly high ceiling in the room? Maybe it was a church of some kind, or a small theater? Frustrated with how little information she was able to gather, Sela tried to discern the smells of wherever she was, but this just made her realize that her nose had taken considerable damage from the blows she'd suffered. The front of her face was too swollen for her to smell anything at all.

Time to take a risk, Sela, she thought to herself, gathering what little courage she had left. The footsteps were moving steadily; when she was sure he'd walked behind her head, she tried peeking a glance at her surroundings. She found that one of her eyes wouldn't open—it must be swollen shut like her nose.

But she blinked her good eye to clear her vision and saw that she was in a poorly lit vacant apartment. There was no furniture as far as she could see, and only one wall in the direction of her feet bore any decoration. The rest were bare.

She wanted to get a better look at that wall, but quickly shut her eye again as the footsteps came back around.

How am I going to get out of this? she thought helplessly, again fighting the urge to panic.

Then, Sela realized: unlike the feeling of being tied down she'd experienced on her Nascent Eve morning when the roses had grown over her bed, she was not currently restrained. The only thing keeping her on the floor was pain; pain, and the fear that Jackson would hit her again.

But this time, she'd be ready for him, wouldn't she? Even with a head injury and a swollen face, wasn't it possible that Sela could take him on, or at the very least get away from him? What the hell was the point of being a witch if she couldn't protect herself?

As he made another round, she opened her eye again to try and locate an exit. There wasn't one in her purview, which must mean it was behind her. She caught a better glimpse of the wall on the end of the room, and saw that it was covered in some kind of chaotic collage. She recognized what seemed to be blown-up photographs among other objects, all hung in a disorganized mess.

"You're awake."

Sela froze at the sound of her captor's voice. She shut her eye for a moment, then forfeited her charade and looked up at Jackson as he approached her.

He wore a ghastly smile on his gaunt countenance. His hair was matted, his face dirty, and he looked thinner than he had in previous glimpses she'd caught of him weeks before. He hadn't shaved in a while either, it seemed—stubble grew unevenly down his neck and up his thin cheeks around a ratty beard.

"Jackson," Sela began, and when his smile grew, her heart dropped. "Jackson, you can't keep me here."

Confusion showed on his face. "I've been here, Sela. I've waited for you to come. We're supposed to come together. Forever."

"But Jackson, I didn't come here." She made an effort to choose her words carefully. This spell had taught her nothing if not that words mattered in the extreme. "You brought me here, remember?"

"To be with me, forever." He was echoing himself, but also the spell she'd written.

"Jackson, you hurt me to bring me here. Were you supposed to hurt me?"

He looked even more confused, and she saw that his eyes weren't tracking normally. They seemed to move about against his will, haphazard like a drunk's gaze. "I was supposed to come to you so we would never part. Never part." He seemed to understand her fear, to a degree, and he held out a hand. "Come look, Sela."

Trembling a little, she allowed him to pull her to her feet. The room spun for what felt like minutes, and she retched and gagged despite an effort not to. Whatever he'd hit her with, it was heavy enough to have messed up more than her nose and eye. Once she'd recovered enough to walk at an uneven shuffle, he led her almost patiently towards the wall.

Through the sickening dizziness, Sela saw image after image of herself. All of the photos were candid; the wall reminded her of stalker shrines she'd seen in movies like the ones Natalie had teased her about when she read Sela's original spell. Sela almost laughed aloud, despite there being nothing funny about her current situation.

There were other things that were unfamiliar included in the collage, too: crumpled tissues, coffee stirrers, hair ties, dead flowers, all tacked up among the photos. As she tried to understand them, she realized with deepening horror that many were items she'd thrown out, while others must have been taken from her home when Jackson had broken in.

"See? I've waited for you. Now we'll be together."

She backed away from him, and he frowned. She paused, scared that if she tried to run for the door, she'd fall. The room was still spinning, so much that she nonsensically felt the urge to scream at it to stop.

Instead, she tried a different approach: "Jackson, you look like you don't feel well. Are you okay?"

"I have you. You're all I need."

"You need food, too, Jackson. And you need water. When was the last time you ate?"

His eyes flickered. "Don't know. I've…I've been looking for you."

"Well, we're together now," she offered, making her voice

as comforting as she could, trying to keep her racing heart from entering her throat.

"No. It has to be forever."

She sank to the floor. Standing was taking too much effort, and she decided to use this to her advantage. "I'm not going anywhere, see? I'm right here. I'm staying."

Even under an enchantment, he was human, wasn't he? He'd need to rest at some point. He'd need sleep. And then she could make a break for it. She just had to distract him until he got tired, to convince him that she was staying with him.

He shook his head. "No, I have to hold your heart, Sela. Otherwise you'll go and we won't be together forever. Within forever."

In the dim light of the ever-spinning room, she saw him take a long chopping knife from the floor and hold it up. He stared at her with his shaky flickering eyes, and it took all the strength she could muster not to begin crying.

"Please, Jackson. Don't hurt me any more than you already have."

He squatted before her. "Sela, everything will be okay. Soon, we'll be one." He reached forward and touched the base of her collarbone.

As Jackson held the knife over her chest, Sela's fear suddenly swept across her, transforming into something else. Her entire body grew cold, and she felt her breathing, which had been shallow, extend so that the moments she existed in became somehow longer. The room finally stopped spinning as she found quiet in her steady breaths, and her heart seemed to beat only every minute or so. In this slow-motion state, she found herself slipping into a dream-like place and finding, of all things, the edges of her magickal seal.

She moved her mind towards the seal, not hoping to

uncover it—there was no time for that—but attempting to use as much of its force as she could to send out a call for help.

I'm here. The words inside of her came more steadily than they would have if she'd tried to speak them aloud. *I'm in trouble and I need help. I can't do this alone. Please find me.*

She blinked back into the present, and saw that vines had formed along the length of Jackson's body. They had wrapped themselves up his torso, binding his arms to his sides, and they'd almost completely covered the knife and the hand that held it.

Jackson, more confused than ever, tried to struggle, but the vines grew thicker with every moment that passed. Because the scene was not bizarre enough, they began flowering, little blossoms opening like hope as Jackson tried to move his limbs, his growing frustration evident.

Sela began to wonder how the plants had appeared without her even casting a spell, but coming back to the incredible dizziness she'd felt before that moment of calm now caused her to start gagging again. She gripped the wall behind her with unsteady hands, hoping that her last moments would not be spent here, in a dark and empty place, a mural of her garbage and candid shots of her face hanging above the crumpled pile that was her agonized body.

Her strength was spent. *Sable's not coming*, she thought in despair. *He couldn't hear me. I didn't even tell him where I am. I don't even know where I'm going to die.*

Again, she felt that bizarre desire to laugh at her own terrifying situation. Just as she was about to drift into unconsciousness and let Jackson escape the vines, a door across the room crashed open, bringing the bright light of the hall outside into the dark apartment.

"Sela!" a woman's voice called to her.

Sela couldn't place it, but like so many things she couldn't place of late, it was indeed familiar. She saw a panther rush towards her, the shape of a tall man right behind him, and then everything went dark once more.

Thirty-Nine

"Are you sure you've healed her internally, as well? She's still knocked out."

"The spell worked—look at her face. That's just dried blood that's left."

"Here, give me that cloth. I'll clean up her forehead."

"She just needs a minute. Her body has been through a lot, never mind the healing spell."

"Her body? What about *her*? She must have been terrified."

A chorus of murmuring voices and the sensation of warm, wet fabric being gently dragged across the bridge of her nose brought Sela back to herself. She blinked, and realized with a start that she could open both of her eyes. She sat up, greeted by the concerned faces of her coven and the comforting sight of Lyla's living room.

"Hey, guys," she managed with a weak smile. Then she added in some surprise, "This room isn't spinning."

"We were really worried!" Sybil told her, throwing her arms around Sela.

"Easy, Sybil," Micah chided her. "Our baby witch almost died tonight—you don't want to finish the job."

"You know, here's a question: why *didn't* I die?" Sela saw now that Sable was sitting on her legs, looking upset. "Did you find me?"

He shook his head. "I could sense your terror, but that was

it. I had no way of locating you."

"That's not your fault," she told him.

"It's not my fault that I'm a shit familiar?"

"You're not!" she told him sternly. "I didn't even know where I was. If I did, I'm sure I could have sent directions. But it's not your fault."

"Actually," Lyla interjected, "none of us found you."

Sela looked at her in confusion. "If you guys didn't, then who?"

Micah, Thackeray, and Sybil stepped aside and made way for two women to come forward. The one who stood closer to Sela had medium-brown skin, thick black curls, and brown eyes graced with impeccable black liner and mascara. Her smile reached all the way to her eyes, and Sela leapt off the couch to hug her.

"Maria!" she cried, thrilled to have found her friend who still looked much the same as she had when they were younger: beautiful and stylish, her warm heart radiating bright as ever through her smile. "You have no idea how badly I've needed to see you!"

Maria's laughter echoed in her ear as she returned the tight hug. "Probably almost as badly as I've needed to find you. You're not the only one who cast ridiculous spells when we were kids!"

"But how did you find me?" Sela wanted to know, pulling back to look her friend in the face. "Like I said, even I didn't know where I was."

"Remember that night I just showed up at your parents' house? The night we cast the spell to always be able to find one another if we were in trouble?"

Sela nodded. "Of course."

"Well, it worked. I was already in the neighborhood—I've

been local for a couple of days. And then I knew exactly how to find you once you got really scared and started calling out."

"But you found me so quickly," Sela said, confused. "At least, it felt that way."

"It wouldn't have been quickly enough," Thackeray chimed in. "We were all out searching in groups, but Maria's spell on Jackson stopped him in time for us to meet up with her and then find you."

"Wait, what spell? And also, who are you?" Sela acknowledged the woman next to Maria, who laughed at her confusion.

"I'm Oria," she introduced herself. She had long, brown hair that was braided over one shoulder, and her violet eyes seemed to sparkle as she spoke, not unlike Maria's did when she smiled.

Sela thought to herself how familiars and witches began to resemble one another, and wondered how long it would take for her to start looking like Sable, who was definitely the pretty one as far as she was concerned. "You're Maria's familiar."

"And you're the reason we've been having so much trouble over the past six months!" Oria laughed again, not unkindly. "I'm glad we got to you in time."

"You used to always like being the older one," Sela teased her friend, "although I guess it's less fun when you're dealing with irreversible spells. But I don't understand: what did you cast tonight?"

"First, a spell to stop whoever was hurting you," Maria replied. "I didn't know who it was or what he was doing, but I didn't need to. I just focused on immobilizing the person trying to do harm."

"The vines," Sela realized. "Of course! You've got the magickal green thumb, too, since we cast that spell together."

Maria nodded in confirmation. "Then, I cast another spell for, well, reinforcements, I guess." She gestured to Thackeray and Micah. "These guys got there right before we did."

"How did you know to look for me?" Sela asked Micah and Thackeray.

"Ritzy and Sybil," Thackeray answered. "They sounded the alarm almost the moment you left the club."

"We tried to warn you," Ritzy told her apologetically. "I'm so sorry we didn't get to you in time."

"You knew he was out there?"

Sybil shook her head. "We just had an awful feeling you were suddenly in danger, and then by the time we all gathered back in the VIP room, Sable was already freaking out because he'd heard you calling for help."

"We figured the best way to find you would be to split up," Alexander told her. "We all felt Maria's spell, but it turned out that Thackeray and Micah were closest to where he had taken you."

"It's a good thing I was there to keep tabs on Micah," Thackeray added. "He looked like he was about to devour your captor."

"I would've stopped myself," Micah retorted. "I was only trying to scare him."

"Pretty effective scare tactic," remarked Maria. "I was sure that was it for Jackson."

Sela turned towards Micah, touched that he'd apparently been so protective of her. He rolled his eyes, saying, "What? I told you: I've been rooting for you."

Sela's smile faded. "Where is Jackson?"

"He's down in the shop," Lyla told her gently. In spite of everyone around her, Sela began to shake.

"He's not going *anywhere*," Alexander assured her firmly.

"Your enchantment on him might have been powerful, but several of us worked together to contain him. We have him totally immobilized for the moment, until you and Maria can reverse the original spell."

Sela turned back to her childhood friend. "Can we? Now?"

Maria held up Sela's Book of Shadows in one hand. "We even went to your apartment with Sable for supplies."

"You brought everything?"

"The sphere and the gossamer chain," Sable confirmed. "We're a go for the reversal."

"The rest of us should head downstairs and keep an eye on our unwanted guest," Alexander advised. "If the reversal works, he's going to be very confused in a little while."

They started heading downstairs, and Ritzy handed Sela her purse. "He left this behind in the alley when he grabbed you." She looked down in shame. "Sela, I can't say enough how sorry Sybil and I am that we didn't make it to you before you left the club."

Sela stood to hug her. "You have nothing to be sorry for. If not for the two of you, Micah and Thackeray might have arrived too late, and Jackson could've hurt Maria, too."

After everyone had left, Sela and Maria stood hand in hand, their familiars discussing the particulars of a two-witch spell reversal.

"Like old times, huh?" Maria said, squeezing Sela's hand.

"Pretty much. It's really good to see you."

"You, too. When did you get the tattoos, by the way? I thought you were terrified of needles."

Sela rolled her eyes, remembering she still had flowering vines running up both legs. "A few days ago. Total magickal misfire, but at least the results weren't terrible."

"They look great!"

"Anyway, what have you been doing with yourself for the last ten years?" Sela asked. "You were always so smart. You must have a great job."

Maria burst into an odd laugh that Sela recognized as a sound she herself began exhibiting a couple of years after college ended, when her temp jobs really began ruling her life. It was a noise somewhere between disbelief and desperation, with a dash of bitterness.

"Guess again," Maria told her. "I'm working on a Humanities PhD."

"That sounds...good?"

Her friend shot her a look. "Try shit pay, shittier people, no sleep, no jobs, and ever-increasing debt. How about you?"

Sela echoed her friend's laugh. "Dog-walking, baby-sitting, waitressing, tutoring, temping, and trying to start my own business in between everything else. I'm amazed I haven't lost my apartment since becoming a witch."

"Yeah," Maria agreed. "I fell so behind in my research after my Nascent Eve, I was shocked they didn't throw me out of the program."

"What kept you safe?"

Maria grinned. "A couple of spells that gave me certain ...powers of persuasion, let's say, although there have been more than few consequences thanks to our magick being a little out of control."

"Tell me more," Sela began, but Sable and Oria called for their attention.

"It's time, you guys," Oria told them. "Let's get this stalker over his fixation once and for all."

"Please," Sable agreed. "I'm already behind on my Netflix queue."

Oria looked intrigued. "What are you watching?"

"Later, you two," Maria chided them, winking at Sela. "We've got serious magick to perform."

They drew the circle in salt, placing within it a bundle of rose stems that Sela and Maria had carefully de-thorned. The two friends sat across from one another, matching gossamer chains on their left hands, familiars to the right of each of them. Oria had taken her animal form, a chameleon, for convenience's sake. The circle itself was intimate: just large enough for two witches to reverse the spell on one heavily enchanted man.

"Ready?" Maria asked, lifting the bundle of stems. Sela nodded, and reached out to hold the bundle with her friend. They shut their eyes and together, they began to chant:

Jackson, feel this magick no more.
Leave this place and forget this day.
Return to life as it once was.
The spell on you we now allay.

Live your life as it was before,
think of Sela never more, and
never harm another soul.
Go and live a life that's whole.

The spell is broken, we say it so.
While you still can, get up and go.
Think of these witches never again,
and we shall no more you detain.

They both took half of the bundle of stems, and each witch snapped her half in two. A tremor ran through Sela's body.

"Did you feel that?" she whispered to Maria.

"Definitely," Maria whispered back.

"I couldn't tell if it was the spell breaking or the effects of all of that awful forced rhyming," Sable remarked dryly.

"Right?" Oria agreed. "I keep telling her it doesn't have to rhyme."

Sela and Maria shared a smile.

"It was for old times' sake," Maria told them.

"And besides, we barely had a chance to prepare," Sela added. "The rhymes could've been better if we had more time."

"Let's head downstairs to make absolutely sure it worked," Sable advised. "I won't feel better until I hear several accounts confirming as much."

"No argument here."

Sela reflected on the night she'd had. Dawn was just starting to creep into the sky, and somehow, she'd lived to see it. Maria looped her arm through Sela's, and she realized: not somehow and not miraculously. She'd survived because she had very good people in her life. And between her coven, Sable, and Pete—

"Holy shit!" she exclaimed, causing Maria to jump almost a mile in the air next to her.

"What?"

"Pete!" Sela told Sable in horror. "He was supposed to meet me outside of Visions." She reached for her purse and dug around, finding her phone. There were several missed calls and text messages. "What do I say?"

"You could go with the truth," Maria suggested, shrugging. "Getting kidnapped by your stalker definitely falls under legitimate things to stand a guy up over."

Sela shook her head. "Jackson already broke into his apartment. He'll definitely call the cops if I tell him I was kidnapped."

"He broke into your man's apartment? We really have a lot

of catching up to do."

"But what do I tell him?"

Sable made the only suggestion that made sense: "Tell him that your phone was stolen at the club."

"There's only one problem with that. How do I explain this?" she asked, holding her phone up. "It's not like I can afford another one. I just bought you yours."

Maria took it from her, examining the beat-up purple case. "How fond of this look are you?"

"Not particularly."

"Good." Her friend smirked conspiratorially. "We'll cook up a new appearance for it—something with more glitter. Then, you can just say you switched your service over to the new device and managed to keep your old number."

"Devious," Sela remarked as she took back her phone and opened Pete's texts, preparing to respond. "And brilliant, and exactly what I'm going to do."

"Just like old times."

Forty

When they walked back into Essential Elements, there were no traces of Jackson anywhere.

"That was one confused formerly-enchanted individual," Micah told Sela. "Do you know he actually asked if *I'd* kidnapped *him*? As if I'd bother."

Lyla and Alexander had decided that business could be delayed after the night they'd all had, and they had put up a sign indicating that, just for today, the shop wouldn't open until three in the afternoon. In the meantime, they'd set out a large spread of food, probably with the help of Idris and Reese, who had both come to see that Sela was safe and well.

But there were four new faces in the shop, and Sela realized that she recognized at least two of them.

"Hi," she said, approaching the strangers. "I'm Sela."

"We've heard," said the man, who was easily the tallest person in the shop. He was muscular, with very dark-brown skin and eyes, and his black hair was shaved close to his scalp.

The woman next to him was nearly as tall as he was. She was curvy, her figure reminding Sela of Natalie, and her hazel eyes were brightened by glitter liner she'd dramatically applied, which Maria immediately complemented. She wore her coiled hair natural and short.

There was something in the way they stood next to one another and exchanged glances that reminded Sela of her sister again, and she observed aloud, "You're family, aren't you?"

"Twins, actually," the woman replied, and there was a general moment of stunned silence at this declaration that took Sela by surprise.

"Couldn't form a boring old ordinary coven, could you, baby witch?" Micah broke the moment, shaking his head. "Witch twins—I never thought I'd live to see the day."

"Is that unusual?" Sela asked the room.

"Blythe and Maddox are, like you, rather exceptional within the magickal community," Idris told Sela. "As are their familiars, Lee and Ruby."

The other couple to whom he referred were also clearly siblings. They stepped forward to stand next to their witches, the man going to Blythe's side, the woman to Maddox's. Lee had brown hair and bright green eyes, the olive undertones in his skin contrasting against his sister's own very pale complexion. She wore her straight red hair past her waist, and while one of her eyes was green like her brother's, the other was brown like her witch's.

"Also twins, of course," Ruby offered in a small voice. Her demeanor was shy, not unlike Ritzy's.

"Look guys, I think we've all established that I'm new," Sela announced. "Why does the fact that people are twins matter so much?"

"Witch twins are particularly powerful, especially when they're part of a coven," Idris explained. "They are as in touch with one another's will during a spell as any of us can get, and they use their ability to act in near-perfect unison to better guide the rest of the coven towards a more unified intent during spells."

"And sometimes we finish each other's sentences," Blythe quipped.

Alexander shook his head. "I'm almost glad to know this is going to be the sum of us," he remarked. "Any more power in this coven and I'd feel downright irresponsible."

"So, you're the covenmaker." Maddox nodded at Sela, and then he shifted his gaze to Maria. "And you're the other witch who was practicing pre-initiation?"

"That's right," she confirmed.

"Well, shit," Lee chuckled. "I thought life was special when we were just two sets of twins walking around and casting together."

"This is a hell of a lot to take in," Sable said, finally joining the conversation. Sela knew he must be feeling left out, the only familiar who couldn't leave his animal form.

Almost as if he'd detected Sela's thoughts, Micah suddenly took his panther form. "I agree with my feline cousin here. And on that note, I'm going to have a drink if we're going to keep on with the deep personal revelations," he announced. "Alexander, where's the good shit?"

And with that, any remaining tension in the room was shattered. Sela was glad to note that, if nothing else, the members of this coven shared a healthy sense of humor. Given all that had happened since her Nascent Eve, she figured they were probably going to need it.

The coven mingled and talked for hours, enjoying the food Idris and Reese had provided. Sela learned more about the four newcomers: that they'd been initiated for about five years, and that they were, like the rest of her friends, down-to-earth and kind. Lee and Ruby took their dog forms and spent a long time getting to know Sable.

"Are you really going to have to open after all this?" Sela asked Lyla as the conversations were winding down and she and Alexander were beginning to clean up. "I can stay and help with customers until you close."

Lyla put an affectionate arm around her. "Sela, take Sable and *go home*. You've been to hell and back in just one night, and you've brought a coven together on top of all that! And don't think I've forgotten the order I placed. I expect it this week, and I won't let you use being kidnapped as an excuse for not bringing it by."

Sela smiled, excited for her new partnership with her not-so-new and now dear friend. "Don't worry. I promise it'll arrive on time."

"I know it will." Lyla looked at her warmly. "You're doing wonderfully for a new witch. And I know you worry about Sable, but he'll be just fine. Now, let Alexander and me tend to the shop, and go get some sleep!"

"I second that," Maria said, coming up beside them. "Oria and I can crash by you, right? We haven't exactly found a place to stay yet."

"Of course! We'd be happy to have you, if you don't mind a small space. I'm going to find Sable and head outside to get the car started."

"We'll be there in a minute. I just have to make sure Oria didn't drown in the sangria—Idris made that shit strong."

Giggling, Sela found Sable. He looked proudly up at her, warmth filling his amber eyes. "Well, it turns out you're not a shit witch after all, covenmaker."

"Guess not. You ready to go home?"

"Fuck, yes—I could sleep for a week. I thought the Nascent Eve was going to be our most exhausting night." He eyed her sharply. "No more stalkers, okay?"

She tried to laugh lightly as they walked out of the shop, waving goodbye to the rest of the coven, but the sound was hollow in her mouth.

"You're still pretty messed up about it, aren't you?" her familiar observed, concern on his face.

"He almost killed me, Sable," she said quietly. "If Maria's spell had kicked in even a minute later, he would have cut my heart out of my chest."

Sable shook his head. "I'm furious with myself that I wasn't there to protect you."

"But—"

"Don't tell me it wasn't my fault. I have one job in life, and that's to take care of you. And it's not just a job," he added quickly, seeming to sense Sela's own guilt. "You're *my* witch, my family."

They were silent for a moment as Sela dug around for her car keys in the huge purse. She suddenly said, "Actually, it won't be your only job."

"What?"

"Well, once you have control of your form, you're going to need to contribute, remember?"

His mouth opened in outraged protest, and then her jest registered in his eyes. "I'm much too pretty to work full-time, Sela. I'll pay my debts, but don't think I'm going to be running around like you, picking up dog shit and changing diapers and who knows what else."

She laughed, and the sound was true this time. "Dude, your ice cream bill alone is going to run you like a week's wages."

"Excuse me," a voice came from behind Sela, taking both her and Sable by surprise. "Is this shop open today?"

Sela turned to find a stunningly good-looking man smiling down at her. He had dark-brown curls, bright blue eyes, and a roguish smile. His accent was distinctly Irish, and he seemed inexplicably pleased upon catching her attention.

"It should be in a little bit," Sela managed.

"I'm lucky enough to have come to a town where the witches are as charming as the shops and houses, I see."

Sela had to fight not to take a step back as he said it. She hadn't read his presence as magickal at all; even now, she was picking up on nothing whatsoever. She glanced quickly down at Sable, who seemed ruffled, as well.

Her familiar met her gaze with a silent question: *Another coven member?*

She gave the slightest shake of her head in reply.

"I'm sorry. That was a bit forward." The stranger nodded his head, smile still on his face, and Sela felt her pulse quicken ever so slightly.

"It's fine." She tried to laugh nonchalantly. "I...I'm late meeting my boyfriend, and I just have a lot on my mind today."

Unperturbed by her deliberate mention of a boyfriend, the stranger continued to gaze at her. "Well, it's been nice to make your acquaintance. Both of you," he added, turning his smile on Sable. "I'm Liam."

"Sable," her familiar introduced himself. "And this is Sela."

"Thanks again." Liam turned towards the shop, and with his smile no longer directed at them, Sela and Sable prepared to go home. Sela had opened the passenger side of the car to let Sable in, and was about to go around to the driver's side when she heard her name.

"Sela."

She started, the sound of her own name causing such a strange sensation that she didn't even know what she was doing for a moment. As if spellbound herself, she turned to see Liam giving her a friendly wave.

"I look forward to getting to know you, Sela."

As she got into her car, she saw Maria and Oria leaving the shop and heading her way. She smiled, forgetting the stranger and never realizing that his voice, the voice that had just called her name aloud, was the same one she'd heard echoing again and again in the backdrop of a familiar alley in many a hazy dream.

Acknowledgements

My parents once told me that when they made the choice to have me later in their lives, they also decided that since I wouldn't have siblings, I should never want for friends. That effort on their part to give me a happy childhood in the company of my peers has followed me into my adult life; much like Sela has the found family of her coven, I am grateful to be able to say that I have incredible people in my corner at all times. Without my cherished friendships, this book would not be in your hands now.

Thank you to Jonathan Alexandratos, Tracy Bealer, Brianna Beard, Maureen Boles, Cesar Bustamante, Camille Lofters, Jessica Lynn, Daniella Pagán, Sabine Pierre, Megan Pindling, Veronica Schanoes, Jamison Standridge, Omari Weekes, and Gabrielle Williams for always cheering me on in my writing endeavors. For getting me through a difficult time with constant support, enough that I could stay focused on this book, I'm throwing heaps of love at Marissa Lieberman and Jen Rebmann. And many thanks to Leah Kramnick for always listening and offering sound guidance, and for encouraging me in my writing and everything else.

Enormous gratitude to Rachel Altvater, Kelly Centrelli, Yanina Goldstein, and John Rice for their enthusiasm to see *Nascent Witch* enter the world. For reading early chapters of the first drafts of this novel and for their encouragement and insights, I am indebted to Rich Pisciotta, Sharon Jackson, Robert Palmer, and Kayleigh Webb.

Love and gratitude to my dear friends Erik Wade and Emily Wasserman for acting as unofficial publicists and getting the word out on both sides of the Atlantic. My books could not ask for better champions!

The biggest hugs to Emily Rosewood for sending witchy gifts, GIFs, memes, and cards to get me hyped for this book release. For surprise writer swag fit for a goblin queen and sending me luck even as she's busy building her career like the jefa she is, thanks and love to my cousin Ginalysse Ingles.

Kate Schnur was the first person outside of my writing group to read this manuscript in full, and she approached it with her usual wisdom, wit, brilliance, and generosity. Shifa Kapadwala brought her own inspiring magic to my novel and gave me the confidence to put it in the hands of readers. Alexis Daria continues to be a guiding light to those writers around her, and I owe her my deep gratitude for emergency calls and writerly wisdom when I've needed it most.

The friends that write together stay together! Thanks to Paige Alena, Catherine Carl, Lennay Chapman, Gwynneth Davidoff, Cristina Guarino, Kaitlin Guertin, Christina Jen, and MaKaila Knight for keeping me company in the Hive and at other write-ins. Thank you to Grant Faulkner and the NaNoWriMo community, especially the NYC Wrimos who make every November fun, memorable, and a total whirlwind. Gratitude to Brian Mooney of Storymatic Studios for the inspiring positivity he offers to every creative soul he meets.

Yin Chang and her vibrant 88 Cups of Tea community have kept that spark of excitement alive in my heart even during the most challenging of times. Special thanks to Fernanda de Ávila, Michelle Reynoso, and Rebecca Villarreal

for celebrating the early behind-the-scenes stuff with me
during tea times and for our inspirational message thread.
Thank you as well to Satchel Buck Jones, Kat Korpi, Cheri
Kramer, Jessica Lemmons, Olivia Liu, Benny Luong, Melissa
See, and Madison Story for being incredible and uplifting
members of this community.

Thank you to the staff at the Seaford Public Library for
always rooting for me and encouraging my writing, especially
Lindsay Eiseman, Kristina Fuessler, Chris Ho, Sabrina Krug,
Olivia Laurendi, Jackie Lopez, Lauren Rosenberg, and
Amanda Tucci. Thanks also to the staff at the Rockville Centre
Public Library, especially Terry Ain for her mentorship over
so many years, and Amy Hayman, Jean Rheingold, and Alene
Scoblete for the enthusiasm they've shown for my writing
endeavors. So much gratitude for the well wishes I've received
from Rachel Altman, Cristina Carter, Diana Carter, Beth Early,
Amera Labib, and Gabrielle Loccisano, all of whom have
grown into incredible women and I'm so proud to say were my
first library kids.

To my new colleagues at the Great Neck Library, thank
you for being excited about my book even though I just started
working with you! Special thanks to Holly Coscetta, James
Grzybowski, and Michelle Minervini for wishing me a happy
early book birthday.

I've received so much encouragement over the past year
from my library school classmates, teachers, and friends.
Special thanks to Margaret Brown-Domenech, Elle Hauschen,
Jess Iannuzzo, Ruth Konigsberg, Maggie Leung, Emily
Macchia, Jen Marroquin, Suraya Saiyan, Joe Sánchez, Lucia
Serantes, and Kaye Spurrell.

Thanks alone will not suffice for Sara Carrero and Eva
Papka, dazzling creative goddesses and the best friends any

writer could ask for. For every page they've read, every comment they've sent, every rejection they've helped set alight, every meal they've been unable to finish, and for all of my favorite memories, they have my love and admiration in addition to my unending gratitude. (Sela says thanks, too.)

When Danny Dupont and I finally found each other, I was able to begin to thrive in my writing. If he has contributed in any way to the character of Pete, it's by demonstrating whole-hearted and endless support for his partner, to the extent that I sometimes have to pinch myself to make sure he's real. He has made it so that every day, I can call myself a writer, and there is no greater gift than that; I love him for it, among so many other things, every single day.

For ensuring I would find this great family of friends, for always encouraging me to keep writing, and for being the people I want to chat with every day, I am ever grateful to my mom and dad. Like Sela, I've sometimes had difficulty facing my roots and home, feeling like I wasn't succeeding in the ways I wanted to. No matter what, I have been received with open arms, and I love my parents for being the family I would willingly choose, even if they hadn't been given to me first.

About the Author

Melissa Bobe is a fiction writer based in New York. After spending more time than anyone should in school pursuing more degrees than anyone really needs, she happily began work as a children's librarian. Melissa is the founder and host of The Writing Hive, a Municipal Liaison with the NYC chapter of National Novel Writing Month, and a cohost for Word Magic Chat on Twitter. When she's not at her writing desk or lost in the stacks, Melissa can usually be found cooking, drinking caffeine in excess, stretching at the ballet barre, reading about bees and wishing she could have hives of her own, and spending time with her fiancé and their four rescue cats.